Moscow Tales

Moscow Tales

Stories translated by
Sasha Dugdale

Edited by
Helen Constantine

OXFORD
UNIVERSITY PRESS

OXFORD
UNIVERSITY PRESS

Great Clarendon Street, Oxford, OX2 6DP,
United Kingdom

Oxford University Press is a department of the University of Oxford.
It furthers the University's objective of excellence in research, scholarship,
and education by publishing worldwide. Oxford is a registered trade mark of
Oxford University Press in the UK and in certain other countries

© General Introduction Helen Constantine 2013
© Introduction, selection, notes, translation Sasha Dugdale 2013

The moral rights of the authors have been asserted

First Edition published 2013

Impression: 1

Published in the United States of America by Oxford University Press
198 Madison Avenue, New York, NY 10016, United States of America

British Library Cataloguing in Publication Data
Data available

Library of Congress Control Number: 2013943773

ISBN 978–0–19–955989–3

Printed in Great Britain by
Clays Ltd, St Ives plc

Contents

Picture Credits

General Introduction

The stories collected in this volume, as in the other City Tales, have been chosen to reflect the nature—and to some extent the changing nature—of Moscow and its inhabitants. In this way they cast a present light on what is still perhaps a society in transition, a society which gives the impression of being on a bumpy road to democracy and still rather unsure of its identity; but, like the previous anthologies, these tales also illumine the past. We cannot compare Moscow with Berlin or Paris or London, for the richness of Russia's cultural past largely belongs to St Petersburg, which was the Russian capital from 1732 until 1918, and is still the most 'western' of Russian cities. But a tradition of short-story writing is emerging in what is now Russia's capital—Sasha Dugdale calls it 'an uneasy, shifting, experimental genre'—and examples of this will be found in this book. Many of these stories are by contemporary writers and are here translated for the first time. In their various ways they will open windows on to a city that, despite being the capital, remains even today mysterious and largely unfamiliar to western tourists and travellers.

This unfamiliarity is no doubt partly due to its relatively recent past. In a newspaper article the journalist Evgeny Lebedev writes: 'It is a very Russian propensity, the desire to wipe the past clean and start from scratch. They did it in 1917; they did it again, to a lesser degree in 1991. Everything people knew was turned upside down.' He describes how when he went back to Moscow as a child at that time, it was not the city that he knew. The street names had been changed and landmarks had vanished. Historic sites had been demolished and replaced by 'monstrous new buildings'; from being a relatively safe city—which is the impression we get, for example, from Larisa Miller's story—Moscow had become a 'wild place' with death and destruction everywhere. His family, like so many others, were divided in their political views: his grandmother was against the coup which ousted Gorbachev, preferring the Soviet Union, which despite the horrors of Stalinism, had offered a certain degree of stability. (This view is still prevalent in many parts of Russia.) His parents, in contrast, took part in demonstrations and protests to make their opinion clear that the old order had vanished and there could be no going back.

The writer goes on to express another very Russian characteristic: 'I am also a patriot. Russia is the land of my birth and I am proud of it.' Perhaps no race is prouder of its heritage than the Russians: most students know their famous poets and Pushkin above all, by heart, as I could appreciate at first hand on a visit to Pushkin's estate a few years ago. Certainly Marina Tsvetaeva knew her Pushkin too; her childhood seems to have revolved around the Pushkin Memorial if we are to believe her autobiographical account in her story: 'My Pushkin'. The imposing statue which she thinks of as 'a black giant' (Pushkin's great-grandfather was an African slave) was for her a place in her own childhood mythology, as well as a monument that established the parameters of her child's world in Moscow in the last years of the nineteenth century. Similarly in Koval's story every child's need for a place to start from, a place to relate to, is epitomized here in the house by the metro station 'The Red Gates' named after the former triumphal arch, which was demolished in 1927 to make way for a station on the city's justly world-famous metro network.

One of the more enjoyable experiences available to children growing up at the end of the nineteenth century, as indeed it is today, must have been the Moscow Circus which Chekhov writes about in his story 'Kashtanka'. Created in 1880 on Tsvetnoy Boulevard by Albert Salamansky, it was nationalized in 1919 after a decree from Lenin. It was managed by Nikulin between 1982 and 1997 and had its last performance in the old theatre in 1985, when it was replaced by a new building on the old site. During the Second World War special performances enacting military activities and involving German soldiers were put on. Since that time the circus has become world famous and regularly goes on tour all over the world. Chekhov's story, compassionate and sobering, gives us an insight into the circus from an animal's point of view.

The somewhat schizophrenic attitude of Russians, the love–hate relationship with their native country which is so frequently expressed in their literature, can be seen in the story by Sutyagin, where, after a graphic and terrifying evocation of his solitary confinement in Lefortovo prison, he urges us to 'find your own Moscow... and you will love it for the rest of your life.' Like many other Muscovites, he loves it despite its faults as well as for its good qualities. One such quality must surely be the Russian talent for folk wisdom and its people's willingness to accept the irrational and the supernatural. Here it is epitomized in the tale by Marina Boroditskaya, the well-known children's writer and broadcaster, where she tells us about Lizaveta, the old woman who has a magic touch with devices like fridges, toasters, cars and any other machine you care to mention. Her way of making them work is simple: she gives them all names and talks to them and hey presto! Her fame spreads throughout the city and her fortune is made.

A feature common to nearly all of the anthologies of City Tales is a certain nostalgia for what life was like there in the past and *Moscow Tales* is no exception. Larisa Miller describes her Moscow as 'a town of a million temptations' when she was growing up there in the 1950s and evokes images of all the different trades that existed in the city at the time—the cobbler, the tinker, the dressmaker, the furrier—trades which have now by and large died out, as they have in so many other countries. The urban atmosphere she recalls, is 'incredibly homely'. Kazakov, by contrast, in 'A couple in December', describes what was and is a very common leisure activity of Muscovites—the trip to the dacha, the cabin some way outside Moscow to which many city dwellers travel for their holidays or for weekends away from the capital. Here we are transported from the cold, snowy streets of the town as we follow two people skiing into a winter fairyland of 'churring bullfinches... in the ice and snow, like tropical birds, scattering little trails of dried seed from their strong thick beaks.'

Readers will find in this collection of stories an engaging and diverse image of Russia's capital. We hope it will provide an insight into a city which may not yet be the easiest for tourists to get to and explore, but which continues to intrigue and fascinate.

Like the other books in the series, this volume is illustrated with photographs and a map and suggestions for further reading. Explanatory notes at the end of the book offer the reader more information on both authors and stories.

Helen Constantine.

Introduction

In Pushkin's great long poem, *Eugene Onegin*, the heroine Tatyana comes for the season to Moscow from the country, and her arrival is the cue for a description of the white-walled city where the gold crosses on the ancient domed churches burn like fire. Pushkin ends the stanza with the most famous words ever written about Moscow:

Moskva... so much flows together
In this sound for a Russian heart...

If you go down into the Moscow Metro, to the knot of stations under Pushkin Square, you will see these words written on the walls of Pushkinskaya station.

Moscow has always exerted a powerful pull on the heart, but it is no longer possible to call it a beautiful city. In fact most of us that love it now love it despite the face it presents to the world. It is choked with traffic: the streets and avenues are wide, but the traffic increases daily and the city's arteries are furred with fumes. Roads of many lanes cut right through the centre and a dark smog fits over the city like a cap. At the roadside the snow is soiled and brown the moment it falls, and the city trees are black and coated in grease. No one in power appears to care greatly for city planning, so beautiful buildings are pulled down and neglected and ugly ones erected at the whim of the wealthy and powerful.

The city pays too much attention to money and power—for Moscow, by virtue of its very structure, is given to the contemplation of authority, consisting as it does of a series of concentric rings around a central fortress, the Kremlin, from which roads extend all the way across Russia. The centre of Moscow always seems to me to exert a centrifugal force: that strange triangle of power with its red walls, flashing gold *kupola* and ruby red stars, and the whirling mass of palaces, shacks, concert halls, metro stations and markets which surrounds it.

For Moscow is also a city of confusion, of sprawling blocks with yards perfect for short cuts, of dusty playgrounds, deserted ice cream kiosks and ants' nests of stalls and shops around metro stations. It has quietly beautiful streets, lit with an eerie light when it snows, and tree-lined boulevards for midnight walks in June. Drifts of fluffy seeds rain from the poplars in early summer and collect under grimy lilac bushes, trams jangle and clatter until late in the evening. In hot weather pyramids of watermelons appear on streetcorners and couples talk quietly on benches until dawn. For all its ugly sides it is a very appealing city, and it has an infectious youthful energy. It is not a city of permanence or convention—perhaps it has had the threat of destruction over it too often. For Moscow is a 'hero-city'—proud of its history of struggle and resistance. It is not a city of comfort either although it can be one of luxury. Above all it is a city of spontaneity and intensity, of conversation and storytelling.

It has always been a city of tales and myths. Every building has its own story, and stories are layered on stories. Storytelling, intimacy, and rhetoric were important currencies in the twilight of the Soviet Union and the freefalling years of the 1990s. Now the city has the sheen of a new millennium: new buses, new trains, new bins... But I doubt that much has changed around the tables of the warm kitchens: the telling of beautifully tall tales must go on because it is the way of things in this town.

Its inhabitants call it a big village and sure enough after a while you discover that everyone knows everyone in Moscow, and then after another while you begin to see people you know at crowded metro stations or in galleries, your purse becomes heavy with business cards and scrawled numbers on scraps of paper. Long before social networking appeared Moscow's inhabitants had perfected the art of connection. It is an odd paradox this—for every stranger to Moscow comes with an expectation of inscrutability:

goose-stepping Soviet parades, or enormous banners with the faces of leaders, motor cavalcades flashing with blue lights—whereas the truth is that Moscow is an accretion of intensely human relations: phone calls that last for hours, parties that never end, meetings in cafes and metro stations, and the giving and receiving of gifts and compliments, insults and bribes.

Like any capital city, Moscow offers a dream of wealth and privilege. During the Soviet period conditions were always better there than anywhere else. In Moscow you could get hold of things that no one else had, and the rest of the empire was jealous. But Moscow has an anxious sense of its status. On the one hand the word 'provincial' when spoken in Moscow is tinged with contempt, on the other hand the city knows it was itself 'provincial' for long periods when St Petersburg was the capital and much of the country's cultural wealth still remains there. There is a sense also that St Petersburg is Peter the Great's 'window knocked through to Europe' (Pushkin's phrase again), whereas Moscow is an eastern city, looking towards the east, once even collecting and paying tribute to the Mongol Horde.

Moscow has always been a magnet for the transient peoples of the region. Now the *gastarbeiter*, as they are known, come to work on building sites from Tadzhikistan and Uzbekistan, and they are a source of great irritation to the city's inhabitants, many of whom are themselves new-comers or the offspring of migrants. Migration to cities and urban growth is a fact of twentieth-century history, but Moscow grew so radically over this period it seemed to squeeze all of the previous century's growth into a few decades: it has doubled in population size since the 1950s and its area has increased fivefold. This exhilarating but unchecked growth shows no signs of slowing down in the twenty-first century: the village is becoming a huge metropolis, a boiling pot of peoples.

What literature can hope to encompass such scale and variety? The fifteen stories presented here do not even attempt to provide a definitive picture of Moscow, although many of the scenes in the stories seem in some way emblematic. Most of them have not been translated before but some of them have. Chekhov's elusive and magnificent short story 'The Lady with the Little Dog' has been translated many times, but deserves its place here. In its central character Gurov, Chekhov gives us a perfect portrait of a man embedded in the big village of Moscow, its social rituals and routines. A man for whom the palms and mountains of the Crimea are all very well, but they aren't home, and the provincial town of S. inspires hatred and boredom. In 'Scar' Evgeny Grishkovets, a contemporary playwright and writer, holds a mirror to Moscow from a town like S.—and dissects the longing of the provincial for Moscow. The parallels are striking, even if the stories are very different: the provincial hotel as a point of contrast between Moscow and the provinces, and the almost identical uncertainness at the end. Will a solution be found to Gurov and Anna Sergeevna's predicament, and will the narrator of 'Scar' understand what he is to do with his life?

There is a compelling strand in a number of the stories which concerns exactly this relationship between city and country or province. The earliest story here is the classic (Russian school-syllabus choice) 'Poor Liza', by Russia's eighteenth-century historian Karamzin. This story, one of the first examples of sentimentalism in Russia, is probably no longer quite to the taste of a twenty-first-century reader with its heightened emotions and descriptions, but in the eighteenth century it proved an enormous hit and was frequently imitated. In many ways its subject is Moscow (corruption, money, greed) reaching out to idealize and then despoil the natural beauty of the landscape. What particularly makes it worth including here is Karamzin's panoramic and historic opening—the light glinting off the golden domes of the churches, the palace at Kolomenskoye, the riverboats and Moscow, the defenceless old widow, whose plight in war anticipates that of Liza's mother in peacetime.

Moscow has long domesticated its surroundings for leisure and recreation, creating an idyll for the continuation of Moscow life in green and pleasant places. Bunin's sultry Musa installs her lover in an equally sultry estate of dachas and comes out from Moscow to visit him every night. The dacha park, reminiscent of the one Lopakhin planned to build in 'The Cherry Orchard', is a controlled environment, brash, half-finished. Only the weather, so powerfully and meticulously described by Bunin, seems wild and beyond their knowing.

The mass exodus of holidaymakers to the countryside around Moscow was a Soviet and post-Soviet phenomenon. Kazakov's story 'A Couple in December' forms a good contrast with 'Musa', although Kazakov's Soviet heroine is disappointingly submissive and desperate to be made a wife and mother. Kazakov's exquisite description of the day they spend skiing from the little railway halt to the dacha has little to tell us that this is a cold-war story, except the little plane they see as the sun sets and the hero's fears that another war must soon come, but the atmosphere is that of Krushchev's thaw, when Russians began thinking about material goods and lifestyle, about new skis and summer holidays.

One other common detail which is worth mentioning for its peculiarity is dogs... There was no plan to produce a guide to literary Moscow for dog-lovers, but for some reason dogs have trotted their way into the lion's share of stories. There is nothing untoward about this. Moscow is a city of many dogs: the large and expensive accessory dogs that live in tiny unsuitable flats and are dragged down to the yards at dusk to stretch their legs, and the packs of yellow-eyed emaciated strays that lie in underpasses and wastelands and roam the streets at night. Maria Galina's wonderful and atmospheric story 'Underground Sea' is set in such Moscow wastelands and backstreets, and amongst the horror-film clichés she uses and discards is that of a huge black dog with red eyes, a terrifying but not uncommon sight for anyone who wanders Moscow at night. There is even a statue of a stray dog at one of Moscow's metro stations, Mendeleevskaya: the homeless dog called 'Malchik' had been a long-term resident of the station until he was killed.

'Kashtanka', the story of another pitiful lost dog who nearly joins the Moscow Circus, is another school classic in Russia which deserves to be better known in English, and the remarkable 'The Red Gates' by the children's writer Yury Koval is a poetic and rhythmical hymn to Moscow, its eccentrics, its teachers and its bag-ladies, and is a story about growing up with a stray dog.

Yury Koval has rarely been translated into English, although his prose, like all great children's writing, reaches far beyond its young readers. Ivan Shmelyov is an equally neglected writer. He left Russia in the early 1920s and his nostalgic description of an Orthodox Russian childhood in Moscow has the fairytale charm of 'The Nutcracker'. It is used now as documentary evidence of a culture that was entirely destroyed: Shmelyov's list of Lenten foods gives names which a hundred years later are quite undecipherable.

The prose piece that stands out rather, for it isn't really a short story and it covers none of the same ground as the others, is Igor Sutyagin's 'Moscow', dedicated to Moscow life behind bars. Igor was convicted of being a spy in 2004, but after a great deal of international pressure he was released and sent to the UK as part of a spy swap in 2010. Igor wrote this description of the infamous FSB prison Lefortovo for *Moscow Tales*. It has the peculiarity of truth, and it is a chilling portrait of a part of Moscow we should hope never to see ourselves. It is also a reminder of the sinister side of Moscow: the prisons and remand centres that hold protesters against the government, and those who have crossed the political elites.

I want to thank Igor for writing this piece, and to thank all those who suggested *Moscow Tales*: Yulia Raikhelgaus, Anna Genina, Natasha Perova, Marina Boroditskaya and those who helped by reading and commenting on the translations: Liz Barnes, David Constantine, Masha

Wiltshire, Paul King, Masha Karp and the Translation Workshop at Pushkin House. I am deeply grateful to the series' editor Helen Constantine for her unending patience and wisdom.

Anna Genina and Michael Pushkin were both wonderful, tireless readers and enthusiasts and I can't thank either of them enough.

Musa

Ivan Bunin

I was no longer a very young man, but I had made up my
mind to study painting—I'd always had a passion for it—
and leaving my estate in Tambov Province I spent a winter
in Moscow. I took lessons with a talentless but fairly well
known artist, a slovenly plump man, who had mastered
the essentials of being a painter: long hair, fat greasy curls
which he tossed back, a pipe in his mouth, a crimson
velvet jacket, dirty-grey gaiters over his shoes (I hated
these especially), a brusqueness of manner, a superior
way of glancing at a pupil's work with narrowed eyes
whilst muttering, as if to himself:

'Interesting, yes, interesting... a definite success...'

I lived on the Arbat near the Praga restaurant in a
room in the Hotel Stolitsa. I worked at the artist's and at
home during the day, and I often spent my evenings in

cheap restaurants with various new bohemian acquaintances, both the young and the more careworn, all of them
equally given to billiards, and beer with crayfish... It was a
dull unpleasant sort of life. That grubby and effeminate
artist, his 'artistically' neglected studio, cluttered with all
kinds of dusty props, the gloomy Hotel Stolitsa... All that
has remained in my memory is this: the snow falling
constantly outside the windows, the muffled rumbling
and ringing of the horse-drawn tram on the Arbat and
the sharp stench of beer and gas in the dimly lit restaurant
at night. I don't know what possessed me to lead such a
desperate life, I was far from poor back then.

But one day in March I was sitting in my rooms,
drawing with pencils, and the winter dampness of snow
and rain no longer came in at the open doubled fanlight
windows, the horses' hooves clopped along the roads in a
way that no longer spoke of winter and the jingling of the
horse-drawn tram sounded more like music. Somebody
knocked at the door.

I shouted out 'who's there?' but there was no answer.
I waited a moment, then shouted again. Once more,
silence, then another knock at the door. I stood up and
opened the door. There stood a tall girl in a grey winter
hat, a straight grey dress and grey boots. She was staring at
me. Her eyes were the colour of ripe acorns, drops of

rain and snow shone on her long eyelashes, her face, and the hair under her hat. She looked at me and she said,

'I'm a student at the conservatory. I'm Musa Graf. I heard you were an interesting man and I thought I'd come and meet you. Do you mind?'

I was fairly amazed, but I answered courteously enough,

'I'm very flattered. But I must warn you that the rumours you have heard are hardly true—there's nothing interesting about me.'

'At any rate let me come in, don't keep me standing here at your door,' she said, still looking straight at me. 'Now I've flattered you.'

And, entering, she made herself quite at home, taking off her hat and patting her rust-coloured hair into place in front of my silver-grey mirror which had tarnished to black in places, and throwing off her coat and dropping it onto a chair. In a checked flannel dress she sat down on the divan, sniffing, her nose wet with rain and snow, and issued orders:

'Take my boots off and fetch me my handkerchief from my coat.'

I gave her the handkerchief, she wiped her face then stretched out her legs towards me.

'I saw you yesterday at the Shor concert.' she said indifferently.

Hiding a silly smile of pleasure and bewilderment—
what a strange visitor this was—I took off the boots
obediently, one after the other. The sweet smell of fresh
air hung about her, and I was excited by the smell, and by
the combination of her boldness and all that was young
and feminine in her face, her frank eyes, her beautiful
large hands, in everything I saw and felt as I pulled off
the boots from below her skirt, under which were her
knees, rounded and firm, her full calves in thin grey tights,
and her long slender feet in open patent leather pumps.

She made herself comfortable on the divan and was
clearly not about to leave. I didn't know what to say, so
I asked her what she had heard of me and from whom,
who she was, where she lived and with whom. She
answered,

'It doesn't matter what I heard about you, or from
whom. Mostly I came because I saw you at the concert.
You're quite attractive. I'm the daughter of a doctor, I live
quite close, on Prichistensky Boulevard.'

She spoke in an abrupt and impetuous way. Again
I didn't know what to say so I asked,

'Would you like tea?'

'Yes,' she answered. 'And if you have any money then
order some reinette apples, from Belov's, near here on the
Arbat. Only hurry. I'm no good at waiting.'

'And you seem so calm.'

'There you're mistaken...'

When the bellboy had brought the samovar and a bag of apples she made some tea and wiped the cups and spoons. Once she had eaten an apple and drunk her cup of tea she sat back on the divan and patted the seat next to her.

'Come and sit with me now.'

I sat down, she put her arms about me and kissed me unhurriedly on the lips, moved away, looked at me, and, as if she had convinced herself that I was worth it, closed her eyes and kissed me again, a long deliberate kiss.

'There,' she said, as if relieved. 'Nothing more now. The day after tomorrow.'

It was already quite dark in the room—only a dreary half light from the street lamps. You can imagine how I felt. Such happiness all at once! She was young and strong, the shape and taste of her lips so extraordinary... I heard the unchanging ringing of the horsecars and the clop of hooves as if in a dream.

'I want to have dinner with you the day after tomorrow in the Praga restaurant,' she said. 'I've never been there and in fact I'm very inexperienced altogether. I can imagine what you're thinking about me. But actually you are my first love.'

'Love?'

'What else could you call it?'

I soon dropped my studies of course, she continued hers after a fashion. We were inseparable, we lived like newly-weds, visited galleries, exhibitions, concerts, even public lectures for some unknown reason. In May I moved, at her request, to an old estate just outside Moscow where some fairly small dachas had been built for hire, and she began travelling out to see me, returning at one o'clock at night to Moscow. I had hardly expected this either. A dacha just outside Moscow. I had never lived a dacha life before, in such idleness and in an estate so different from our estates on the steppe, in a climate so different.

Pine trees surrounded the house, it rained the whole time. White clouds often piled up in the bright blue above the trees, thunder rolled high above and a glittering rain began scattering through the sunlight, soon becoming a fragrant pine vapour in the intense heat... Everything was wet, sticky, shimmering... In the estate park the trees were so tall that the dachas built here and there looked tiny, like huts under trees in the tropics. The pond was a huge black mirror, half covered with green duckweed... I lived at the edge of the park, near the woods. My log hut was not quite finished. The walls had not been caulked, the floors were rough, the stoves had no doors and there was hardly any furniture. My boots, lying under my bed, grew a velvet mould in the constant dampness.

At night it only grew dark towards midnight. The twilight hung in the west above the silent still wood. On moonlit nights this twilight merged strangely with the light from the moon which seemed just as magical, just as motionless. And the calm which reigned, the clear skies and the air, all gave me to believe there would be no more rain. But as I was falling asleep after walking her to the station I would suddenly hear the rain drumming on the roof and rolls of thunder, darkness all around and lightning falling like a plumb line. In the mornings dappled light and blinding spots of sunlight fell on the purple earth of the chill paths under the trees, flycatchers chittered and thrushes called with hoarse trills. By midday it was sultry and oppressive again, the clouds had reappeared and the rain began pattering down. Before sunset the sky cleared and the low sun's luminous golden web quivered on the walls of my log hut. It was then that I went down to the station to meet her. The train arrived, disgorging countless holidaymakers onto the platform, the smell of coal fire from the engine and the damp freshness of the woods was in the air, and there she was, holding a string bag heavy with parcels of fruit and snacks, a bottle of Madeira. We dined companionably and alone. Before she left late in the evening we wandered in the park. She walked as if in her sleep, her head resting on my shoulder. The black pool, the ancient trees rising up to the star-filled sky... The magically light night, so infinitely silent, the infinitely long shadows of the trees across the silver meadows which looked like lakes.

In June she travelled home with me to my village, and lived with me without marrying me, but as my wife. She ran the house. She spent the long autumn busying herself with the household and reading.

Our most frequent visitor was a neighbour by the name of Zavistovsky, a poor landowner who lived on his own about two versts from us. He was a feeble little man, red-haired, nervous, callow—but not a bad musician. In the winter he began to appear almost every evening. I had known him since childhood, and was so used to him that an evening passed without him seemed odd. We played draughts, or he played duets with her on the piano.

Just before Christmas I went into town. The moon was already up when I returned. I went into the house and couldn't find her anywhere. I sat down by the samovar.

'Where is she, Dunya? Has she gone out?'

'I don't know, sir. They went out at breakfast and haven't been back since.'

'They put on their coats and went out,' said my old Nanny sombrely, walking through the room with her head lowered.

'She's probably gone to Zavistovsky's,' I thought. 'And she'll probably be back soon with him. It's already seven o'clock...' And I went and lay down in my study and fell asleep suddenly—I had been on the road in the cold all day. I came to just as suddenly an hour later with the clear, incredible thought: 'She's left me. She hired a man in the village to take her to the station and she's left for Moscow—there's no telling what she's done. But maybe she's come back?' I walked through the house. No. She hadn't returned. The servants must have known.

Around ten, not knowing what to do, I put on my fur jacket, picked up a gun for some reason and set off along the road towards Zavistovsky's, thinking, 'And even he didn't come round this evening and I have a whole terrible night ahead! Surely she can't have gone away and left me? No, it can't be true!' I walked along the rutted road, my boots squeaking on the snow, high drifts on either side, and the snowy fields to the left of me glistening under a low and meagre moon. I turned off the main road towards Zavistovsky's pitiful estate: the avenue of bare trees which led towards it across the fields, the driveway into the yard, the old, rundown house on the left, the windows dark... I climbed up to the ice-covered porch, opened the heavy door with its tatters of wadding on the back. In the hallway the fire smouldered red in the open stove, warmth and darkness... But it was dark in the drawing room as well.

'Vikenty Vikentich!'

He appeared in the doorway of his study, noiselessly, in felt boots, illuminated only by the moon through the window.

'Oh, it's you... Come in, please, come in... As you see I'm sitting here in the darkness, spending the evening without a candle...'

I went in and sat down on the lumpy divan.

'Musa's vanished, can you believe it?'

He said nothing. Then, almost inaudibly,

'I do understand, you know.'

'What, what do you understand?'

And then, just as noiselessly and also in felt boots with a shawl over her shoulders, Musa came out of the bed-room adjoining the study.

'You have a gun,' she said. 'If you want to shoot someone, then shoot me, don't shoot him.'

And she sat down on the divan opposite me.

I looked at her felt boots, at the knees under the grey skirt, everything was very clear in the golden light which fell from the windows. I wanted to cry out: 'I can't live without you... Your knees, that skirt, those felt boots, I'd give up my life for them alone.'

'It's all quite finished,' she said. 'No point in making a scene.'

'You are monstrously cruel,' I managed to say.

'Give me a cigarette,' she said to Zavistovsky.

He went and cowered by her, offering his cigarette holder, and began rifling in his pockets for matches...

'You're so cold towards me,' I said, struggling to breathe. 'Could you not be less familiar with him, at least in front of me?'

'Why?' she asked, lifting her eyebrows, holding the cigarette away from her.

My heart was tight in my throat, my temples throbbed. I stood and, staggering, I left.

A Couple in December

Yury Kazakov

He waited a long time for her at the station. It was a bright frosty day and everything gave him pleasure: the crowds of skiers, the squeaking underfoot of the newly fallen snow that hadn't yet been cleared in Moscow. His own self gave him pleasure: the tough ski boots, the woollen socks which came nearly to his knee, the thick furry sweater, the peaked Austrian cap, but most of all his skis, his wonderful laminate skis, bound together with a strap.

She was late, as always, and at one time it used to anger him, but now he was used to it, because, when you thought about it, it really was her only failing. Now he leaned his skis against the wall, stamped his feet a little to stop them from freezing, and looked in the direction from which she would come. He was contented. He wasn't full of joy, no—he was merely contented, and it gave him calm pleasure when he considered how he was liked at work, how everything was going well there, and at home, too, and how good the winter was. December, and yet it looked just like March with the sun, the glistening snow. And, best of all, things were going well with her. They had come through that difficult period of arguments, jealousy, suspicion, distrust, unexpected telephone calls when all you could hear was breathing down the line and silence, and it near broke your heart. Thank God it was all passed and now there was something different: now there was calm, trust and fondness between them. Yes, that was how it was.

When she at last arrived and he saw her face and her figure close by him, all he said was,

'Well then, here you are.'

He took his skis and they went slowly so she could catch her breath. She had been hurrying and was breathing hard. She was wearing a red hat, locks of hair had escaped onto her forehead, her dark eyes darted about and flickered when she glanced at him, and her nose was covered in pretty freckles.

He hung back slightly and fished some change from his pocket, looked at her from behind, her legs, and thought suddenly how beautiful she was, how well dressed, and how she had probably been late because she wanted to look beautiful and those locks of hair, so carelessly escaping, perhaps weren't careless at all, and how touching she was, how attentive.

'That sun! What a winter!' she said as he bought the tickets. 'You haven't forgotten anything?'

He merely shook his head. He reckoned he'd probably taken too much, his pack was a good weight.

The train was crowded with skis and rucksacks and it was noisy. Everyone was shouting, calling to each other, finding places noisily, banging skis together. The windows were cold and clear, but the heaters under the benches gave off a dry heat and it was good to look out at the sun on the snow and listen to the rapid muffled clatter of the wheels when the train set off.

Twenty minutes or so later he went out to the end of the carriage to smoke. The glass was missing from one of the sliding doors and a chilly wind was chasing through. The walls and ceiling were feathered with hoar. There was a sharp smell of frost and steel, and the clatter of the wheels had become a loud roar, the rails hummed.

He smoked, looking through the glass door back into the carriage, transferring his gaze from bench to bench, feeling a certain pity for everyone sitting there, because none of them, as he saw it, would have quite as good a time as he would these two days. He also looked at all the girls, their animated faces, and felt the slight prickle of agitation he always felt when he saw a young beautiful woman passing with another man, and not with him. Then he looked at her and he was glad. He saw that even there, amongst all the young and beautiful women, she was still the best. She was looking out of the window, her face was soft, her eyes dark, the lashes long.

He looked out of the open window at the frost and the air, and he wrinkled his face against the bright light and the wind. Rickety wooden platforms covered in snow flew past. Sometimes the platforms had wooden station buffets, painted all blue with a steel pipe on the roof and a little blue smoke issuing from it. And he thought how good it would be to sit in a little buffet like that, to hear the thin whistling of the trains racing past, to warm himself by the little stove and drink a mug of beer. And how wonderful everything was anyway: what a winter, what joy that he had someone to love, that his beloved was sitting in the train and he could look at her and catch her answering gaze. He for one knew exactly how good that was: how many evenings had he spent alone, at home, when she had not been with him, or aimlessly wandering the streets with friends talking philosophy, the theory of relativity and other pleasingly clever matters, and when he got home he would feel sad. He even wrote poems, and a friend of his liked the poems, because he didn't have anyone either. And now that friend had married...

He thought, how strange people are. There he was, a lawyer, and already thirty, and he hadn't achieved anything, he hadn't invented anything or become a poet or a sportsman as he had dreamed in his youth. How many reasons he had to be disappointed because he hadn't succeeded in his life's plans, but he wasn't, the fact that his work was ordinary, he hadn't garnered any glory, none of that cast him down, or horrified him. He was actually contented and calm, and lived much as if he had had all the success of which he'd dreamed.

He had only one constant anxiety—the summer. He began back in November to plot where he would go on his summer holidays and how he would get there. His summer holidays always seemed so endless, and at the same time so short that he had to think ahead, choose the most interesting place, make no mistakes or bad choices. All winter, all spring he worried at it, finding out where was good, what the countryside was like, the people, how to get there, and all his enquiries and the laying of plans may even have given him more pleasure than the holiday itself.

He was thinking about the summer even now, about how he would go and find a little river. They'd take a tent and when they got to this little river they'd blow up the inflatable canoe and it would be like a Red Indian kayak.

And then farewell to Moscow and its pavements, and legal procedures and consultations!

And then he remembered the first time they had left Moscow together. They had gone to Estonia to a tiny town where he had had some sort of business. He remembered how they'd travelled on a bus and arrived in the late evening in Valdai where everything was dark and a single restaurant still had its lights on and was working. He'd had a glass of vodka and was drunk and happy on the bus because she was beside him and she drowsed from time to time through the dark night, leaning up against him. And they arrived at dawn, and although it was the middle of August and the rain was pouring down in Moscow, here it was clean and light, the sun came up, there were little white houses and pointed red-tiled roofs and gardens everywhere, it was quiet and a long way from anywhere, the grass curled up between the cobbles on the streets.

They had taken a clean, bright room. Ripe apples were spread on all the windowsills, in the cupboard and under the bed, scenting the room. There was a market with plentiful supplies. They went together and chose some smoked pork fat, honeycomb, butter, tomatoes and cucumbers (so cheap you could barely believe it). And then there was the smell from the bakery and the constant cooing of pigeons and the beating of their wings. And best of all—her: constantly surprising, almost a stranger to him, and yet at the same time, intimate and beloved. What bliss it had been, and might be again, if there was no war.

He had begun thinking about the war a lot recently, and he hated the thought of it. But now, looking out at the glinting snow, the trees, the fields, listening to the clatter of wheels and the hum of rails, he felt quite certain that there would be no war, just as there would be no death. Because, he thought, there were moments in life, when it was impossible to think about horrors, or believe in the existence of evil.

They were nearly the last to leave the train at a remote station. The snow squeaked noisily under their feet as they walked along the platform.

'What a winter!' she said again, wrinkling up her face. 'Hasn't been one like this for ages!'

They had to ski about twenty kilometres to his dacha where they would stay overnight, and then they would have another day's skiing and return to Moscow on a different railway line.

He had a little orchard and a summer cabin with two beds, a table, some simple stools and a potbellied iron stove.

He put on his skis and jumped up and down a few times, banging the skis on the ground, scattering the soft powdery snow, then he checked her bindings and they set off. To start with they wanted to travel fast so they could reach the dacha sooner and rest and warm themselves through, but travelling fast through these meadows and woods was impossible.

'Just look at the trunks on those aspens!' she said, stopping. 'They're the colour of cats' eyes.'

He stopped too, and looked, and she was right—the aspens were a greeny-yellow colour, exactly like a cat's eye.

Smoky rays of light slanted through the forest. Here and there the snow had caught between trunks like a shroud and the firs, freed of their snow burden, waved their paws about.

They went from one ridge to another, and sometimes saw villages beneath them, houses with white roofs. Stoves were alight in all the homes and smoke rose from the villages. It rose in pillars to the sky and then collapsed, dispersed, drifted and wound itself around the near hills like a blue transparence. Even a kilometre or two away from a village they could smell the smoke and it made them want to get to the dacha quicker and light the stove.

Sometimes they crossed tracks covered in manure, which had been so worn by sledge runners they shone, and even though it was December, on these tracks, with their scraps of hay and the blue shadows of the ruts there was something spring-like, they smelt of spring. Once a black horse with gleaming flanks galloped past on a track towards a village, his muscles rippling and the snow and ice flying up from under his hoofs, and they heard the snorting and the staccato crunching of snow. They stopped again and watched him disappear.

Or an anxious and very preoccupied jackdaw flew past with ruffled feathers, and another jackdaw hurried after him, and from a little way off a curious magpie dived down, never letting them out of its sight: *what have they found?* And you simply had to watch. Or churring bull-finches rocked and scrambled busily about a thistle poking up above the snow—how strange they looked in the ice and snow, like tropical birds, scattering little trails of dried seed from their strong, thick beaks.

Sometimes they came across the prints of a fox which stretched in an even, and at the same time curving, line from tussock to tussock, mound to mound. Then the trail turned and vanished into the glare of the snow. On they went and saw hare and squirrel prints in the birch and aspen groves.

These traces of the mysterious nocturnal life of the cold and deserted fields and woods made the heart tremble and thoughts turn to the evening samovar before a night hunt, the sheepskin coat and gun, the slow course of the stars, the haystacks where the hares feasted at night, and to where from afar the vixens came, sometimes lifting their front legs off the ground to rise up and sniff in the air. In the mind's eye a flash of light, a thundering shot and the faint echo breaking against the hills, the barking of nervous dogs in the surrounding villages and the eye of the stretched out hare glassy and cold, the stars reflected in those eyes, and the whiskers thick with frost and the warm weight of the hare's carcass.

In the valleys and ravines the snow was deep and dry and the skiing was difficult, but on the lower slopes of the hills lay a thick marbled crust of snow with only a little powder on it, and when they climbed to this the skiing was fine.

The forests on the hills at the horizon had a pink tinge, the sky was blue and the open space seemed endless.

And so they went on climbing and then dropping down again, resting on fallen tree trunks, smiling at each other. Sometimes he took her around the neck from behind and kissed her with cold wind-chapped lips. They barely spoke a word to each other, just the occasional 'look!' or 'listen!'

If she seemed sad and distracted, he didn't register it, and when she kept falling behind he simply thought she was tired. He would stop and wait for her, and when she caught him up and looked at him with a sort of reproach, a strange expression on her face, he would ask carefully, knowing how unpleasant such questions can be from a companion,

'You're not tired? We can always rest.'

'Not at all,' she would answer hurriedly. 'I was just... in a dream.'

'I see,' he answered then and carried on, but at a slower pace.

The sun was lower in the sky, and only the snow at the top of the hills still shone, the woods, valleys and ravines were already deep in grey shadow, and the two small figures kept moving through the boundless white of the field and the forest, he in front and her behind, and he liked listening out for the rustling of snow beneath her skis and the scratch of her ski poles on the snow.

Once, in the pink glow beyond the trees where the sun had already set, the even growl of an engine could be heard and a plane appeared high in the air a moment later. The plane was the only thing still illuminated, the sun flashed on the fuselage, and it was a good sight from down below in the silence and twilit frost, and good, too, to wonder about the passengers sitting up there and thinking about the end of their journey, Moscow, and who would be there to meet them.

At last they arrived in near darkness. They stamped their icy boots on the cold veranda, opened up and went in. It was quite dark inside, and seemed even colder than it was outside. She lay down straightaway and shut her eyes. She was hot and damp from the journey and now she began to cool down and a shudder went through her, she couldn't move. She opened her eyes, saw in the darkness the planked roof, saw the strong flame behind the steamed up glass of the kerosene lamp, pressed her eyes closed and the colours began swirling in her head: yellow-green, white, blue, crimson—all the colours she had seen over and over all that day.

He got firewood out from under the veranda, threw it down with a crash beside the stove, rustled some paper, lit the fire, grunting, and she didn't want anything, she wished she hadn't come with him this time.

The stove heated up, it became warm enough to take off clothes. And he took off his shoes and socks and hung them by the fire and sat in his undershirt, contented, stretching out his toes, his eyes half-closed, smoking a cigarette.

'Are you tired?' he asked. 'Take your clothes off.'

And although she didn't want to move, she wanted just to fall asleep in chagrin and sadness, she got undressed obediently and hung her jacket, socks and sweater to dry, and sat down on the bed wearing only a man's long plaid shirt, her shoulders drooping, and she stared at the lamp.

He stuck his feet back into his shoes, threw on a jacket and took the metal bucket, which rang out like a song from the veranda. When he returned he put the kettle onto the stove, began rummaging in his rucksack, got out everything he had in there and laid it out on the table and the window sill.

She waited silently for tea, poured herself a cup, then sat quietly, chewed some bread and butter, warmed her hands on the hot mug, sipped the tea and still stared at the lamp.

'Why are you so quiet?' he asked. 'What a day it was, eh?'

'I'm... I'm just very tired today...' She stood and stretched without looking at him. 'Time to sleep.'

'Yes, good idea,' he agreed. 'Wait a moment, I'll put some wood ready by the fire, or it'll get cold.'

'I'm going to lie down over here by the fire on my own, if that's alright. You won't be angry?' she spoke rapidly and lowered her eyes.

'What is it?' he said in surprise, and immediately remembered her sad, distant expression that whole day, and then he felt bitter and his heart lurched painfully.

He realized all of a sudden that he really didn't know her, he didn't know much about her studies at university, or who she knew, or what she talked about. She was as mysterious and unknown to him as at their first meeting, and he probably seemed stupid and coarse to her, not understanding her needs, not capable of making her happy always, needing nothing and no one beyond him.

And now the whole day filled him with shame, this poor dacha and stove, and even the frost and the sun, and his sense of calm. Why on earth had they come here, why had it all seemed so important? And where was this cursed happiness everyone praised so?

'Well then,' he said indifferently, and breathed in deeply. 'Sleep where you like.'

Without looking at him, without undressing, she lay down straightaway, covering herself with her jacket, and stared at the fire in the stove. He went to the other bed, sat down on it, lit a cigarette, then he put out the lamp and lay down. The hurt filled him: he could tell she was leaving him. Something always spoiled their chances of happiness, but what it was he couldn't say and it angered him.

After a moment he could hear her crying. He sat up and looked over the table at her. The stove made it fairly light in the room, she was lying on her front, looking at the smouldering firewood and he could see her unhappy face, awash with tears, her pitiful lips and chin, trembling and crooked, her wet eyes, which she kept wiping with her thin little hand.

Why had she suddenly become so unhappy, so weighted down today? She didn't know. She just felt that that period of first love had passed and something new had taken its place, and the life that had gone before no longer interested her. She was fed up of being nobody in front of his family, his parents, his friends and their girlfriends, she wanted to be a wife and a mother, and he couldn't see it. He was quite happy with what they had. But she felt such acute sorrow for the passing of that first stage of their love, full of trepidation, when everything was unclear and indefinite, but strange, passionate and full of a sensation of novelty.

Then she began to fall asleep, and she had her old dream, the story she had always fallen asleep to as a child. In it he was a strong brave man, and he loved her and she loved him, but for some reason she said, 'no!' and he left and travelled to the far north where he became a fisherman, and she pined for him. He went hunting along the sea cliffs, jumping from stone to stone, composing music, going into the sea to catch fish, thinking always of her. And then one day she realized that her only chance of happiness was with him, and she dropped everything and went to him. She was so beautiful that on the way all the men admired her, the pilots and drivers and sailors, but she had eyes only for him. Their meeting would be so extraordinary that it was terrifying even to think of it. And she made up more and more reasons to put off this moment. Usually that was when she fell asleep, without having met up with him.

She hadn't had the dream or anything like it for a long time, but today she wanted to dream a little, for some reason. And even today, when she was on the motorboat on her way, her thoughts began to drift into each other and she fell asleep.

She woke in the night because it was cold. He was crouching, relighting the cold stove. His face was sad, and she felt sorry for him.

In the morning they said nothing at first, they ate breakfast silently and drank their tea. But then they became more cheerful, they took the skis and went skiing. They climbed up to the hills, skied down, choosing increasingly steep slopes and dangerous places.

Back at the dacha they warmed up, made small talk about this and that, what a wonderful winter they were having. And when it began to get dark they packed up, locked the dacha and skied to the station.

They arrived back in Moscow in the evening. They dozed, but when the blocks with their rows of lit windows appeared, and he thought about how they would have to part, he suddenly imagined her as his wife.

Why not? He was no longer very young, that time when everything seems simple, dispensable—a home, a wife, a family—had passed, he was thirty, and the thought that, 'well, there she was next to you and she was all very nice and everything, but you could always leave her for someone else because you were free...' That thought no longer brought him any cheer.

Tomorrow he would spend the whole day in the lawyer's office, writing appeals, declarations, thinking about human misfortune, families in trouble, and then home, to whom? And then the summer, the long summer, all those trips, the canoeing, the tent... and again—with whom? And he so wanted to be better, a better human, and to do everything to make her happy.

When they got to the square outside the station the streetlamps were on, the city roared, and the snow had been cleared and taken away, and they both had the feeling that their trip had not really occurred, that these two days together had not really happened, that now it was time to say goodbye, go their separate ways and they would meet perhaps in a day or two. They both became quite matter-of-fact, calm, easy with it, and they said goodbye as they always did, with a quick smile, and he didn't see her home.

Kashtanka

Anton Chekhov

Chapter One: Bad Behaviour

A young rust-coloured dog—a cross between a dachshund and a mongrel—with a muzzle very like a fox's, ran back and forth along the pavement, looking about anxiously. From time to time she stopped and, whining, lifted up first one frozen paw, then the other, trying to work out how it could have happened that she was lost.

She remembered very well how she had spent the day, and how she had ended up on this unfamiliar stretch of pavement.

The day had begun when her master, the joiner Luka Alexandrych, had put on his hat, put under his arm some wooden thing wrapped in a red scarf and shouted,

'Kashtanka, come on!'

Hearing her name, the dachshund mongrel had come out from under the work bench where she had been sleeping on a pile of shavings, had had a really good stretch and run after her master. Luka Alexandrych's customers lived an awfully long way away, and before he reached them all, the joiner usually had to make several visits to inns to fortify himself. Kashtanka remembered that she had behaved very badly on the way. She had jumped about in joy at being taken out for a walk, barked at the horse-drawn tramcars, run into all the yards and chased dogs. The joiner kept losing sight of her, and he would stop and shout angrily at her. Once, with a rapacious look, he had even seized her fox's ear in his fist, tugged it and spoken, emphasizing each word,

'Bloody... cur... bloody... kill... you... I will!'

Once he had visited his customers, Luka Alexandrych dropped in to see his sister, where he would usually have a drink and a bite to eat; from his sister's he went round to visit a bookbinder he knew, from the bookbinder's he went to an inn and from the inn he went to his godfather and so it went on. In short by the time Kashtanka had reached this unfamiliar stretch of pavement it was already dusk and the joiner was as drunk as a lord. He was waving his arms about, sighing deeply and muttering,

'Born in shin I was in my mother's womb I was. Oh my shins... sins... walking along the street here we are, and all the streetlamps burning... and then we're dead and gone and we'll be burning in the fires of hell...'

Or he would take a kinder tone, calling Kashtanka over and saying,

'You, Kashtanka, you're an insect, no better than an insect. Compared to a person, you're like a carpenter compared to a joiner...'

He was speaking to her like this, when there was a sudden roar of music. Kashtanka looked round and saw a regiment of soldiers bearing down upon her along the street. She couldn't stand music, it worked on her nerves and she began chasing about and howling. To her great surprise the joiner did not seem afraid, nor did he begin yelping and barking, but gave a wide grin, drew himself up and saluted smartly. Seeing her master unprotesting, Kashtanka howled even more and, quite distracted, she dashed across the road to the other pavement.

When she recovered her senses the band was no longer playing and the regiment had gone. She crossed the road to where she had left her master, but alas, the joiner was no longer there. She raced forward, then back again, crossed the road once more, but it was as if the joiner had been swallowed up by the earth...

Kashtanka began sniffing the pavement, hoping to find her master by smelling his traces, but some scoundrel had passed by earlier in a pair of new rubber galoshes and now all the slighter smells were mixed into the sharp rubbery odour and nothing could be made out.

Kashtanka ran back and forth, unable to find her master, and meanwhile it was getting dark, the streetlamps lit up on both sides of the road and lights appeared in the windows of buildings. Large, soft snowflakes were falling, whitewashing the road, the horses' backs and cab drivers' hats, and the darker it became the whiter everything seemed. Unfamiliar customers passed by (for Kashtanka divided all humanity into two unequal groups: owners and customers. There was a significant difference between these groups: the first had the right to beat her, and she had the right to seize the second by the shins), they passed back and forth ceaselessly, obscuring her view and knocking her with their legs. The customers were all hurrying and paid her no attention.

When it got quite dark Kashtanka was gripped by horror and despair. She pressed herself against the entrance to a building and began to cry bitterly. Her day's travels with Luka Alexandrych had exhausted her, her ears and paws were frozen and she was terribly hungry as well. Only twice the whole day had she had something to chew on: at the bookbinder's she had eaten some glue, and in one of the inns she had found the skin of a sausage by the counter—and that was all. If she had been a person she might have reflected, 'I can't live like this. I should shoot myself.'

Chapter Two: A Mysterious Stranger

But she did not reflect, she merely cried. When the soft, feathery snow had completely covered her back and head and in her exhaustion she had fallen into a heavy drowse, the entrance door suddenly clicked, squeaked and hit her on her flank. She jumped up. A person came out, a person of the customer variety, and as Kashtanka yelped and fell straight into his path he could hardly fail to notice her. He bent down to her and asked,

'Where have you come from then, girl?' Did I hurt you? Poor little thing... There, there, don't be angry... It's my fault.'

Kashtanka looked at the stranger through the snow-flakes hanging on her eyelashes and saw before her a short, plump little man with a puffy shaven face, wearing a top hat, and his fur coat flung open.

'Hey, why are you whining?' he continued, knocking the snow off her back with his fingers. 'Where's your owner? You must be lost, is that it? Poor little dog. What are we going to do with you?'

Hearing a warm friendly note in the stranger's voice, Kashtanka licked his hand and whined even more piteously.

'You're a nice little thing, a funny thing,' said the stranger. 'Just like a fox. Well I suppose there's nothing for it, you'd better come with me. Perhaps you'll even come in handy for something or other... Come on then!'

He clicked his tongue and made a gesture which could only mean one thing: let's go. And Kashtanka went.

No more than a half hour later she was sitting on the floor of a large, light room, and, with her head on one side, she was watching the stranger with affection and curiosity as he sat at his table eating dinner. He ate and threw her morsels. First he had given her bread and the green rind of the cheese, then a piece of meat, half a pie, some chicken bones, and she, in her great hunger, had eaten all this so fast that she hadn't even been able to distinguish the separate tastes. And the more she ate, the hungrier she felt.

'Your owners haven't been feeding you very well, have they!' the stranger said, watching her swallow down the pieces without even chewing them in her ravenous hunger. 'What a skinny thing you are! Skin and bones.'

Kashtanka ate a lot, but not her fill, the food only made her feel intoxicated. After dinner she lay out in the middle of the room, stretched her legs, and feeling a very pleasant fatigue throughout her whole body, she wagged her tail. Whilst her new master sprawled in an armchair and smoked a cigar she wagged her tail and settled in her mind the question of whether it was better at the stranger's, or at the joiner's. The stranger had a poor, unattractive set-up: apart from the armchairs, the divan, lamp and carpets there was nothing there, and the room seemed empty. The joiner's flat was completely stuffed with things: he had a table, a workbench, a pile of shavings, planes, chisels, saws, a cage with a siskin in it, a tub... The stranger's home smelt of nothing, but there was always a fug in the joiner's flat, and a wonderful smell of glue, varnish and wood shavings. Still the stranger had one very important point in his favour: he fed her well, and in all justice Kashtanka had to concede that when she had sat before the table and gazed at him tenderly, he hadn't hit her once, or kicked her, nor had he shouted, 'Get out of it, you cur!'

Her new master finished smoking his cigar and went out, and in a minute he returned, carrying a little mattress.

'Hey, come on girl, this way!' he said, putting the mattress down in the corner by the divan. 'Lie down here. Go to sleep!'

Then he put out the lamp and went out. Kashtanka stretched out on the mattress and closed her eyes. From the street came a barking, and she wanted to answer it, but all of a sudden and quite unexpectedly she was over-whelmed by sadness. She remembered Luka Alexandrych,

his son Fedyushka, the cosy spot beneath the workbench...
She remembered how, during the long winter evenings,
when the joiner was planing, or reading the paper aloud,
Fedyushka used to play with her. He would pull her out
from under the bench by her front paws and make her do
such tricks, that she saw stars and her whole body ached.
He made her walk on her hind legs, or he pretended she
was a bell by tugging on her tail so hard that she began
yelping and barking, or he would give her tobacco to sniff.
But this next trick was the most painful: Fedyushka would
tie a piece of meat to a thread and give it to Kashtanka,
and then, when she had swallowed it, he would pull it back
out of her stomach with loud laughing. And the more
vivid the memories, the louder and sadder grew Kashtanka's whining.

But soon her exhaustion and the warmth overcame her
sadness. She began to fall asleep. In her imagination dogs
were running about—and running amongst them was
the shaggy old poodle she had seen that day on the street,
with one white eye and clumps of fur around its snout.
Fedyushka, with a gouge in his hand, was chasing the
poodle, and then all of a sudden was himself covered with
shaggy fur; barking happily he appeared by Kashtanka's
side. He and Kashtanka sniffed at each other's noses in a
friendly manner and ran out onto the street...

Chapter Three: A New, Very Pleasant Acquaintance

When Kashtanka awoke it was already light and the sort of noise came from the street that you only hear during the day. There was not a soul in the room. Kashtanka stretched, yawned, and angry and morose, trod a path around the room. She sniffed all the corners and the furniture, she glanced into the hallway, but found nothing of interest. Apart from the door into the hallway there was one other door. After a moment's thought, Kashtanka scratched at it with both paws, opened it, and went into the next room. There on the bed, covered in a felt blanket, lay a customer asleep, in whom she recognized yesterday's stranger.

'Gggrrr...' she growled, but then, remembering yesterday's meal, she wagged her tail and began sniffing about.

She sniffed at the stranger's clothes and boots and found that they smelt strongly of horse. Another door led out of the bedroom, and it was shut too. Kashtanka scratched at this door, pushed on it with her whole chest, opened it and immediately smelt something strange and very suspicious. Anticipating something unpleasant, Kashtanka, growling and looking about her, went into the small room with its dirty wallpaper, and then fell back in fear. She saw something both unexpected and terrifying. A hissing grey goose, its head and neck pressed down to the ground, its wings spread wide came right at her. A little to the side, a white cat lay on a mattress; when it saw Kashtanka it jumped up, and arched its back, its tail shot out, its fur stood up on end and it began hissing too. The dog was seriously frightened, but not wishing to show her fear, she barked loudly and rushed at the cat. The cat arched its back even higher, hissed and hit Kashtanka on the head with a paw. Kashtanka leaped back, crouched down on her four paws, and stretching her snout towards the cat, she barked and barked, loudly and shrilly; just then the goose came up from behind and gave her a painful shove on the back with its beak. Kashtanka jumped up and rushed at the goose...

'What's all this?' rang out a loud angry voice, and the stranger came into the room in a dressing gown, with a cigar between his teeth. 'What's all this about? Back to your places!'

He went to the cat, flicked him on his arched back and said,

'Fedor Timofeich, what's all this then? Have you been starting a fight? You old rascal! Lie down.'

And turning to the goose he shouted,

'Ivan Ivanych, back to your place!'

The cat lay down on his mattress obediently and closed his eyes. Judging by the expression on his face and whiskers, he was himself not best pleased that he had lost his head and got into a fight. Kashtanka whined in a hurt manner and the goose stretched out his neck and began talking fast, heatedly and very distinctly but entirely incomprehensibly.

'Indeed, indeed,' said their master, yawning. 'Peace and harmony is what we're after.' He stroked Kashtanka and continued, 'Now don't be scared, my little fox... You're in good company, they won't hurt you. But wait a moment, what are we going to call you? We can't have you going without a name.'

The stranger thought a little and then said,

'I know. You can be Tyotka. Understand? Tyotka!'

And after repeating the word 'Tyotka' a few times he went out. Kashtanka sat down and began watching. The cat lay motionless on the mattress, pretending to be asleep. The goose, stretching out his neck and stamping up and down on the spot, continued to talk rapidly and heatedly. It was clearly a very clever goose: after a particularly long tirade he would step backwards in surprise, as if admiring his own speech... Listening to him, and answering 'Rrrrr', Kashtanka began sniffing in the corners. In one of the corners was a little trough in which she saw some soaked peas and some dampened crusts of black bread. She tried the peas, but they didn't taste good, she tried the crusts and began to eat. The goose was not in the least offended that a strange dog was eating his food, but actually began talking even more heatedly and, to show his trust, came up to the trough and ate a few peas.

Chapter Four: Small Wonders

A little while later the stranger came back into the room, carrying an odd-looking thing in the shape of a door-frame, or the letter П. On the cross-bar of this wooden clumsily-made shape hung a bell, and a pistol was attached. A piece of string hung from the bell's clapper, and the trigger of the gun. The stranger placed the structure in the centre of the room, spent a long time untying something, and then tying it back up, then looked at the goose and said,

'Ivan Ivanych, please.'

The goose went to him and stopped expectantly.

'Well,' said the stranger, 'we'll start right at the beginning. First of all a bow and a curtsey. Quick sharp!'

Ivan Ivanych stretched out his neck, nodded in all directions and pawed at the ground.

'Good boy! Now die!'

The goose lay on his back and stuck his feet in the air. After a few more such antics, the stranger suddenly clutched his head, put on an expression of horror and shouted,

'Help! Fire! We're on fire!'

Ivan Ivanych ran over to the wooden cross-bar, took the string in his beak and rang the bell.

The stranger was very pleased. He stroked the goose on the neck and said,

'Good boy, Ivan Ivanych. Now, imagine that you're a jeweller and you sell gold and diamonds. And now imagine that you arrive at your shop and you find some thieves in it. What would you do in a situation like that?'

The goose took the other piece of string in his beak and tugged it, and immediately a deafening shot rang out. Kashtanka liked the ringing bell a great deal, but she was so delighted by the shot that she began running round the wooden shape and barking.

'Tyotka, back to your place!' The stranger shouted at her, 'Quiet!'

Ivan Ivanych's work was not done with the shot. For a whole hour more the stranger made him run round in a circle on a piece of cord, whilst he cracked a whip. And if that were not enough, the goose had to leap over a little jump and through a hoop and sit up and beg—on his tail, that is, waving with his feet. Kashtanka did not take her eyes off Ivan Ivanych, she howled with delight, and once or twice even took up chasing him with a loud bark. When he and the goose were quite exhausted, the stranger wiped the sweat from his brow and shouted,

'Marya, call up Khavronya Ivanovna!'

After a minute a squealing could be heard... Kashtanka began growling, put on a very brave expression, and slunk nearer to the stranger, just in case. The door opened, an old woman looked in, said something, and then let in a very ugly black pig. The pig took not the slightest bit of notice of Kashtanka's growl, but lifted its little snout high and squealed merrily. She was clearly very pleased to see her owner, the cat and Ivan Ivanych. When she went over to the cat and nudged him gently on the belly with her snout, and then exchanged a few comments on some matter with the goose, a warm friendliness could be felt in her movements, her voice and the quivering of her tail. Kashtanka immediately realized that growling and barking at such creatures was quite pointless.

The owner removed the wooden shape and shouted,

'Fedor Timofeich, please!'

The cat got up, stretched lazily, and went unwillingly over to the pig, as if he were performing a great favour.

'Well then, let's start with the Egyptian Pyramid!' said the stranger.

He spent a long time explaining something and then gave the command:

'One, two, three!' At 'three' Ivan Ivanych stretched out his wings and jumped up onto the pig's back. He found his balance, using his wings and neck, and once he had settled on the bristly back, Fedor Timofeich, listlessly and lazily, with obvious disdain, and looking as though he despised his art and thought it negligible, climbed up onto the pig's back, and then reluctantly up onto the goose where he sat up and begged. This was what the stranger had called this 'Egyptian Pyramid'. Kashtanka yelped with delight, but at the same time the old cat yawned, lost his balance and fell off the goose. Ivan Ivanych staggered and fell, too. The stranger shouted, waved his arms and began explaining something again. A whole hour was spent on the pyramid, and their indefatigable owner then began teaching Ivan Ivanych how to ride on the cat, and then started teaching the cat how to smoke, and so on.

The lesson ended with the stranger wiping the sweat from his brow and leaving the room. Fedor Timofeich snorted contemptuously, lay down on his little mattress and closed his eyes. Ivan Ivanych went to his trough, and the pig was led away by the old woman. After so many new impressions, Kashtanka barely noticed the day passing and in the evening she and her little mattress were already placed in the little room with the dirty wallpaper and she passed the night in the company of Fedor Timofeich and the goose.

Chapter Five: Real Talent

A month passed.

Kashtanka was already used to being fed a delicious meal every evening and being called Tyotka. She was also used to the stranger and her new companions. The days slid past like butter in the pan.

Every day began in the same way. Ivan Ivanych usually woke up first and went straight over to Tyotka or the cat, stretched out his neck and began to talk heatedly and persuasively, but as incomprehensibly as before.

Sometimes he lifted his head high and spoke long monologues. In the first days of their acquaintance Kashtanka thought that he spoke so much because he was very clever, but after a while she lost all her respect for him—when he approached her with his long speeches she no longer wagged her tail, but treated him like an annoying chatterbox who wouldn't let anyone sleep, and she answered him very unceremoniously with a Grrrrr.

Fedor Timofeich now, was quite another sort of gentleman. When he awoke he made no sound, barely stirred and didn't even open his eyes. He would willingly have stayed asleep, because it was quite clear he had little love of life. Nothing interested him, he had the same weary disdain for everything, he despised it all, and even ate his delicious dinner with a contemptuous snort.

When Kashtanka woke up she began inspecting the rooms, sniffing the corners. Only she and the cat had the run of the whole apartment. The goose was not allowed to cross the threshold of the room with dirty wallpaper and Khavroniya Ivanovna lived somewhere out in the yard in a sty and only appeared at lesson time. Their owner woke up late and once he'd drunk his tea he would immediately begin his tricks. Every day the wooden shape, the whip and the hoops were brought into the room and every day they went over one and the same thing, more or less. The lesson lasted about three or four hours, so that sometimes Fedor Timofeich staggered like a drunkard with exhaustion, Ivan Ivanych opened his beak and panted, and their owner went pink in the face, and couldn't keep up with wiping all the sweat from his brow.

The lessons and the dinners made the days interesting, but the evenings were fairly boring. Usually their owner would go out in the evenings, and take the goose and the cat with him. Left alone, Tyotka would lie down on her mattress and mope... The sad feeling crept up on her almost without her noticing and came over her slowly, like the twilight in the rooms. It began with the dog losing all desire to bark, eat, run about, or even look around, then shadowy figures would appear in her imagination, neither dog, nor yet human, with kindly, nice but indistinct faces. When they appeared Tyotka would wag her tail and it seemed to her that she had seen then once before and loved them... And as she fell asleep she always had the feeling that these figures gave off a smell of glue, varnish and wood shavings.

Tyotka had become completely accustomed to her new life, and had been transformed from a skinny bag of bones to a sleek and well-fed dog, when her owner one day stroked her before the lesson and said,

'Time to get down to work, Tyotka. You've been playing around long enough now. I'm going to turn you into an *artiste*. How would you like to be an *artiste*?'

And he began to teach her different skills. In the first lesson she learnt to stand and walk on her back legs—and she liked it terribly. In the second lesson she had to jump up on her back legs and seize some sugar that her teacher held high above her head. Then, at later lessons, she danced, ran on a long lead, howled to music, rang the bell, shot the gun, and after a month was quite comfortably able to replace Fedor Timofeich in the 'Egyptian Pyramid'. She was a willing pupil and she was pleased with her successes: running around on the long lead with her tongue hanging out, jumping through the hoop, riding old Fedor Timofeich—all these gave her the greatest pleasure. Every successful trick was accompanied by loud and delighted barks, and her teacher was amazed, he was delighted too, and he rubbed his hands.

'You've got talent.' he said. 'Real talent. You'll be a definite success!'

And Tyotka grew so used to the word 'talent', that whenever her owner said it, she would jump up and look round, as if it were her name.

Chapter Six: A Night of Disquiet

Tyotka dreamed a doggy dream: a sweeper was chasing her with his broom, and she woke up in fear.

It was quiet, dark and very stuffy in the room. The fleas were biting her. Tyotka had never before been afraid of the dark, but now for some reason she was terrified and wanted to bark. In the next room her owner sighed loudly, and then, a little later, the pig snorted out in its sty, and then everything was quiet again. The thought of food always calms the spirit, and Tyotka began thinking about how she had stolen a chicken claw from Fedor Timofeich that day and hidden it in the living room, behind the dresser, where there were a lot of cobwebs and dust. It wouldn't hurt to go and have a quick look: was that chicken claw still whole or not? It was very likely that their owner had found it and eaten it. But she mustn't leave the room before morning, that was the rule. Tyotka shut her eyes so she would fall asleep soon, as she knew from experience that the quicker she went to sleep, the quicker the morning came. But suddenly there was a strange cry from close by which made her shudder and jump up on all her four paws. It was Ivan Ivanych crying out, and his cry was not talkative and confident as it usually was, but somehow wild, piercing and unnatural, like the squeak of a gate opening. Unable to make anything out in the darkness and uncomprehending, Tyotka felt even more fearful and she growled,

'Gggrrrr.'

Some time passed, the time it might have taken to chew a good bone; the cry was not repeated. Little by little Tyotka calmed down and then dozed off. In her dreams she saw two big black dogs with clumps of last year's fur on their sides and haunches. They ate scraps hungrily from a large trough, from which rose white steam and a very good smell; they glanced round at Tyotka occasionally, showed their teeth and growled: *you're not having any!* But a man came running out of the house wearing a fur coat and carrying a whip and he chased them off. And then Tyotka came to the trough and ate, but as soon as the man had left through the gates, both the black dogs attacked her with a roar, and suddenly again there was a piercing cry.

'Kkkgggg! Kkgg!' cried Ivan Ivanych.

Tyotka woke, jumped up and without leaving her mattress she started howling. By now it seemed to her as if it were not Ivan Ivanych crying out, but someone else, someone quite apart. And for some reason, the pig snorted again out in the sty.

Now there was the sound of shoes shuffling and their owner came into the room in a dressing gown and carrying a candle. The flickering light played across the dirty wallpaper and the ceiling and chased away the dark. Tyotka saw that there was no one else in the room with them. Ivan Ivanych was sitting on the floor quite awake. His wings were spread out and his beak was open and he looked as if he was very weary and wanted a drink. Old Fedor Timofeich was not sleeping either. He must have been woken by the cry too.

'Ivan Ivanych, what's wrong?' their owner asked the goose. 'Why are you crying? Are you ill?'

The goose was silent. Their owner touched him on the neck, stroked his back and said,

'Funny animal. You can't sleep, so you don't want anyone else to.'

When their owner had gone out and taken the candle with him, the darkness returned. Tyotka was scared. The goose did not cry out, but once again she felt as if a stranger was standing there in the darkness. The most frightening thing was that she couldn't even bite this stranger because he was invisible and shapeless.

And for some reason she thought that something very bad was sure to happen. Fedor Timofeich was restless too. Tyotka could hear him moving on his mattress, yawning and shaking his head.

Somewhere on the street someone banged at a gate, and the pig snorted in her sty. Tyotka whined, stretched out her front paws and lay her head on them. The banging on the gate, the snorting of the strangely sleepless pig, the darkness and the quiet seemed to her to be just as eerie and frightful as Ivan Ivanych's cry. Everything seemed restless, uneasy—but why? Who was this stranger who couldn't be seen? And now, right beside Tyotka, two muted green sparks flashed for a moment. For the first time in the whole of their acquaintance Fedor Timofeich had come over to her. What did he want? Tyotka licked his paw, and without asking what he wanted, she began howling softly, the pitch ever-changing.

'Kkkgg!' cried Ivan Ivanych. 'Kkkggg!'

The door opened once more and their owner came in with a candle. The goose was sitting just as before, with his beak wide open and his wings stretched out. His eyes were shut.

'Ivan Ivanych,' called their owner.

The goose did not move. Their owner sat down on the floor in front of him, stared at him for a minute silently and said,

'Ivan Ivanych. What is this? Are you dying, is that it? Oh! Now I remember. Yes!' he screamed out and seized his head in his hands. 'I know why this is. It's because the horse stepped on you today. Oh Lord. Lord.'

Tyotka didn't understand what her owner was saying but she saw in his face that he was expecting something terrible. She stretched her snout towards the dark window, where, it seemed to her, something strange was looking in, and she howled.

'He's dying, Tyotka.' said their owner and flung up his hands. 'Yes, he's dying. Death has come, come into this room. What can we do?'

Their pale and agitated owner, sighing and shaking his head, went back to his room. Tyotka was terrified by the thought of remaining in the darkness and she followed him. He sat on his bed and repeated a few times,

'Oh Lord, what can we do?'

Tyotka pattered about by his feet, not understanding her own sadness, nor why they were all so restless, but in her attempt to understand she followed his every movement. Fedor Timofeich, who rarely left his mattress, came in to his owner's room too and began rubbing himself against his owner's legs. He shook his head as if he wished to shake off his heavy thoughts, and looked suspiciously under the bed.

Their owner took a saucer and poured water into it from a hand basin and went back to the goose.

'Drink, Ivan Ivanych,' he said gently, putting the saucer down in front of him. 'Drink it up, my friend.'

But Ivan Ivanych didn't move and didn't open his eyes. His owner bent his neck down towards the saucer so the beak was in the water, but the goose did not drink, he opened his wings even wider, and his head lay in the saucer.

'No there's nothing more to be done,' their owner sighed. 'It's all over. Ivan Ivanych is done for.'

And shining drops slid down his cheeks, like the ones that slide down window panes when it rains. Tyotka and Fedor Timofeich pressed close to him, not understanding what was the matter, and staring with horror at the goose.

'Poor Ivan Ivanych,' said their owner, sighing sorrowfully. 'And there I was, dreaming of taking you to the dacha in the spring and taking you for walks in the green grass. Sweet creature, my good friend, and now you've gone! How will I manage without you?'

To Tyotka it seemed that the same thing would happen to her, that she too, for some unknown reason, would close her eyes, stretch out her paws, stretch her mouth, and everyone would look at her with horror. It seemed that the same thought was going through Fedor Timofeich's head. The old cat had never looked so grim and gloomy as he did now.

Dawn was breaking, and that invisible stranger who had so frightened Tyotka was no longer in the room. When it was quite light the caretaker came and took the goose by the feet and carried it off somewhere. And a little later the old woman came and took away the little trough.

Tyotka went into the dining room and looked behind the dresser. Their owner hadn't eaten the chicken claw, it lay in its place in the dust and cobwebs. But Tyotka felt sad and empty and she wanted to cry. She didn't even sniff the claw, instead she went under the divan, sat there and began whining quietly.

Sku... sku... sku...

Chapter Seven: An Unsuccessful Debut

One fine evening their owner came into the room with the dirty wallpaper and rubbing his hands said,

'Well then.'

He wanted to say something more but he didn't, he went out. Tyotka who had studied his face and intonation intently during their lessons, could tell that he was agitated, troubled and, it seemed, angry. After a little while he returned, and said,

'Today I'm taking Tyotka and Fedor Timofeich. You, Tyotka, will replace Ivan Ivanych in the Egyptian Pyramid. What a mess! Nothing ready, nothing learnt, not enough rehearsals! It'll be a disgrace! A miserable failure!'

Then he went back out and after a minute came back in his fur coat and top hat. Going over to the cat he took him by the front paws, lifted him and tucked him into the breast of his coat. Fedor Timofeich seemed entirely indifferent and did not even bother to open his eyes. It was clearly all the same to him whether he lay there, or was lifted by the paws, whether he sprawled on his mattress or was curled up at his master's breast under the fur coat.

'Come on Tyotka,' said their owner.

Bewildered, but wagging her tail, Tyotka followed him. After just a minute she was sitting at his feet in the sledge and could hear him, huddled with cold and nervousness, muttering,

'It'll be a disgrace! A miserable failure!'

The sledge stopped by a large strange building, like an up-ended soup tureen. The long entrance to the building, with three glass doors, was lit by a dozen bright lights. The doors opened with a clang, and like mouths they swallowed the people darting about by the entrance. There were lots of people and even horses frequently came trotting up to the doors, but there no dogs to be seen.

Their owner picked Tyotka up and tucked him into the fur coat at his breast, to join Fedor Timofeich. Here it was dark, and stuffy, but warm. Two green sparks flashed for a second—this was the cat opening his eyes, upset by the dog's cold, hard paws. Tyotka licked his ear, and trying to settle more comfortably, shifted about, pressed on him with her cold paws and her head stuck up suddenly out of the coat. She immediately growled angrily and dived down under the coat. She thought she had seen a huge, dimly lit room, full of monsters. From behind the partition walls and cage doors stretching down both sides of the room, peered terrifying faces: horses' heads, horned and long-eared faces, and one particular great enormous head with a tail in place of a nose, and two long bones, chewed clean, sticking out of its mouth.

The cat had just begun mewing hoarsely under Tyotka's paws, when the fur coat suddenly flew open, their owner said, 'down you go!' and Fedor Timofeich and Tyotka jumped down to the ground. They had reached a small room with grey boarded walls. Apart from a small table with a mirror on it, a stool and some cloth hanging in the corners, there was no furniture in here, and instead of lamps or candles, there was a bright fan-shaped light fixed to a pipe coming out of the wall. Fedor Timofeich licked his coat, which had been ruffled by Tyotka, went under the stool and lay down. Their owner, still very nervous and rubbing his hands, began to get undressed. He got undressed in the same way that he usually got undressed at home, ready to lie down under the felt blanket—that is, he took off all his clothes except his underclothes, and then he sat down on the stool and looking in the mirror, he began to do the most extraordinary things to himself.

First of all he put on a wig with a parting and two curling points of hair, which looked like horns, then he smeared something white thickly onto his face, and over the white paint he drew brows, a moustache and red cheeks. This was not all: once his face and neck had been smeared, he began to dress himself in a strange and entirely peculiar costume. Tyotka had never seen anything like it, not in any house, nor out on the street. Imagine the widest pantaloons, sewn from chintz patterned with large flowers—the sort used for curtains and upholstery in bourgeois households. Pantaloons which tied up under the armpits. One leg was made from brown chintz and the other was bright yellow. After immersing himself in these, their owner then put on a jacket of the same material with a large collar, all points at the edge, and a gold star on the back; stockings of many colours and green slippers.

The colours swam before Tyotka's eyes and troubled her soul. The white-faced baggy-looking creature smelt of her owner, it had a familiar voice—their owner's voice, but there were moments when Tyotka was beset by doubt, and then she wanted to run away from the brightly-clad creature and bark. This new place, the fan-shaped light, the smell, the metamorphosis which her owner had undergone—all this put in her an unidentifiable fear, and a foreboding that she was about to meet with some horror like the fat-faced creature with the tail in place of a nose. And somewhere outside the room, far off, hateful music was playing as well, and from time to time she could hear an inexplicable roaring. The only thing that calmed her was the imperturbable Fedor Timofeich. He dozed in the most placid way under the stool and did not open his eyes, even when the stool moved.

A man in a tailcoat and white waistcoat looked in the room and said,

'Miss Arabella's on now. Then you're next.'

Their owner said nothing. He pulled a small suitcase out from under the table, sat down and waited. It was clear from his lips and hands that he was anxious, and Tyotka could hear the trembling of his breath.

'Mr George please!' shouted someone from outside the door.

Their owner stood, crossed himself three times, then pulled the cat out from under the stool and put it into the suitcase.

'Come on, Tyotka,' he said quietly.

Tyotka, quite bewildered, came to his arms. He kissed her on the head and put her in the suitcase next to Fedor Timofeich. Then it went dark. Tyotka stamped on the cat, scratched the walls of the suitcase and in her horror she was unable to utter a sound. The suitcase meanwhile bobbed about like a boat and shook.

'Here I come!' shouted their owner loudly. 'Here I come!'

After this shouting Tyotka felt the suitcase hit some-thing hard and it stopped moving. There was a loud and full-throated roar and the sound of something being pat-ted and clapped—probably the face with the tail instead of a nose—and it roared and guffawed so loudly that the catches on the suitcase rattled. In answer to this roar, their owner laughed in a piercing, screeching way he had never laughed at home.

'Ha!' he shouted, trying to make himself heard above the roaring. 'Ladies and Gentlemen, boys and girls, I've just come straight from the railway station. Grandma's popped her clogs and she's left me something in her will! Something very heavy in this case! Must be gold! Haa! What if there's a million in here? Let's open it up and have a look!'

The catch on the suitcase clicked. A bright light struck Tyotka full in the eyes: she jumped right out of the suitcase and, deafened by the roaring, she ran as fast as she could round and round her owner, barking shrilly.

'Ha!' shouted their owner. 'Uncle Fedor Timofeich and dear Auntie Tyotka! My dear relatives, curse the lot of you!'

He fell on his belly in the sand, seized Tyotka and the cat and hugged them. Tyotka, squeezed in his embrace, surveyed in an instant the world fate had brought her to, and froze for a moment in wonder and excitement, overcome by its grandeur. Then she tore free of her owner's embrace and ran round and round on the spot like a wolfcub, so intense were her impressions. The new world was huge and full of bright light; wherever she looked, everywhere, from the floor to the ceiling, all she could see were faces, faces, faces, and nothing else.

'Tyotka, sit down please!' shouted her owner.

Remembering what this meant, Tyotka jumped up on a chair and sat down. She looked at her owner. His eyes, as always, had a gentle and serious look in them, but his face, especially his mouth and teeth, were distorted by a wide and rigid smile. He laughed, leaped about, twitched his shoulders and pretended that he was having lots of fun in the presence of these thousands of faces. Tyotka believed in his merrymaking, she suddenly felt with all her body that the thousands of faces were looking at her and she lifted her fox's face and howled with joy.

'You stay sitting there, Auntie,' said her owner, 'and the old man and I will dance a jig.'

Fedor Timofeich was standing, waiting for the moment when he would be made to do silly tricks, and glancing indifferently around. He danced wearily, glumly, without much care, and it was clear from his movements, his tail and whiskers, that he had utter contempt for the crowds, the bright lights and his owner, and himself. Once he had danced his bit he sat down and yawned.

'Well then, Tyotka,' said their owner. 'We'll have a little song together, and then we'll dance. Alright?'

He took a little pipe out of his pocket and began to play on it. Tyotka couldn't bear the music and she moved restlessly on her chair and began to howl. From all sides came roars and applause. Their owner bowed and when everyone had quietened he continued to play. Just as he played a very high note, there was a loud gasp somewhere towards the top of the auditorium.

'Da!' shouted a child's voice. 'That's our Kashtanka there!'

'So it is!' affirmed a drunk and quavering tenor. 'Kashtanka! Fedushka, well I'll be blowed, it's Kashtanka! Here, girl!'

There was a whistle from the gallery and two voices, a child's voice and a man's, called,

'Kashtanka! Kashtanka!'

Tyotka shuddered and looked up to where they were shouting. Two faces, one hairy, drunk and smirking, the other puffy, red-cheeked and frightened, struck her full in the eyes, just as the bright light had struck her before.

It all came back to her, she dropped down from her chair and crouched in the sand, then she leaped up and with joyful yelps she rushed towards these faces. There was a deafening roar and through it came a whistle and a child's high-pitched cry,

'Kashtanka! Kashtanka!'

Tyotka jumped over the barrier and then, jumping over someone's shoulder, she found herself in the stalls. To get up to the next level she needed to climb over a high wall; Tyotka jumped, but not high enough, and she slid back down the wall. Then she was passed from hand to hand, licking hands and faces, moving higher and higher until at last she reached the gallery.

Half an hour later Kashtanka was walking along the street behind two people who smelt of glue and varnish. Luka Alexandrych was staggering, and instinctively, through long experience, was attempting to stay as far away as possible from the gutters.

'In the depths of sin, I am, in the womb...' he muttered. 'See—you Kashtanka... you beat me, you do... Compared to a person you're no better than a carpenter is compared to a joiner.'

Fedyusha walked alongside him in his father's cap. Kashtanka looked up at their backs, and it felt to her as if she had been following them now for a long time and she was happy that there had been no break in her life, not even for an instant.

She remembered the room with the dirty wallpaper, the goose and Fedor Timofeich, the delicious meals, the lessons, the circus, but it all seemed to her now like a long, confused and heavy dream...

The Red Gates

Yury Koval

My brother Borya, my dear brother Borya, and I, were rowing a boat down the Sestra river.

I was idle. I sat at the back of the boat, dangling my bare feet, kicking gently at the still-moving bream, which we'd baited with semolina. The still-moving bream shifted by my feet in the water, which always collects in any boat worth its salt.

I was idle, kicking at the still-moving bream, but my brother Borya, my dear brother, was leaning on the oars with all his might.

Borya was in a rush, Borya was in a hurry, he was afraid of missing the bus.

At the place where the Sestra passes under the canal— that most remarkable place where the river and the canal cross, and the canal and the bed of the canal, all housed in concrete, pass over the living river—at that very place I saw a small white dog on the riverbank.

The dog was running along the bank, and Borya and I were rowing down the river.

I was idle, Borya was hurrying, and the little dog was running along.

On a whim, for no other reason than that I had nothing to do, I beckoned to the dog with my finger and then pursed my lips and made that special doggy sound, that sound that people always use to call dogs. It would be quite a job to write it down, it's pretty much like a big smacking kiss. If you were to try and write it down, it might look like this: *ptsoo-ptsoo*.

So I made this ridiculous *ptsoo-ptsoo* sound, sitting all the while idly at the back of the boat.

The small white dog heard this indescribable sound, looked at me from the riverbank, and then suddenly jumped into the water.

How could I have known that would happen?

I made that ridiculous *ptsoo-ptsoo* sound in an ironic way, a humorous sort of way. I called the dog knowing full well that it couldn't get to me. The very *ptsoo-ptsoo* of the sound made the difference in our circumstances quite clear: I was in a boat, and the dog was on the bank. We were separated by the abyss—the river water. No ordinary dog would have jumped into the water, not without having been pushed by its owner.

But the little white dog was no ordinary dog. It jumped in at the first invitation and crossed the abyss without a second's thought. It swam towards me. When it reached the boat I grabbed it by the scruff of the neck and pulled it in. The little white dog stood amongst the half-dead bream and gave itself a mighty shake.

My brother Borya let go of the oars. He knew he had to say something. But he was silent. He didn't know what to say. My unwarranted *ptsoo-ptsoo*, the dog's reaction, the swim, the dragging it out by the scruff of the neck, the mighty shake—it had all happened in an instant.

Borya didn't know what to say, but he knew he had to say something. An older brother always has to say something in a situation like this. I don't know what other older brothers would have said in a situation like this, but my genius brother didn't think for long.

Looking the dog over gravely, he pronounced,

'Smooth-haired fox terrier.'

My brother Borya was in a rush, Borya was in a hurry.

In an instant we had steered the boat over to where its owner stood on the bank, handed over three roubles, and in another instant we had added a rouble, tied our rods together and thrown our bream into a sack.

And now we were running to catch the bus. The little white dog ran along behind us.

The bus came rushing down the road, we ran along the track. We and the bus would meet at a certain point where a crowd had already gathered. This point was called Karmanovo.

The bus got there before us. It was waiting there and we were still running, but the kindly driver saw us running along, and he was in no hurry to be off.

We ran up, we leaped into the bus, we threw down our rucksacks, we made ourselves comfortable on those very particular springy bus seats, we settled ourselves, and all the other passengers settled themselves, and we were ready to leave.

But the driver was in no hurry. He might have been having a smoke.

I looked through the open doors and saw out there, on the edge of the road, the little white dog Borya had given such precise name to.

It was looking into the bus. The driver was taking his time, or having a smoke. We had already thrown down our rucksacks; we were sitting on those very particular springy bus seats. We were wiping the sudden sweat. Borya was no longer hurrying. He was on the bus. The driver was still smoking. The dog stood looking into the bus at me.

And then for no reason, out of boredom really, I made that same unwarranted and indescribable noise with my lips, that same *ptsoo-ptsoo* I've already mentioned.

The small white dog charged onto the bus and in an instant had hidden itself under the very particular springy bus seat I was sitting on, and had crept close to my legs.

The bus passengers noticed, but pretended not to. The driver lit up again and the doors shut and we were off.

My brother Borya felt the need to say something. He was amazed by my second unwarranted *ptsoo-ptsoo*, which had led to this state of affairs. He was amazed by the behaviour of the little white dog sitting by my feet under the very particular springy bus seat.

My brother Borya, my only brother, spoke.

'Smooth-haired fox terriers,' he said, 'are not as common as wire-haired fox terriers.'

Borya said nothing more all the while we bumped along in the bus. For a long time he remained the author of these two phrases of genius.

But when we got into the train at Dmitrov, and the little white dog had settled by my feet under one of those very particular wooden train seats, Borya asked a question of lesser genius.

At first I didn't even hear him, I hoped he wasn't going to repeat it. I thought he knew that there was no place for questions of lesser genius in his life.

But funny old Borya did repeat it.

'What will Dad say?' he asked again.

Everyone knew what Dad would say of course. I knew, and my brother Borya knew. All the inhabitants of our block at Krasniye Vorota knew what Dad would say.

My father, my dear father, who has long since departed this world, did not like pets. He didn't like any animals, except horses, of course. He adored horses, and his love of horses had occupied all the room in his heart for other animals. He liked no other domestic animal, and he especially hated pigs.

My father in his youth, his far distant rural youth, when he hardly even knew what a town was, back then my father owned horses.

Well of course he didn't own them himself, his father, my grandfather, owned them. But my father grazed these horses and led them to pasture at night. He would lead them out of the village and into the woods or the meadows to graze, and at dawn he would lead them back to the village. He was not meant to sleep when he did this, he was supposed to be watching over the horses, but he longed to sleep.

So he would tie the horses to a rope, and tie the other end around his wrists and he would go to sleep like this, and the horses would graze, and drag my father about the meadows and pastures. And he slept. He even liked to sleep like that, on the grass, with grazing horses dragging him along on a rope.

But one day he woke and pulled on the rope, and although the horses were surely there, they were standing very stiffly. So he rubbed his eyes, took hold of the rope and followed it, hand over hand, towards the horses. And he saw that the rope had been tied to an oak tree and the horses weren't there. The horses were gone, stolen by gypsies, and the gypsies had tied the rope to the oak whilst my father slept on the grass.

This episode proved fateful for my father.

The horses were lost, and my father, who was still very young, took fright. Two horses, breadwinners for an enormous family, were gone, and my father was not brave enough to appear before his father, my grandfather. He ran away and after long travels reached Moscow, where he met my Mother.

Later on my father was forgiven, and he tried to help my grandfather from Moscow, but all the same there was no going back. No help from Moscow could ever replace those two horses, breadwinners for an enormous family.

And so my father liked no domestic animals, and he especially hated pigs. He adored horses, but he no longer had the right to adore them from close up, he adored them at a distance. His heart was gladdened by the sight of the mounted police riding through the Moscow streets.

My Father laughed with joy when he saw the mounted police. He was amazed: the police, horses, they just didn't belong together. But there they were on the Moscow streets, and particularly when CDKA were playing a match against Dinamo. Then there were, for some reason, an awful lot of policemen on horseback.

When Spartak played Torpedo there were never any mounted police. And no one in Moscow knew why this was.

My father adored horses. There was room for no other animal in his heart, and everybody knew what my father would say when he saw the little white dog. The little white dog he hadn't yet seen, which sat close by my feet on the train from Dmitrov to Moscow.

My father said nothing. It was almost as if he hadn't noticed the little white dog. He was astonished by the astonishing things that were going on back then in the world. And he was astonished by the things that were going on in our family.

Astonished by all these things my father didn't even notice the white dog. Or rather no one noticed that he had noticed it, apart from me of course. I could see that he saw the little dog, but he, astonished by so many astonishing things, had no time for noticing dogs.

Everyone was waiting for my father to pronounce on *that dog*, which should be *got right out of his sight*, but instead he came over to me and said quietly,

'By yourself.'

Then he turned his back on me and went into his study.

Expecting my father to pronounce on *that dog* he wanted out of his sight, no one quite understood what he meant when he said 'by yourself.' It wasn't a phrase we much associated with owning pets.

But I understood everything. I knew that when he said 'by yourself' he meant me, my self. I'd never had a self before, and now I had one, and all because of the astonishing things going on in the world and in my family.

Up until now I had been the youngest child, and now I was a 'self', and the little white dog was the first sign of my new position. Now I was a self I had the right to own anything, from a little white dog to a stallion, but it was all up to me. I had to feed and water and look after it and be responsible for it myself. Myself.

My father said 'by yourself', turned and went into the study and my family wondered what he meant by such a short and simple phrase for a couple of minutes. But by the third minute everyone had forgotten about me, the 'by yourself' and the little white dog, which was standing in the corridor, pressing against my leg.

By the third minute we were forgotten. Everyone in our family was occupied by what was happening just then in the world, and in our family. Everyone knows what was going on in the world just then, and in our family Borya was getting married. It was three days until his wedding.

They forgot about us. They sent us to bed, and carried on discussing around the kitchen table what was going to happen in three days' time.

In the middle of the night Borya came into the room where I was trying to sleep, and where the little white dog lay asleep and snuffling, under my bed.

'What are you going to call it?' he asked. 'What name have you chosen for your little white terrier?'

'You know what,' I said. 'I want to call it Milady.'

'Milady?' Borya was surprised.

'Milady,' I admitted.

At that point in my life I loved 'The Three Musketeers', and I had long since decided that if I had a dog I would call it Milady.

'Milady,' said Borya. 'It's a nice name. Only I'm afraid, it really doesn't suit this little dog.'

'Why?' I asked, my heart in my mouth.

'Because it's clearly a Milord.'

Wondrous things were happening to my brother Borya, my dear brother. He grew paler and paler, he raced about town, and he ran around the flat, he spoke in English on the phone. He barely noticed me, or the dog, and I realized that I would have to be patient, I would just have to wait until his genius wedding was over and Borya came back to normal and back to the little white dog and me.

I looked after the little dog, which had so unexpected acquired the name of Milord.

I had always hated little white dogs. Especially the ones with little pink eyes covered over by their brows.

Little pink eyes, little pink eyes!
I've been to the nurse again
She's bandaged me up
And you're to blame!

I could never understand why anyone would need bandaging over nonsense like that.

I didn't think that little white dogs with red eyes were dogs at all. To me they were just jumping button mushrooms.

I had a passion for racing dogs, noble setters, Irish Setters and Gordon Setters. I had a lot of respect for Drahthaars, and I paid homage to West Siberian Laikas.

Actually Milord wasn't so very small and white. You could never have called him a button mushroom. He was quite a size for a fox terrier and his white coat was covered in black and brown spots. One ear was black and a brown patch spread round his eye and then slipped down to his nose in a very amiable way. And definitely no pink eyes. His were intelligent, brown with a dart of gold.

Still, to my sense of all things canine, Milord was on the small side. He fitted the description of 'doggie', and that annoyed me. Why a 'doggie', when all I'd ever wanted was a 'dog'?

Borya, my dear brother, was talking in English on the phone for secrecy's sake. But I knew he was talking to his ethereal bride who also spoke the language, and I would just have to wait. So I waited, wondering all the while how Milord fitted into my sense of all things canine. Was he, after all, a button mushroom? I came to the decision that he might have been called a doggie but he was no button mushroom.

How strange it was that Milord had turned up like that.

My unwarranted *ptsoo-ptsoo* must have seemed so wonderful to him that he jumped into the water without a second's thought. Had I perhaps promised something I couldn't deliver when I produced that indescribable sound?

But what is it a person promises a dog when he makes that *ptsoo-ptsoo* sound? Nothing at all, except a bit of dry bread and a little scratch behind the ear. And Milord got that straight away in the boat. And then he ran after me to the bus, just in case something else came his way.

And a second *ptsoo-ptsoo* came his way, the decisive one. And he charged into the bus.

He chose me. He broke with his past. And I accepted him. The sure fingers of fate had flicked us to the same small spot.

But most extraordinary was my father's 'by yourself'. This phrase made good fate's finger flick. Fate's fingers had flicked us together, to the same spot at the exact moment when Milord needed me and I needed him, and my father could say nothing against it.

The fingers of fate had flicked us both to the same small spot and now this spot needed a little enlarging. My brother Borya was busy talking in English and we were busy enlarging the spot. Not as yet to any huge size. We went walking out by Krasniye Vorota, the Red Gates. Our home was right by the Red Gates—it was a grey six-storey modernist building. But its greyness and its six storeys were of little interest. What was important was that it stood by Krasniye Vorota.

I was proud that I lived by the Red Gates.

When I was younger I even played a game: I would run out to the metro and ask passers-by:

'Where do you live?'

On Zemlyanoy or on Sadovoy, they would answer.

'Well I live by the Red Gates.'

That told them!

It was a shame that there weren't really any gates. They didn't exist. They must have stood there a long, long time ago, but now a metro station had been built in their place. The station, which had been completed in an age of grey modernism could have passed as a set of gates, but only as underground gates, and no underground gates could ever replace gates above the ground.

There were no Red Gates, none at all, and yet there were. I don't know where they came from but they had always been there. It was even as if they had grown and grown and now stood high above the metro and our block.

My brother Borya's genius wedding was no trivial matter.

The table was laden with a hitherto unseen quantity of chicken legs and salads. Fruit shone everywhere.

Lyonechka, guitarist and wild boy, famous in Moscow in those days, strummed Mendelssohn's 'Wedding March' on his guitar. The maestro Solomon Mironych played with stern fury on the grand piano.

There were gladioli.

The bride, who had the divine name of Lyalya, looked ethereal.

A roar of 'kiss the bride' went up with the regularity of the incoming tide, flowing seamlessly from time to time into the song 'Slender Rowan'.

Goodness, the whole world was at this gobsmacking wedding. Golub and Litvin were there, of course. The greatest man in our block, and later in the diplomatic world, the brilliant Seryozha Divilkovsky was there. Tanka Menshikova was there, so was Mishka Mednikov and Vovochka Andreev... No, hang on. I don't think he was... So who was it playing the accordion, then?

Boba Morgunov wasn't there. Boba should have been at my wedding a long time after, but my wedding didn't happen.

But Vitka was definitely there! Vitka, who went by the name of Old Man, wouldn't have missed it for the world! He was there for certain!

The bag lady's whistling came in through the open windows from the yard below. The old bag lady whistled all evening and it was quite beyond a joke! I had already carried out three bottles of fortified wine to her, and some pies and porkfat.

After midnight the shout went up: 'The Merry Boy! The Merry Boy!'

They were calling me to perform. That meant that they had exhausted 'Dark Night' and 'Bésame Mucha'. The 'Merry Boy' was being called for and I was thrown into the wedding spotlight. The maestro Solomon Mironych struck up the introduction and the guitarist and wild boy began strumming. Borya smiled fondly at me.

I was always forced to sing this 'Merry Boy' song. Everyone said I sang it wonderfully and especially from the bit that went 'ai-yai-yai'. I hated this song with a fierce hatred, and especially from the bit that went 'ai-yai-yai'.

But the introduction had been played, Borya had smiled, and I could never have let him down in a million years.

'My horse's hooves are ringing out

Jauntily I wear my cap,'

I began in a thin voice, in which you could feel a certain oncoming beat of horses' hooves.

'*Yes I am known hereabouts*

As the Merry Boy from Karabakh!'

And after that came the 'ai-yai-yai', monstrous in its wild, confounding force.

People listened in a dim suspicion, as people mostly listen to performing teenagers, who have passed their performing years. But I knew well that once I reached the penultimate 'yai' they would fall about laughing. And the suspicious audience knew this too and wanted, in a dim sort of way, to fall about laughing, if only I could do it. And I did it, and they fell about.

And they were still falling about when I proposed:

'*Drink well, my horses!*
Drink well, my horses!'

And the fallen were lifted from the floor and given drink. For indeed they themselves wanted to be lifted and given drink, if only I could do it. And I did it, and they got up and drank again, and every second one of them felt himself to be a glossy steed.

There was deafening applause, the horses galloped to their watering place, gladioli flashed before my eyes, and I no longer quite knew what was going on myself. I knew only that it was the morning, dawn, and that Lyonechka, famous in Moscow in those days as a guitarist and wild boy, was clutching a bottle of Madeira and leading me and Milord off to his place to sleep.

Borya, my only brother, left us for good. He went to live at his ethereal bride's home, where we had been rushing that day with the bream and with Milord. But no one told me that Borya had left forever. I thought he'd gone for a short while, like going to army camp for retraining. And I waited for him every day, because I couldn't have lived without him in a million years.

Borya sometimes came round and gazed at me lovingly and asked me all about Milord, and about the important things that lay ahead of me, but my parents soon stole my brother away and talked to him for a long time, and then he went.

And everything was quite changed. Everything was changed but I hadn't yet realized that everything was changed, I carried on telling myself that it was just like when Borya went to army camp for retraining.

But Borya now lived with Lyalya. And that was a long long way away from the Krasniye Vorota. He now lived on the Smolensk Boulevard.

If you were to walk for a long long time, a morning or an afternoon, leftwards along the Garden Ring, then you would get to Smolensk Boulevard. And if you were to walk for a long long time, a morning or an afternoon, rightwards along the Garden Ring then you would also get to Smolensk Boulevard.

I wasn't allowed in the metro or on a trolleybus with Milord so we walked along the Garden Ring, sometimes leftwards, sometimes rightwards, and we always got to the Smolensk Boulevard.

Strangest of all was that there was no boulevard at Smolensk Boulevard. There, on the Garden Ring, stood only grey and yellow buildings. But all the same it was there, the boulevard was there. There were trees and leaves, only they just weren't visible, just as our Red Gates weren't visible.

Borya always greeted me fondly, and Lyalya fed me an ethereal sort of lunch, and then it was time to go home. The afternoon was left for my walk home.

I walked from Smolensk Boulevard around the Garden Ring to Krasniye Vorota and it seemed to me as if I had lost my brother. I hadn't yet realized that it is impossible to lose a brother.

It was Milord who cheered me up. He was a clever dog, and he had his wits about him. You never had to ask him twice, and he never asked me for anything, or to go anywhere. He just lived with me, like a small shadow by my right shoe.

In the early morning, rising from bed I lowered my bare feet onto the floor, and straightaway Milord climbed out from under the bed and licked my heels. He never rushed madly about the room, delighted that I was awake, he just sat by my bare foot, as it was slowly shod.

After that we moved as one. Me, and Milord by my shoe. Up till then I had been a shadow by my older brother's shoe, and now, with Borya gone, Milord had appeared by my shoe.

There had been a change-around and I wasn't yet sure what was better: to shadow another's shoe, or to move my own shoe and have another shadowing it.

Really I still wanted to be moving alongside Borya's shoe—and at the same time, Milord might as well shadow mine. But this was not an option and only the thought of retraining at army camp saved me.

After breakfast Milord and I went down to the yard.

There were no bag ladies in the yard in the morning, and Milord and I walked by the fountain.

Out of sheer boredom I taught Milord to balance on my head.

It was a tricky thing. Milord couldn't jump straight onto my head—he couldn't jump that far, and in the end I would lift him up onto the highest plaster rose on the fountain and Milord climbed from there down onto my head. Back then I wore a tough old cap, which helped in such experiments.

With Milord on my head I walked about by the fountain waiting for something, even the bag lady, to appear.

But then my aunt would begin shouting my name from her second floor window. She would make reference to all those important things which would soon happen to me, and which would draw a distinct future line between me and a bag lady.

My head and my shoe—the two objects I placed at Milord's disposal, although my head was partly occupied with other matters. I was preparing to go to college.

Everyone in the block saw that there was no way I would ever get into college. I saw it, my brother Borya saw it, my teachers saw it, perhaps only Milord didn't see. Although even he must have guessed that a person who wore a smooth-haired fox terrier on his head was unlikely to ever get into teacher training college.

But there was a man whose name was Vladimir Niko-laevich Protopopov and he refused to see that I wouldn't get in to college. He saw that I would and I was uncom-fortable with the thought that I would fail and let down Vladimir Nikolaevich Protopopov.

Protopopov was a great teacher. For him turning a failing student into a C-grade student was nothing. The mere sight of Vladimir Protopopov, his furious beard and his piercing gaze turned a failing student into a C-grade student instantaneously.

When Protopopov opened his mouth and relentless rolls of thunder came forth then the recently qualified C-grade student had no other choice but to make a last desperate attempt to become a B-grade student.

'And the rest is in God's hands,' Protopopov would usually say.

My brother Borya, who had been a hopeless case, would tell of how Vladimir Nokolaevich Protopopov came into their classroom for the first time in late autumn nineteen forty-six.

To start with, the classroom door began to shake of its own accord. It shook in nervous terror. It felt someone approaching, but who it was it didn't know. Its teeth chattered, a shiver ran down its spine, and at last with a crash it was flung open.

In the doorway appeared a shaggy, shaggy hat pushed right down over a brow, under which glittered steely piercing eyes—Protopopov had arrived.

He was, as I have already stated, in a hat, and a rucksack hung on his right shoulder. That aside, he was wearing a black suit and a tie, but it was the rucksack and hat which were remembered afterwards, and the black suit and tie were quite forgotten.

Protopopov half-stepped, half-leaped to the teacher's desk with a noble, decisive movement, and spoke a terrible prophecy:

'The traitorous pupil fell from the bough like a fruit...'

Those pupils who had managed to stand to greet their teacher stood stunned by their desks, and those who hadn't yet managed froze where they were, half-sitting, half-standing.

Protopopov fell into a long silence. His gaze was extremely bright. He was clearly following the fall of the traitorous pupil from the bough and into the abyss.

The abyss was depthless and how long the silence might have lasted, no one knew. It was obvious to everyone that until the falling traitor struck against something that would shatter him into tiny pieces, Protopopov would watch his descent.

And then there was an awful blow. It was Protopopov throwing his rucksack down onto the desk.

And it was clear to everyone that the traitor had struck against that thing and had been shattered into tiny pieces. It was an instantaneous but terrible death.

Protopopov reached up for his hat, to take it off, but changed his mind.

After the death there was an emptiness.

And in this emptiness something slowly began scrabbling about and rustling, but what it was no one knew.

'The devil flew to him,' whispered Protopopov, 'and over his face he stooped.'

And Protopopov turned away from this image, the sight was too unpleasant.

Still he did need to explain what was happening and he did this with impressive and powerful words:

'Blew life into him, and soared high with his rotten prey And threw the living corpse into the hungry mouth of hell...'

Protopopov rummaged meaningfully in his bag and drew out of it an Austrian double-edged bayonet blade, then a hunk of bread, and then at last he took off his hat. He cut into the bread with the blade and began to eat.

The pupils were completely and utterly stunned. They understood nothing, except for the fact that the familiar word 'pupil' had been unhappily coupled with the word 'traitor'. And some of the children decided right out that if they didn't learn their lesson then the 'devil' would 'blow life' into them as well. Protopopov's beard, into which the piece of bread was disappearing, appeared to all of them without exception to be the gate to the 'hungry mouth of hell'.

Protopopov, chewing on the bread, glanced craftily at the pupils and muttered, nodding here and there at pupils:

'Not for those birds, not for the loons, was the excitement of life's battle...'

The stunned pupils immediately felt themselves to be loons, and many of them had the desperate desire to be allowed the excitement of life's battle.

Protopopov looked about the class and winked unexpectedly at a few of the pupils. He winked at my brother Borya. And Borya realized that all was not lost, and that he perhaps would be able to drag his way up and out of the species of loon.

Some of the pupils, probably some of those at whom Protopopov had not winked, became annoyed that a teacher was eating in lesson time. So then Protopopov stood and mightily crushed their annoyance:

'Who are these judges? Since ancient times their hatred of freedom has been implacable.'

Protopopov worked a miracle.

He dragged my brother out of the company of failing loons, and sent him up into the higher feathered orders, more on the level of the woodcocks and swans.

He worked a miracle and then he left the school where dear Borya was a pupil, and then I was.

My parents' gladness that Borya had dragged himself out of the subspecies of loon was mitigated by the fact that I still hung around with them. It was decided that only Protopopov could set me on the wing, and so he undertook this difficult business.

Late at night, at about eleven o'clock I would leave home, on my way to Protopopov.

I walked along Sadovoy-Chernogryazskoy from Krasniye Vorota, the red gates which stood high above the metro and our block. I walked towards Zemlyanoy Val and then turned off to the left and the school was right there on Gorokhovoy Street. This was where Protopopov broke through the ceiling of my *loonacy*, and brought me to the flight levels of a woodcock.

He did this by night. He had no time to do it during the day and besides he believed the loons had a weaker hold on me by night. When I got there Protopopov was usually sitting in the empty staffroom marking books.

When he saw me he laughed with joy, a laugh which came right from the heart, and he pummelled my chest with his fist. And I would laugh, turning away from the really quite hard blows with which my teacher greeted me.

Once he had thumped on my chest and in so doing had opened my soul to learning, Protopopov would brew some very, very strong tea and would fill his pipe with a mix of two different types of tobacco, *Golden Rune* and *Naval*.

And we began drinking tea.

Vladimir Nikolaevich taught me how to fill a pipe and brew very, very strong tea, and he was pleased with my progress in these sciences of daily life.

Then Protopopov resumed his marking and I helped him as well as I could.

And here was the trick of these nightly lessons: this great teacher would trust me, a potentially failing student and friend to the loons, with the marking of essays by writers who were possibly older and more educated than me.

Protopopov killed many birds with one stone.

He didn't just stretch to breaking point my paper-thin knowledge, he heightened my attentiveness, my sense of responsibility, awoke my decisiveness and even drove into me some bits of information from the books I marked. And when I had improved then Protopopov killed another bird: I reduced his pile of marking, even by a little.

He even trusted me to put marks in the books: Ds and Bs. He wouldn't let me give Cs or As. And this constituted his curious idea.

He knew of course that for me, a companion of loons, a D grade went against the grain. I really did hate Ds, and always tried to stretch to a C grade. It seemed criminal to award Ds to poor loons from another school. And if I was forced to award a D, then it was a tragic, but unavoidable fact of life, and all that was left was to take off my hat to the recipient.

Protopopov checked all my C grades, and as As were a gift from God, Protopopov was obliged to look over those himself.

But Bs I was welcome to. Bs he trusted to me and here our opinions never differed and I was proud of this fact.

Once I had marked the books I would lay them out in piles: Ds, Cs, Bs and As.

'Teacher,' teased Protopopov at that and he would pummel me on the chest with his fist. 'Let me humbly kneel at the sound of your name...'

And then he would check over the Cs and As, and if he found some or other instance of my stupidity or confusion he would grumble crossly,

'Loons...' And he would dig his nail into that place in the exercise book where my stupidity or confusion had been displayed.

My stupidity or ignorance were never accompanied by Protopopov's fist. His fist was used for joy and gladness and his fingernail came into force at these other moments. He would press down into the exercise book where *loonacy* had been exhibited and if I didn't understand, some hard nail-like words would come my way too.

Then I would fall asleep at last on the leather staffroom sofa, and if I sometimes woke up I would see my teacher sitting at the table, drinking tea, smoking his pipe and marking, marking the endless exercise books, and his kind, kind, steely eyes sparkled. Vladimir Nikolaevich Protopopov never slept.

One winter night when a blizzard raged I couldn't sleep, and in my sleeplessness I knew a sudden glimmering of inspiration and I made up some poetry.

'*The blizzard blew*
The blizzard flew
The blizzard whistled
Down so low...'

Protopopov laughed like a child, pummelled me on the chest with his fists and then all of a sudden he jumped up and made his way around the staffroom in a monstrous and precipitate jig, chanting:

'*Fly, blizzard*
In your pink tricot!'

I was stunned. Protopopov's sudden dance startled me. And I was surprised too that someone else had already written about a blizzard and so my sudden moment of inspiration couldn't be counted, and all of this felt like the worse excesses of *loonacy*.

It was once late May.

Protopopov woke me in the early morning. He led me, half-asleep, to the window. Through the grey-blue school window the poplar branches could be seen, dark in the morning gloom, leaves slippy with dew.

We looked out of the window.

Protopopov was sunk in thought, and had even put his arm around me, something he had never done before. Then he remembered himself and thumped me on the chest with his fist.

'*A morning frost,*' he said. He fell silent. He continued. '*I clenched my jaw...*'

I already awaited a blow to my jaw, but received instead another thump on the chest.

'*... And the leaves rustled like a voice in a fever*
The dawn glittered beyond the Kama's shore
Bluer than a mallard's feather.'

Another blow to the chest to mark the end of the stanza.

And that was how Vladimir Protopopov thumped poetry into me.

Anyway, everyone in our block saw I was never ever going to get into college. I saw it, my brother Borya saw it, my school teachers saw it, only Protopopov refused to see it. He saw that I would get in—and I did.

And then I was caught up in a whirlwind. My heart fairly cracked under the family's joy, my chest hummed with blows from Protopopov's fist, the bag lady whistled up at the windows, my brother Borya smiled fondly, the wild boy strummed on his guitar, the Maestro Solomon Mironych was a stern fury at the grand piano, and Milord, who had by this time learnt to fly, kept jumping up onto my head.

I must note here that I had never been particularly bothered by the whole flying pets issue, and when I was preparing for my exams I couldn't spend any time on the matter at all.

But now and then I'd throw aside my books and go out with Milord to the fountain.

We had been joined by a third party, a thin leather lead, which I fastened on to the dog's collar. I fastened the lead on at home and took it off at the fountain.

This lead was not necessary. Milord walked by my shoe without any asking. But all good dog owners had leads. A lead was an important link between man and dog, and I owned such a link.

This leather link, thin but tough, was hated by Milord. He couldn't see the point of it. He thought that something bigger linked us.

As soon as I took the lead off by the fountain Milord would begin to gnaw at it instantly.

This made me cross. I couldn't afford to buy a new link between us every day. And I would attempt to take the lead away from Milord.

The normally obliging Milord, was on these occasions extremely stubborn. I couldn't drag the lead from between his teeth. Fox terriers are famous for their death grip and Milord rehearsed this claim to fame with all his might.

It was this death grip that was responsible for Milord's extraordinary flight.

Once by the fountain he gripped the lead with a particularly deadly death grip. I tried everything I could think of to prize open his teeth and save the lead. Lots of our neighbours popped their heads out of the windows, when they heard the terrible barking and my shouts of: 'Put it down! Let go!'

The spectators annoyed me. I grasped the lead even more firmly. Milord gripped tighter and bellowed through his clamped teeth.

I stamped on the spot, pulled the lead tight and then began swinging round. Milord was forced to run in a circle around me. I stamped even faster, Milord could hardly keep up, his legs dragged behind and all of a sudden they left the ground.

Low, just above the ground, flew Milord. Round and round me. He growled, but would not let the lead go.

I turned faster and faster and Milord lifted up in the air and was soon at chest height. I was dizzy but I lifted him in the air even higher and there he was flying high on the lead, right above my head.

The spectators froze at their windows. No dog had ever flown around the fountain in the yard before.

At last the overwhelming centrifugal force undid the death grip, Milord let go of the lead and like a shaggy bellowing stone issuing forth from a sling, he sailed over the fountain.

He dashed bottom first against a ground floor window, over which a thick steel anti-football mesh had been placed.

Bouncing off the mesh Milord charged back to me and gripped the hated lead between his teeth again, and I swung him up again around the fountain.

The unusual flying exploits of a smooth-haired fox terrier became the favourite spectator sport of the smaller dwellers in the yard and the vast bag lady. Whenever we went walking by the fountain shadowy creatures would cluster around with incessant requests to 'spin Milord'. I often gave in to their requests, stupefied as I was by our success.

I would tease Milord with the lead, gave him the chance to grip on tightly enough and began spinning him on the spot like a spinning top, slowly lifting the dog off the ground.

Sometimes I could anticipate the moment when the overwhelming centrifugal forces were just about to overwhelm the death grip and I could slowly lower the dog to the ground. But most of the time I couldn't see it coming and the overwhelming centrifugal force overwhelmed the death grip and, like a stone from a sling, Milord sailed away over the fountain and crashed bottom-first into the ground floor window covered by steel mesh.

There, behind the metal mesh sat prize student El-lochka, always, even in the summer, doing her homework, and many people thought I aimed deliberately at her window with my flying dog.

But although I did always have a secret interest in Ellochka, I never aimed Milord at her window.

The deep secret interest I had in Ellochka was rather made manifest in the dog's flight itself, which must have amazed Ellochka, when, as she lifted her eyes from the pale exercise books, she suddenly saw a smooth haired fox terrier flying straight at her window, bottom-first.

The flying Milord did not always fly into this wonderful window. Sometimes he flew off and crashed against some passers-by or knocked over a bin. The sweet dog never once paid any attention to what he had hit. He clearly liked flying, and when he crashed into something he immediately jumped back onto his feet and rushed back at me, ready to exert his death grip against the overwhelming centrifugal force.

September came and I entered college under the vaults of the Moscow State Pedagogical Institute.

'Under the vaults' is the right expression here. The Institute had a particularly large number of arches, more than any of the other colleges in Moscow. And a central glass dome crowned the enormous main hall. A five-storey modernist block would have fitted comfortably in the main hall of our college.

Space and coolness, those are the two words which come to mind when I remember the main hall. No ray of sun ever pierced the glass ceiling, there was always a half-light in there, but the half-light was clear and sober. Something Roman, something of Ancient Greece drifted in the very air of this hall and only that particular silvery half-light washing over it told of the northernness of this temple of learning.

And on the galleries wrought with columns and balus-trades, the galleries which had something of the colonnade about them, there were even more vaults and under these vaults were... Goodness, what *wasn't* there under them—faces bright with inspiration on the galleries, and shining in the lecture halls, free spirits thronging around the columns and crowding around the legs of the most important sculptures of the time. A simple list of all their glorious names would take up a hundred closely-written sheets and I don't have the energy to draw up a list like that, but it's so very hard to resist.

Take, for example, Yury Vizbor; or Yuly Kim; or even Pyotr Fomenko, for instance. Or take Yurka Ryashentsev, Leshka Mezinov or Erik Krasnovsky... No I won't carry on, or I'll never escape the thrall of these great and so familiar names, I'll carry on remembering, carry on listing them to the end of my days, and to hell with my duty to children's literature. And anyway how could I forget those faces, illuminated by that eternal half-light which flowed down from our northern skies and deep into the Main Hall. Alik Nenarokov for instance? And not just him. How about Grisha Feldblyum? Or Valerka Agrikolyansky?

And what about the girls? What about those wonders who ran along the endless galleries and up the endless stairs? Lord, would I not have offered up my life for Rosa Kharitonova at one time. It is impossible, unbearable, to speak such names casually, without *tremor cordis*, those names which once lit up the silvery half-light under those glass ceilings. And I tremble in my rememberings, and my eyes are genuinely full of tears... There, that's enough of tears in the eyes. But there is one more name: Marina Katsaurova.

She was the reason why I dragged Milord into college.

Right there in the middle of the Main Hall under our silvery northern glassy ceiling I spun Milord. The overwhelming centrifugal forces overwhelmed the fox terrier death grip and Milord went roaring over the heads of lecturers slap-bang into a notice board over which was written *Stalin's Glorious Academic Eagles.*

It looked like expulsion.

About two days later I was asked to come to see the well-known Dean of Studies Fyodor Mikhailovich Golovenchenko. The report file with the record of my behaviour had come to him. Amongst all the many expressions in it was the line:

'... So this student threw a dog on the board.'

'So this student,' read Fyodor Mikhailovich, wrinkling his brows meaningfully, 'threw a dog on the board.'

And Fyodor Mikhailovich raised his philosopher's eyebrows at me magnanimously.

'What on earth is that?' he said. 'Threw a dog? What were you doing? Wrestling? So why "threw a dog on the board"? It should be "at the board". Or was the student lying on the boards himself? What do you say to that?'

I panicked and couldn't speak. I couldn't think of an answer worthy of the great professor.

'Still,' ruminated Fyodor Mikhailovich, 'no signs of chewing or any damage to the board itself. The board, thank the Lord, is untouched... But the turn of phrase is remarkable, "So this student threw a dog on the board". What is that?'

'Excuse me but I think it could be trochaic,' I recovered at last.

'Trochaic? In what way?'

'Tetrameter.'

'What do you mean? What trochee are you talking about?'

'So this student threw a dog on the board. I was suggesting it was a trochaic tetrameter, Fyodor Mikhailovich, but with an anapaest at the end.'

Fyodor Mikhailovich lifted his hands towards the vaults and laughed out loud.

'A divine trochaic tetrameter!' he exclaimed. 'Divine trochaic tetrameter! And here he is telling me about trochees! Be gone with you, you trochaic expert. I'll hear no more of this dog and its board!'

I stumbled and tripped on an armchair and then hung around by the door wondering whether I'd been forgiven or not.

'Oh cover your pale legs!' the dean shouted then, and, pale, I shut the door to his office.

It turned out that I had been forgiven, but more than once I remembered this last phrase of the professor. I couldn't make out why the great man had, in forgiving me in so terrifying a way, quoted the classic example of a one-line poem: *'Oh cover your pale legs.'* Possibly my pathetic appearance had not brought to mind any other poem than this.

I didn't bring Milord to college again, of course. How he sobbed and howled when I went out of the house, and he hid away under the bed and lay there in misery, pressing himself fondly against my old shoe. My heart broke, but I couldn't do anything—a dog was a dog and a student was a student.

By the end of September Milord was fading away. A profound disappointment had come into his life. He had thought that he had found a shoe beside which he could move his whole life long, and now this shoe moved away every morning to teacher training college.

The first Sunday in October I took Milord out to the forest hunting.

It was a strange autumn.

The gold which should have long since taken hold of the forest was late to come. There were neither flecks of gold on the birches, nor red tips on the aspens. The birch leaves fluttered oddly, awkwardly in the wind. They felt uneasy, so young and green, when they should have been turning gold.

I walked along a swampy stream, slowly gaining the bank.

I was waiting for ducks and they rose up from time to time, the drake first, and then the hen, and only after that, already in the air, did they reorder themselves, hen flying first and behind her the drake. Although it was always hard to work out which was the hen and which the drake in the autumn, the drake's startlingly green head was hidden and you could only guess by the way they rose up and flew.

It was a strange autumn. The ducks had separated into pairs for some reason, when they should have been gathering themselves into flocks to fly south.

The ducks, separated into pairs, and the leaves with no desire to turn gold, holding on to the summer with all their might.

I fired my gun occasionally. Milord leaped high out of the grass at the sound of the shots and watched the prey fly away. He didn't understand me, or my firing gun, because in his heart he was no duck hunter. He was drawn to the forest. I wanted to kill a duck of course, just to show Milord once and for all that he was justified in worshipping my boots and shoes.

I was curious: how would he behave when I killed my duck? Would he understand that his job was to fish it out of the water or not? I was positive he would.

At last a drake was slow off the mark. He had only just lifted his wings to pull himself up out of the water when I fired my shot under his wing. The hen, wings creaking, flew away.

The mallard beat its wing on the water only a little way off, it was a mere leap across the stream to reach it. In my excitement I forgot that I had decided to allow Milord this job and I leaped.

I jumped off the boggy bank and the foot I pushed off with caught, the bog clung to the boot, lifted it half from my foot and as I flew from one bank to the other my boot fell from my foot and into the unpleasant rust-coloured swamp.

There on the other side I couldn't immediately work out what to do: save the boot or make a run for the drake which was still beating on the water with its wing.

Milord worked it out immediately. He rushed into the rust-coloured swamp and seized the boot, dragged it out of the swamp and laid it beside my right foot, where it belonged. Then he ran along the bank and quickly retrieved the duck, laying it beside my booted left foot.

Towards midday we reached the forest, a proper mighty pine forest. The pines grew on little mounds, and there were no other sorts of trees at all—pines, pines and on the sandy slopes of sunlit clearings strange junipers rose to the skies, beaded with frosty blue berries.

I laid a fire. I wanted to feed Milord with duck soup, but whilst I was busying myself round the fire, and blowing it to a flame, Milord disappeared.

This had never happened before. Milord was always circling somewhere near my boot. I was suddenly very frightened, I began whistling, shouting, running in the forest and then, when I came back to the fire, I heard a far off barking.

It was Milord's bark, and it came from somewhere underground.

And only then I saw a hole in the sand under the roots of a pine. A hole going deep into a mound.

I fell on the pine-needle covered ground, threw down my harvest of Slippery Jacks and Milk Cap's which were stopping me hearing properly, and pressed my ear to the mound. It was very odd to hear a dog barking from deep underground.

The barking suddenly stopped and there was a growling. It was the same growl as when Milord gripped the lead between his teeth and I guessed that he had engaged his death grip, he was clinging on to something underground and he would not let go for anything, not until the overwhelming centrifugal forces did their bit.

I lay there on the ground a few hours and listened to his growls, but I could do nothing. I had no spade with me of course, and even if I had, well what point would there have been in digging and where would I dig?

'Milord!' I shouted from time to time in despair. 'Stop this nonsense!'

He could hear me of course, but he had no intention of letting go of the badger, for that's what it most likely was.

'I'm going! I'm going to get the train!' I shouted in despair, but he knew that I wouldn't go anywhere, I would hang around on the badger's mound until evening, and then all night and all the next day, and at least until the matter was resolved by overwhelming centrifugal forces.

I decided to go. Milord would hear my footsteps from under the ground and he would know then that I really was going. He could choose: me or the death grip.

I stamped the fire out furiously. Stamping loudly I walked towards the stream. And how I stamped and cursed the sand because it resounded less under my heel than I wished.

Milord appeared without warning, quite as if nothing had happened, he just suddenly jumped out of the grass at one side. His ear was ripped, his whole face was covered in blood. But he paid it no attention at all, he was simply delighted to have caught me up.

I dragged him to the stream all the same, washed his face a little and prized open a cartridge to sprinkle gunpowder on his wounds.

The evening was coming on and we walked to the station, straight across the bog. In one very particular green and damp spot Milord suddenly sprung up high. He dropped back to the ground and then jumped again, oddly, to one side. I ran to him and until I reached him he kept jumping on the spot.

It was a snake. A black viper. I fired and broke its neck with my shot.

The next morning as usual I lowered my bare feet onto the ground and Milord immediately licked my heels.

'Thank goodness,' I thought. 'It didn't manage to bite him'. I went to get washed and Milord set off after me. He pulled himself along the ground using his front paws. His back legs were useless.

From the Red Gates which stood above our block I ran down the ring road towards Zemlyanoy Val. I held Milord in my arms, he licked me on the chin.

'Hold him tightly,' said the vet. 'Hold his muzzle closed.'

I pressed Milord down on the plastic table, squeezed his muzzle with all my might and the vet put a blunt syringe into his belly.

My Mother rang and rang the Veterinary Institute, but could not find anyone who knew how to cure a fox terrier of a snake bite. At last she found someone who recommended manganese baths.

Every morning Milord crawled out from under my bed and went off in search of my mother. He whined piteously, begging her to prepare him his usual bath of manganese solution.

For twenty days I ran with him along the ring road to the vet's. The injections were awful, the syringe blunt. I could barely hold Milord down.

The baths and the injections worked. His paws slowly began moving. Soon he could shuffle himself along, then he could make limited hops, and finally he was back to normal. Everything seemed to be back how it was more or less. Only one thing had changed: he no longer licked me on the heels in the morning; he had stopped moving alongside my shoe.

I had become just another dog owner, a person who had a fox terrier living with him.

I suffered terribly. I understood that it would pass and one day Milord would forget the appalling pain of the vet's syringe. But Milord was frightened of me. He thought I might suddenly seize him and run off for another injection.

Yes, it was a strange autumn. The trees in Moscow only lost their leaves at the end of October. Our yard was full of ash leaves, poplar and box elder leaves.

Natasha, the yard-sweeper, swept the leaves with a broom into huge heaps, and Milord liked to climb into these heaps. He thought someone was rustling inside them.

He dug down through the leaves with his paws, snuffling and growling and diving into the ochre depths. But the leaves of course were rustling only with age and they hid no one.

I also pretended there was someone there, and threw myself onto the heaps of leaves beside Milord, digging at them, tossing them in different directions.

Sometimes I hid a sugar cube or a piece of dry bread in the leaves, and we found it again ecstatically.

I don't know what helped, time, or the leaves, but perhaps the leaves. One day I lowered my heels from the bed onto the ground and felt my heels being licked. I was so pleased that day that I even thought about skipping college, I should have taken Milord and gone out to the countryside somewhere, somewhere on the Moscow River, Ubory perhaps, to dig through all the fallen leaves and sort them out.

But I—stupidly—went to college and when I returned Milord met me in the yard.

We rummaged through all the heaps of leaves and found a couple of pieces of sugar, and I rushed upstairs to the second floor to eat lunch. I left Milord down in yard, walking about. After all everyone in the block knew him and loved him and Milord never went out onto the street without me.

I was still eating when I heard the bag ladies calling my name loudly.

I ran down to the yard.

'A man!' a bag lady shouted. 'A man in grey trousers! He put a lead on him! Put him on a lead and dragged him off!'

'That way! That way! Along Sadovoy!'

I ran along Sadovoy from the Red Gates which stood high above our block, towards Zemlyanoy Val. The bag ladies ran ahead of me and behind me.

'There he is! There he is! There he is!' they shouted.

I kept running, but nowhere did I see Milord or the man in grey trousers. Trolleybuses and cars passed me by, the traffic of an enormous city, a thousand, thousand men in grey trousers flew in different directions.

I realized that it was over and that I would never again see Milord, but still I kept running, and a cold grey dust flew at me and into my eyes, and I hardly realized that it was snowing already. I ran along Sadovoy towards Zemlyanoy Val. From the Red Gates.

Transition

Tatyana
Shchepkina-Kupernik

I

Firsova saw the actor Zaretsky, he walked past her—and didn't recognize her. The words rushed out as if of their own accord,

'Andrei Pavlovich!'

And then she immediately regretted calling him, and was even ready to turn away into a side street, but it was too late, he had already looked around, stopped and, in his actorly voice, lifting his top hat, he said,

'Excuse me... I don't...'

And then in a completely different voice he exclaimed,

'Nadezhda Sergeevna! Is it you? Well, it's been years and years!'

'Three years, that's all,' she objected timidly.

'No... Four... I last performed at Roman Petrovich's four years ago.'

'Yes, I suppose that's right...'

'Haven't you changed, goodness me...'

'I've aged!' answered Firsova in a voice both sad and ironic, avoiding his eyes and looking away to the side. And there he stood, handsome, clean-shaven, wrapped magnificently in a beaver coat, and he spoke condescendingly,

'Come come... Not at all... You look a little plumper, that's for sure! What have you been up to? How is your husband?'

'Vanya died a year ago.'

'Oh... I'm sorry. I didn't know. Well, well.' He felt it necessary to show some interest. 'He was still a young man, was he not?'

'It was tuberculosis.' She felt the barely courteous indifference with which he questioned her, and it became twice as painful to talk about it.

'Do you have children?'

'Two. Little boys.'

'I see... So will you be going back to the stage?'

'I never stopped. I still act... with Roman Petrovich... but I'm afraid...'

She became suddenly angry with herself. Why on earth should she share her anxieties and fears with this sleek man? What did it matter that he had once courted her with sweet words? She had looked quite different then. Slim, sweet, the *ingénue*—never, it is true, a beauty, but young and fresh with eyes that burned and laughed, white teeth, and so infectiously mischievous that they had called her 'the little demon' in the theatre. Where had it all gone?

The answer was obvious, you only had to look at the two baby boys squealing away back in her poor rooms... But Zaretsky had not seen them and could not imagine what had happened to the poor 'little demon', and in his eyes she read only pity—insulting, unfeeling pity... 'Well, even standing beside me must be unpleasant for him... Just look at him in his beaver coat—and me in my shabby jacket.'

She left him suddenly and abruptly,

'Goodbye. I'm in a hurry.'

And without giving him any time to collect his wits, she turned off to the right and disappeared down a side street.

'To think she was a handsome girl, dammit. But now look at her... sickening really. How quickly they go off and run to fat,' reflected Zaretsky, continuing on his way.

He forgot his chance meeting soon enough, and melted into smiles to greet a sixteen-year-old blonde coming out of a music school, with the clear eyes of a cherub, wearing a little hat of cat fur and carrying a music case. The cherub smiled back at him, blushing, and they went on in animated conversation, contented, full of the joys of life. But Firsova took a long time to get over the meeting. Walking the frozen pavements she bit her lip anxiously, and the past, the so very recent past, circled before her eyes like a kaleidoscope.

How was it possible? She had been predicted great success, she'd been told she had talent and compared to her famous grandmother, Rumyantseva... To this day she kept the newspaper cuttings of reviews:

'The young actress brings to mind her famous grandmother, Rumyantseva with her liveliness and natural presence: the same irregular features, the same fire in her eyes. We hope also, given the young actress's promise, soon to be able to bear witness to the same talent.'

A respected elderly critic from the best paper had written that about her...

And perhaps it might have come to pass, had it not been for the ill-fated love affair which had lasted several years and taken from her all ambition to succeed, all desire to work; for the marriage she had been finally brought to with a poor bank clerk, and then two children in three years (the second had not been born until after her husband's death), and her husband's illness... Then his death, when she couldn't even cry because she had to think about the two babies, had to make sure they had milk and chopped firewood and countless other needs.

And even at night she couldn't press herself into the pillow and weep her heart out because a pitiable little squealing was always coming from either the pram, where two-year-old Tosik slept, or the linen basket in place of a cradle for Vanya, and she had to rush to change them, or feed them, or rock them to sleep with a lullaby.

She fed Tosik herself. She wanted to feed Vanya but her milk disappeared before the second month had passed and she had to find a wet nurse.

She had no idea how she would survive on fifty roubles a month and feed the children and find a decent wet nurse, but she had a stroke of luck—she found a good wet nurse, a kindly easy-going woman. She was content with her ten roubles, she had a good grasp of her mistress's situation and didn't try to extract any more from her. But in fact it was she who was mistress and not Nadezhda Sergeevna Firsova, who fulfilled her every request and order without demur, and made every effort to keep hold of her. At least she could quite happily leave the children with her on the rare evenings when she was working in the theatre.

Rarer and rarer were those evenings now.

Roman Petrovich kept her on, she didn't herself understand why—respect for her grandmother, or pity for her... But her wage remained fifty roubles. She had earned fifty roubles in her first year as an actress and she still earned it now. She was given fewer and fewer parts. Well, it was true, she hardly suited vaudeville: her figure, stout and puffy, counted against her, it made an unhappy impression and more and more frequently directors would look at her in just the same way that Zaretsky had looked at her today.

Oh, that look of half-dismissive pity! It had scalded her like the lash of a whip. Not because it had insulted the woman in her—she was well past that. But because it frightened the mother in her. The mother who realized with terror that her last chance of work might be taken away at any moment, and then... But even the thought of what would happen then filled her with horror, and the light-hearted *ingénue* of a few years before began to pray and cross herself like a peasant woman, sobbing.

II

Firsova barely noticed how she found her way back to the low fence, she pushed the gate open unthinkingly, and only then realized she had reached home.

She opened the door from the yard and didn't ring. The door was padded inside with ripped cellophane; bits of sponge showed through the rips. She climbed about ten steps of a narrow, crooked staircase and pushed open the second door.

That door opened directly into a tiny hall, part of a single room, in which a partition wall, lower than the ceiling, divided the room into four unequal parts: the hallway, a kitchen and two tiny rooms. For this 'three-roomed apartment with kitchen', as the landlord called it, she paid twenty roubles a month without firewood.

From behind the door she could hear a child's squealing and the wet nurse's monotonous:

'Ah-ah, ah-ah, ah-ah, a... Shhh... Shhh... Shhh.'

Firsova was immediately enveloped by the smell of the cramped space: the smell of nappies, milk, something gone sour, the inescapable smell of a wet nurse from the country, and her charges. She was used to the smell, but after the fresh frosty air, it hit her and she staggered.

'Nurse! You didn't open the top windows again!'

'Well really! What will you think of! Open the windows? With Tosik's cough, and what am I going to do with Vanya? Those walls are only partitions: if I open the windows in one room everyone will catch cold!' growled the wet nurse indignantly. She was sitting on the old divan which doubled as Firsova's bed, and rocking Vanya.

Tosik was wearing only a little shirt and was making huge efforts to stuff his little plump pink foot into his mouth, holding it with both hands and groaning when he couldn't quite manage it. The wet nurse's son, five-year old Syomka didn't know what to do with himself, he stood there in a knitted jacket and Firsova's old boots, tugging at the nurse and whining,

'Mum... I want to go out... I want to go out...'

From time to time she would give him a silent slap on the back of the head and then her 'bye-bye... baby-bye... bye-bye...' would begin again.

There was nothing whole in any of the rooms. At a first glance it appeared that everything was broken, odds and ends, remnants. Wobbly chairs, some odd wooden drawers out of which bits of material hung, a lamp with a broken glass shade, cups without handles, saucers without cups and so on.

The first room maintained a semblance of order. It was clear someone had intended to make a parlour of sorts out of it. The table had a cheerful table-cloth on it, there was a mirror on the chest of drawers, there were even two armchairs, covered in cretonne, and strips of the same cretonne had been cleverly used for curtains at the window, although even here, on the table and by the photographs, her memories of the past, lay some wet woollen bootees and a baby's bottle of milk and a nappy had been hung over the mirror to dry.

But the next room, a slightly larger room, where the wet nurse had her bed, the pram stood and the children's basket lay, was impossible to describe. Total chaos reigned in there.

'You haven't tidied up your room again, nurse. Not at all today!' Firsova reproached her mildly.

'Ha, if I'd had the time to clear up...' the wet nurse growled. 'What with the three of them, they've fairly pulled my arms out of their sockets. Now you, you're wide awake... Not a thought of sleep! Sh-sh, sh-sh... Have you brought any back, then?'

'Three and a half... They won't give any more. And they took out the interest.'

'Never mind. We'll buy some firewood tomorrow.'

'Have we got enough to last until then?'

'Plenty, plenty! Now you come and rock him and I'll see to the soup. You could do with a square meal!' the wet nurse said, with coarse kindliness, and she handed the wrapped bundle to Firsova, who took it obediently. She had managed to take off her 'smart' coat—the only intact coat in the wardrobe and she had hung it so the wet hem would dry by the stove. Now she sat in the nurse's place, in her bombazine blouse with its worn elbows, and began the familiar:

'Bye-baby-bye-bye...'

She must have sat there a good half hour, dreaming and rocking the already sleeping baby quite without thinking. The nurse was frying potato and stirring cabbage soup, the smell spread through the flat. Syomka was hanging around her, looking hungrily in her mouth, she thrust a scrap in his mouth between tasks, and chased him away. Tosik had apparently found some private source of interest and was quietly and incomprehensibly burbling to himself.

Suddenly the door creaked, and on the other side of the partition there was the sound of heavy boots shuffling, and someone clearing his throat.

'Who is it, nurse?'

The wet nurse looked out of the door.

'It's Fyodor Ivanovich, ma'am.'

Fyodor Ivanovich was the theatre courier. His appearance always caused Firsova some anxiety, and now she even flushed. She put the baby straight down onto the divan where it began squealing again, and she went out to the courier, doing up her blouse over her breast.

'What is it, Fyodor?'

'Sign here please,' he answered, pushing an end of pencil attached to a book at her. 'Come to the theatre today for three o'clock.'

What could it be? Firsova's heart skipped a beat.

'Fyodor, darling, you don't know what it's about, do you?'

'How should we know,' answered Fyodor, breathing in deeply through his nose. 'We never get told nothing.'

'Is it a rehearsal?'

'No. Rehearsals are at ten o'clock nowadays... I expect it'll be something...'

'I'll be there, I'll be there,' she said, hurriedly signing her name.

The messenger left and she dropped down onto the divan helplessly, paralysed by her sense of foreboding. Her heart was in her throat, it beat rapidly, her hands were cold. The wailing of the children sounded as a dull pain in her ears, her heart ached with it, and she was engulfed by a terrible helplessness.

'They've called me in... After a rehearsal... Zamayev has called me in. It will be... I know what it will be... They'll say they don't need me. They'll get rid of me. It isn't as if there's a shortage of pretty young things with nice dresses to play the supporting actresses... From wealthy homes. And probably with wealthy patrons, too. Like Orlyntsina, with her sparkling diamonds, or Ramskaya, whose mere hats cost more than two months' of my salary. They would act even if you didn't pay them. And there's another who'd even pay, just to get on a stage... And she's young and beautiful... Oh Lord! My children, my little children, what will I do with you then...!'

She threw herself down on the threadbare rolled arm of the divan and, hiding her head, she began to cry without making a sound, her whole body shaking with her sobs.

'Come on now, what is it...' The wet nurse bent over her and attempted to comfort her. 'Don't fret yourself now. You'd be better off eating something. That potato is nice and ready.'

But seeing that her words were having no effect she made a resigned gesture and went away.

Tosik looked at his mother. He couldn't yet speak, but he understood everything that was said to him. He was at that mysterious stage when a young child is amongst us and in the world, and yet still inexplicably bound to that other world from whence he has come.

His large grey eyes were clear and piercing, and he smiled when his mother or the nurse said something to him, a strange, gentle and childish smile, as if he wanted to say, 'wait a bit, be patient, I'll speak soon, and then I'll answer you all... Just wait a bit.'

But now he saw that his mother was crying and his lips quivered, and stretching out his little hands to her, he began crying bitterly himself. The little child's weeping did what the nurse's coaxing could not do. Firsova at once came out of her dazed state, she seized the little boy and covering him with hungry kisses she said,

'There... there... don't cry my darling, my little treasure... I'll work as a maid, I'll wash floors, but you won't go hungry, my little darlings, my sweet children...' But despite these words of comfort, the tears kept coming. Tears of fear and helpless despair.

III

Varvara Petrovna Radina-Streletskaya was sitting in her spacious dining room, where the oak walls were covered with tapestries in faded colours. She sat in her *empire* armchair and drank coffee. Streletsky was sitting opposite her in a light jacket, and was reading the paper. A tightly corseted maid in a white mob cap was serving them, stepping noiselessly about the room.

It was a lovely picture. The first breakfast between two young people recently married and *enfin seuls*! Everything had an air of elegance, order and domestic warmth. And it was all of a piece: the light blue—*bleu pastel*—baize of Radina-Streletskaya's hood showed off her golden hair to perfection; his navy smoking jacket; the blinding white tablecloth and the blue china, the glinting of the silver cutlery on the table and the faded figures of shepherds and shepherdesses, smiling their naïve and indistinct smiles up on the tapestries...

Too lovely for words, this picture, if it hadn't been for the sun, the merciless sun. Sunlight flooded into the dining room, and in its rays, as always, the truth shone out clearly and insistently. The sunlight illuminated the walls of the dining room: not real oak, but mere panelling, not real tapestries, but imitations. The silver was not silver at all, but nickel silver, and the beautiful gold of Streletskaya's hair was obviously purchased from Mothiron. The sun illuminated her weary eyes, the wrinkles around her eyes and on her neck, and the grey tinge to her skin, worn out by greasepaint, and the constant rubbing to remove it.

The sun also illuminated in some indefinably clear way the boredom and displeasure, which hung like a shroud over this apparently intimate and cosy scene. It sounded its note in every word the couple exchanged, even though he never addressed her without a 'sweetheart' or a 'dearest' or even 'my angel', and she called him 'Misya'.

They were both actors with Roman Petrovich and had been for more than fifteen years. Their marriage was one of those considered to be exemplary in the artistic world. They endeavoured always to behave with correctness, and it was their conceit that drove this endeavour. They had a horror of being confused with the 'Bohemian set' as they put it. They allowed themselves neither late night meals, nor drinking sprees. They lived a good while in the same flat, they always ate at the proper times, kept a strictly trained servant, only paid visits to family homes and saved their money in a bank.

Varvara Petrovna was older than her husband. Even before her career with Roman Petrovich she had had about ten years of huge success in the provinces, and she had been captivating Petrovich's audiences now for fifteen years with her gaiety, those eyes which seemed so naïve from the stage and her little snub nose.

Although it is true that in recent years the audience had begun to notice that the feather light tread of Varvara Petrovna had become heavier, that her laughter no longer sounded so tinkling and silvery; that after she had danced and tripped merrily about the stage like a butter-fly she had to spend a moment or two getting her breath back; and her extraordinary waist had begun to lose its softness and even the artistic skills of Voitkevich could not conceal this fact.

But who else could say in such an inimitable way,

'And didn't the silly little girl come up trumps!' in *Tomboy.* Or call out in *Secret*:

'I'm going to be the fat old Muchkina and drink *kvas* and eat biscuits and watch the barges come past from the jetty.'

Where else to find such an infectious gaiety, such a 'sweet flippertigibbet', such 'flighty charm', such a 'naughty thing' and so on and so forth?

But three years had passed with ever fewer light come-dies in the repertoire. Playwrights were writing and trans-lating less of them, it was all melodramas, dramas, even, terrible to relate, tragedies. And Varvara Petrovich was less and less called upon, there was no need for her birdlike twittering... And she was irritable, and anxious, and she was working herself up for a row with the director Zamayev. This season she had only played one new part: a young widow, mad about the races, not even a major role, but second fiddle to that slip of a girl Muranova, whose only advantage lay in the fact that she was as skinny as a stray cat, and her eyes occupied half her face.

And the audiences were strangely different. The old-timers and the regulars had thinned out entirely, younger audiences had appeared like mushrooms in the grass, demanding dramas and making something of that Muranova, who was barely out of school... Varvara Petrovna could see it all clearly.

All this explained the unhappy, brooding silence between the couple, whose appearance had suggested such marital bliss.

'Misya, another coffee?'

'Merci, my angel.'

A pause. The rustle of newspapers. The hissing of the samovar.

'Orlitsyna got another bouquet yesterday.'

'That's her oil baron again... I'd like to know how an honest woman would get on in the theatre nowadays...'

A long pause.

'Don't forget Misya that we're engaged to play cards at the Sinitsyns tonight.'

'How could I forget, my sweetheart?'

Another pause.

At last the maid entered noiselessly and brought a book and a parcel to her mistress.

'Please sign, ma'am. Aleksei brought it.'

'A part!' screamed Varvara Petrovna, forgetting all her reserve, and throwing herself on the little book like a cat. 'In a new play... Zamayev didn't mention it at all! And you've got one.'

Streletsky rose from his place, too. They both quickly scribbled by their names in the little book and once the maid had been dispatched they seized the books.

The boredom and languor disappeared straightaway. A new energy ran through them both like an electric shock. Varvara Petrovna's eyes sparkled, her cheeks were flushed...

'"Nina's Marriage",' she read the title. 'This sounds rather interesting. The role of Polina Mikhailovna Ustyuzhskaya, a coquette—'

She suddenly stopped. Her eyes widened, she staggered backwards, as if from a blow and looked at the words, which jiggled about in front of her eyes, her hands were shaking so. For a few minutes she couldn't say a word. Her throat was constricted. Then, panting, she whispered almost inaudibly,

'What, what is this?'

'What is it, my darling?' asked Streletsky anxiously, noticing his wife's agitation.

She handed him the paper with an involuntary gesture.

He looked, and he, too, froze. Before his eyes, in black letters on the white sheet, the words: 'The role of Polina Mikhailovna Ustyuzhskaya, a coquette, aged nearly fifty, but pretending to be younger.'

He lowered his eyes, then, not looking at his wife, he murmured, 'I expect it's a mistake, my angel.'

Varvara Petrovna found her voice at last. She leaped up from her seat, quite forgetting her elegant reserve and paced around the room like a panther.

'A mistake!' she screamed hysterically. 'A mistake! No! I know what this is. This is Zamayev up to his tricks! That Muranova put him up to it! Oh yes! They think they can have a good laugh at me! Well I'll show them! Yes I will! Think they can push me into old lady roles without asking me first! Oh! What a despicable lot they are! I won't forgive them making fun of me! I'm going to write to all the papers! I'll rip up my contract! I'm going back to the provinces! Then they'll see what it's like without Radina! Oh yes! They'll come to me on bended knees then and you see if I give in! The rogues...'

She put her hands to her breast and gulped, unable to finish her speech, then fell onto the divan.

'My angel, calm down!' muttered Streletsky, rushing to the carafe and giving her water. She pushed him away roughly. Drops of water like tears rained onto the blue skirts of her dress.

'Go away! Get out!'

She got up again. Real tears coursed down her cheeks, washing away the powder. Her hair was dishevelled and the pitiful grey strands could be seen under the golden curls.

'You don't care! I know they've sent you another lover role! A handsome lover! It's only me they send this slap in the face! As a reward for all my... Oh God, oh God!'

And she wept real despairing tears, she sobbed and wailed and groaned and banged her head on the back of the divan. After a few minutes the maid was sent for a doctor and Streletsky was sent to Zamayev and the shepherds and shepherdesses watched all this from the tapestries and continued their naïve smiling.

IV

Firsova went through the stage door and backstage.

After the day's sun, it seemed quite dark on the stage. Shadows scuttled past pulling heavy scenery. Lamps burned dimly here and there. The curtain was lifted and the auditorium looked mysterious, in some of the boxes the doors were open and the dead blue daylight had crept in in an unpleasant way.

A hole yawned in the floor of the stage like a black grave.

For the first time ever Firsova felt frightened in the theatre. It seemed to her to be something alive, merciless and indifferent—like fate itself. She seemed to hear its dark walls saying,

'I'll devour everything I need in you... and then throw you away like a worn out rag...' and the gaping doors smiled darkly, mockingly.

Shivering, feeling slightly sick and dizzy, Firsova went into the directors' room with the feeling of someone throwing herself into deep water. Her fate was about to be decided. She knew she would hear rejection. She could even predict the explanations:

'There's just no parts for you. You don't suit vaudeville...' and so on and so forth.

'Well then,' with a sort of dull desperation she attempted to collect her wandering thoughts. 'I'll ask if I can stay on in costumes. Something or other... Just so as not to die of hunger...'

Zamayev nodded to her from behind his books and papers. His kindly, tired face looked at her as usual with some disdain and a good deal of pity.

'Hallo, my dear. I wanted you to come in...,' he began.

Zamayev made a point of being equally courteous with everyone, he had by now seen most things, and always maintained a weary calm.

'Whatever you want, Petr Ivanovich,' she whispered.

He stared at her worn face in silence, at her hat with its raven's wing, her stained cape. Then he cleared his throat.

'Oh Lord, oh lord! He's going to say it...' thought Firsova.

A terrible pallor spread over her face, she held onto her chair so as not to fall. It was immediately as if her legs were full of warm water or stuffed with cotton wool, she couldn't have taken a step.

He began speaking, trying to be delicate.

'I thought it necessary to call you in, my dear. I have a little part for you here, but I wasn't sure whether you would like to take it. I do understand that you are still young... but you see, we need to find an old lady, a comedy role. I know how able you are... I remember your grandmother well... Of course it's very early for you to make this shift. But I do recommend it. It's a very good part... You'll stand out... And of course Roman Petrovich will add to your salary...

He lifted his eyes to look at her and was amazed. Two eyes looked at him raptly. Firsova's cheeks glowed, she smiled and tears hung on her eyelashes. She murmured incoherently,

'Oh Lord! Well of course! I'm so grateful to you... So grateful... Let me try... You'll see... I can do it... Thank you for your faith in me...'

And she shook his hand with feverish energy, forgetting her usual timidity.

He looked at her with pleasure and gave her the book. On it was written:

'Polina Mikhailovna Ustyuzhskaya, a coquette, aged nearly fifty, but pretending to be younger.'

'Thank you, thank you.'

Firsova, barely conscious of her movements almost ran out of the theatre and flew home as if on wings, hugging the little book tightly to her chest. The shift had been made. Survival was possible. This elderly coquette might have saved the lives of two small creatures. And looking into Tosik's grey eyes, his mother spoke in a joyful rapturous whisper,

'We'll have enough food to eat. We'll survive. My sweet babies, I can bring you up and, with God's help, set you on your feet. I'll act so well! My sweet babies! God has provided.'

And Tosik surely understood her. His eyes smiled back at her and he laughed: a quiet joyous laughter, like the cooing of a dove.

Poor Liza

Nikolai Karamzin

Perhaps none of those living in Moscow know the outer reaches of this town as well as I do, because no one comes so frequently to the fields, no one has wandered as much as I have, aimlessly, without any design, following where my eyes take me, through the meadows and copses, over the hills and through the levels. Every summer I find new pleasant places, or new things of beauty in the old places.

But most pleasing of all to me is the place where the gloomy gothic spires of the Simonov Monastery rise. Standing on this hill you can see to the right almost all of Moscow, that terrible accretion of houses and churches which presents itself to the eye in the form of a majestic amphitheatre: a magnificent picture, especially when the sun shines on it, when its evening rays flare on the countless golden domes, the countless crosses reaching up into the sky. The intense concentrated green of the flowering meadows is spread out below, and beyond them, through the yellow sands, flows a bright river, flurried by the light oars of fishing boats and roaring under the rudders of the flat-bottomed goods boats that come from the fertile countries of the Russian Empire to bestow bread upon insatiable Moscow. On the other side of the river there is a copse of oak trees, where numerous flocks of sheep graze. There, young shepherds, sitting in the shade of the trees, sing simple, sad songs to while away the unvarying summer days. A little further in the dense green of ancient elms, gleams the golden head of Danilov Monastery, and further still, almost on the very horizon, is the blue mass of the Sparrow Hills. To the left are the wide fields covered with corn, little woods, three or four tiny villages, and Kolomenskoye a way off with its tall palace.

I often visit this place and I come here almost every year to see spring in. I come here, too, in the dark days of autumn to grieve together with nature. The winds howl horribly within the walls of the deserted monastery, between the gravestones, overgrown with tall grass, and in the dark passageways between the cells. There, leaning on the ruined gravestones, I listen to time's hollow moan rising from the abyss of the past. A moan which wrings my trembling heart. Sometimes I enter the cells and imagine those who lived here—doleful pictures indeed. I see a grey-haired monk, kneeling before the crucifixion and praying that he soon be relieved from his earthly bonds, for all his pleasure in life is gone, all feeling, except the feeling of weakness and sickness, has died within him. A young monk with a pale face and languishing eyes looks out at the fields through the bars on his window and sees the happy birds, swimming freely in the sky's sea. He sees them, and weeps bitter tears. So he pines, withers and fades, and the dull tolling of the bell tells me of his untimely death.

Sometimes I look at the images on the cathedral gates of miracles that came to pass at this monastery, fishes falling from the sky to feed the inhabitants when it was under siege from countless enemies, or the image of the Mother of God, who put enemies to flight. And these refresh in my memory the history of our land—the doleful history of the times when fearsome Tartars and Lithuanians laid the outskirts of the Russian capital to waste with fire and sword, and when unhappy Moscow, like a defenceless widow, looked only to God for help in her cruel misfortunes.

But I am drawn to the walls of the Simonov Monastery more often by the memory of the lamentable fate of Liza, my poor Liza. How I love those things that touch my heart and make me weep tears of tender sorrow!

A deserted hut, without doors or windows or floor, the rotten roof long since fallen through, stands about seventy fathoms from the walls of the monastery, by a little birch copse and in a green meadow. Near on thirty years ago beautiful, kind Liza lived here with her elderly mother.

Liza's father had been a fairly wealthy peasant, as he had loved his work, ploughed the earth well and always lived in a sober manner. But soon after his death his wife and daughter fell on hard times. The lazy hireling worked the land less well, and the corn gave a poor harvest. They were forced to rent out their land, and for very little money. To add to this, the poor widow would weep almost continuously over the death of her husband—for peasant women also know how to love! She became weaker from day to day and was not able to work at all. Only Liza, who was fifteen when her father left them, only Liza, with no thought to her tender youth, no thought to her rare beauty, worked day and night, weaving canvas, knitting stockings, picking flowers in the spring and berries in the summer and selling them in Moscow. The kind-hearted, sensitive old woman, seeing her daughter's tireless work, often pressed her to her feeble heart and called her God's mercy, her provider, the joy of her old age, and she prayed that God might reward her for all she did for her mother.

'God gave me hands that I might use them in work,' Liza said, 'You fed me from your own breast and looked after me when I was a child, and now it's my turn to look after you. Only don't grieve any more, weep no longer. Our tears will not bring Father back.' Still, often sweet Liza could not hold back her own tears when –oh!—she recalled that she had had a father and had one no longer. But for her mother's peace of mind she tried to hide her heart's distress and appear calm and cheerful.

'In heaven, my dear Liza,' the grieving old woman would reply. 'I will stop my tears in heaven. I have heard that everyone will rejoice there, and I too will rejoice when I see your father. But I don't want to die yet—what would happen to you without me? Thrown on the mercy of others? No, first of all, God willing, we must find you a home. Perhaps a good man will be found, and then I will bless you both, my sweet children, make the sign of the cross and lay myself down calmly in the cold earth.'

Two years had passed since the death of Liza's father. The meadows were covered with flowers and Liza went to Moscow with lily-of-the-valley. A young well-dressed man with a pleasant face came up to her on the street. She showed him the flowers and she blushed.

'Are you selling them?' he asked with a smile.

'Yes,' she answered.

'What do you want for them?'

'Five kopecks.'

'That's too little. Here's a rouble for you.'

Liza, amazed, stole a glance at the young man, blushed even more, and then lowering her eyes to the ground, she told him she wouldn't take a rouble.

'Why ever not?'

'I don't want more than I asked.'

'I think that lovely lilies-of-the-valley, picked by the hand of a lovely girl are worth a rouble. But if you won't take it, here's five kopecks for you. I would like to buy flowers from you always, I would like it if you only picked flowers for me.'

Liza gave him the flowers, took the five kopecks, bowed and wanted to go, but the stranger took her arm and stopped her.

'Where are you going now?'

'Home.'

'Where is your home?'

Liza told him where she lived, she told him and then she left. The young man did not stop her from going. Perhaps because passers-by were beginning to stop and watch them with sly grins.

When she got home Liza told her mother what had happened.

'You did well not to take the rouble. He might have been a bad sort.'

'Oh no, Mother. I don't think so. He had such a kind face, such a voice.'

'But still, Liza, it is better to provide for oneself by one's own labours, and never accept anything offered for free. You don't yet know, my girl, how bad people can hurt a poor girl. My heart is never quite at peace when you are in town. I always place a candle before the icon, and pray to our Lord God that He might protect you from all misfortune, and from any attack upon you.' Liza's eyes filled up with tears at this, and she kissed her mother.

The next day Liza picked the very best lilies-of-the-valley and went with them into town. Her eyes sought something quietly. Plenty of people wanted to buy her flowers, but she told them that they were not for sale, and she looked this way, then that way. Evening came, it was time to return home, and the flowers were thrown into the Moscow River.

'No one will have you,' said Liza, feeling a sadness in her heart. The next day, towards evening, she was sitting by the window spinning, and singing sad songs in a quiet voice, when suddenly she jumped up and cried out:

'Oh!'

The young stranger stood beneath her window.

'What is it?' asked her frightened mother, who was sitting beside her.

'Nothing, Mother,' answered Liza timidly. 'It's just that I saw him.'

'Saw whom?'

'The young man who bought flowers from me.' The old woman looked out of the window. The young man bowed to her so politely, with such an obliging expression, that she could think nothing but good of him.

'Good day to you, my good woman,' he said. 'I am very tired. Do you have any fresh milk?'

The obliging Liza, without waiting for her mother's reply, perhaps because she already knew what it would be, ran to the cellar and brought a jug with a clean wooden tankard over it, seized a glass, washed it, wiped it with a white cloth, poured the milk and handed it through the window, but as she did so she looked down at the ground. The stranger drank, and nectar from the hand of Hebe could not have seemed sweeter to him. You may guess how he thanked Liza after this, and thanked her not so much with words as with looks. The kindhearted old lady had managed by then to tell him all about her grief and her consolation—about the death of her husband and the sweet nature of her daughter, her daughter's love of work, her fondness, and so on, and so forth. He listened to her attentively, but his eyes were upon—need it be said upon whom? And Liza, shy Liza, glanced now and then at the young man, but her blue eyes, when they met his gaze, looked down faster than lightning flashes before vanishing in the clouds.

'I would like it,' he said to her mother, 'if your daughter were to sell her work to me and to no one else. In such a way she will no longer need to go so often to the town, and you won't have to part with her. I will come here to you myself from time to time.' At this Liza's eyes sparkled with joy, which she tried in vain to conceal; her cheeks blazed like the sunset on a bright summer evening, she looked at her left sleeve and pinched it with her right hand. The old woman accepted this offer willingly, suspecting no bad intention, and she assured the stranger that the canvas which Liza wove, and the stockings knitted by Liza were the best and lasted longer than any others. It was getting dark, and the young man wanted to leave.

'But what should we call you, kind sir?' asked the old woman.

'My name is Erast,' he answered.

'Erast,' whispered Liza quietly. 'Erast.' She repeated his name five times or so, as if trying to impress it upon her heart. Erast said farewell to them and left. Liza's eyes followed him as he went, and her mother sat in thought and, taking her daughter by the hand, said to her,

'Oh Liza, How kind and good he is. If only your husband were to be such as he.' Liza's heart was troubled.

'Mother! Mother! How could that be? He is a lord, and between peasants and...' Liza did not finish her speech.

The reader should know at this point that this young man, this Erast, was a fairly wealthy man, of good birth, with good sense and a kind heart, kind by instinct, but weak-willed and inconstant. He led a life without purpose, thought only of his own pleasure, looked for it in society's amusements, but often did not find it, and so he was bored, and complained of his lot. Liza's beauty had made an impression on his heart at their first meeting. He was a keen reader of novels, of idylls, had a fairly lively imagination, and was often transported to those times (past or imagined) when, if we are to believe the poets, people walked carefree in the meadows, bathed in pure springs, kissed like turtledoves, rested beneath the roses and myrtles and spent their days in happy idleness. It seemed to him that in Liza he had found that which his heart had long sought. 'Nature is calling me into its embraces, to partake in its pure joys,' he thought and made a decision, at least for the moment, to abandon society.

We will return to Liza. Night had fallen, her mother had blessed her and wished her sweet dreams, but on this occasion her wish was not granted. Liza slept very badly. The shape of Erast, her soul's new inhabitant, came to her mind in such a lively fashion, that she woke almost every moment, she woke and sighed. Before dawn, Liza got up and went out to the bank of the Moscow River, sat melancholy on the grass, looking at the white mist, which drifted in the air, leaving shining drops on nature's green shroud as it rose. Silence reigned. But soon the light of day rose and woke all creation. The copses and the bushes came to life, the birds fluttered and began singing, the flowers lifted their heads to drink in the rays of life-giving light. But Liza still sat melancholy. Oh Liza, Liza, what has happened to you? Until this day you woke early with the birds and rejoiced with them, and your pure, joyous heart shone out from your eyes, as the sun shines in the drops of heavenly dew, but now you are filled with thought, and the joy of nature, shared by all creatures, is a stranger to your heart.

But now the young shepherd chased his flock along the riverbank, playing on his pipe. Liza looked at him and thought, 'if only the one who occupied my thoughts had been born a simple peasant, a shepherd, and if he were now chasing his flock past me, oh, how I would bow to him with a smile and say in greeting, "Good day, dear shepherd, where do you lead your flock? There is green grass here for your sheep, and crimson flowers, to weave a crown for your hat." And he would look at me tenderly and perhaps he would take my hand... Dreams!' The shepherd playing on his pipe passed by and was hidden over the brow of a near hill with his bright flock.

Suddenly Liza heard the sound of oars. She looked at the river and saw a boat, and in it Erast.

Her heart raced, but surely not through fear. She stood and wanted to leave, but couldn't. Erast jumped onto the bank, went to Liza—and her dream came partially true—*because he looked at her tenderly and took her hand...* And Liza, Liza stood with her eyes downcast, her cheeks burning, her heart quivering. She couldn't pull back her hand, she couldn't turn away when he came close to her with his rosy lips... Oh! He kissed her, he kissed her with such passion that all the universe seemed to her to be on fire. 'Sweet Liza!' said Erast. 'Sweet Liza, I love you!' and these words resounded deep in her heart like rapturous heavenly music, she hardly dared believe her ears and... But I will put down my pen. I may only say that in this moment of exultation all Liza's shyness disappeared, Erast found that he was loved, passionately loved by a new and pure open heart.

They sat on the grass and sat so that between them there was little space and they looked into each other's eyes, saying to each other, 'Love me true,' and so two hours passed in an instant. At last Liza remembered that her mother might be worried about her. They must part.

'Oh Erast', she said. 'Will you love me always?'

'Always, my dear Liza, always!' he answered.

'Will you give me your word?'

'Yes, dear Liza, I will!'

'No I don't need a vow. I believe you, Erast, I believe you. Could you ever deceive poor Liza? That could never be.'

'Never, never, sweet Liza!'

'How happy I am, and how my Mother will delight, when she hears you love me, Erast.'

'No, Liza! You must not tell her.'

'Why ever not?'

'Old people can be suspicious. She will imagine something bad.'

'That cannot be!'

'Nonetheless, I beg you not to speak one word of this to her.'

'Very well, Erast, I will obey you, although I do not like to hide anything from her.'

They said farewell, kissed one last time and promised to meet every evening on the river bank or in the birch copse, or somewhere close to Liza's hut, but promised faithfully they would always meet. Liza left, but a hundred times her eyes looked back to Erast who stood on the bank, watching her go.

Liza went back to her hut in quite a different mood to the one in which she had left it. A heartfelt joy could be seen in her face and in all her movements. 'He loves me,' she thought, and exulted in the thought.

'Mother!' Liza said to her mother, who had only just woken. 'What a wonderful morning! How alive everything is in the fields. The larks have never sung so well, the sun has never shone so brightly, the flowers have never had such scent!'

The old lady, supporting herself on a stick, went out to the meadow to enjoy the morning, which Liza had painted with such beautiful colours. It really did seem to her extremely pleasant, her lovely daughter had brought all of nature to life with her own liveliness.

'Oh Liza!' she said, 'How God sets all to rights. I have lived more than three-score years and yet I can never have my fill of the sight of God's creation, of the clear sky like the roof of a high tent, or the earth which is covered anew each year by grass and flowers. The Lord of Heaven must have loved man a great deal that he made such beauty for him on earth. Oh, Liza, would any of us want to die, if we hadn't known grief at one time or another... It seems it must be so. Perhaps we would forget our own souls if tears never fell from our eyes.'

And Liza thought, 'I would rather forget my own soul, than my sweet friend!'

After this Erast and Liza, fearing not to keep their word, met every evening (after Liza's mother had gone to bed), either on the river bank, or in the birch grove, but more often in the shade of the hundred-year-old oak trees (about eighty fathoms from the hut). The oaks overarched a deep clear pool, dug in ancient times. There the quiet moonbeams fell through the green branches and shone silver in Liza's fair hair, ruffled gently by the west winds, and her friend's hand, and often these moonbeams lit a sparkling tear of love in Liza's eyes, dried always by Erast's kiss. They embraced, but chaste and modest Cynthia did not hide herself behind a cloud—pure were their embraces, and innocent.

'When you...' Liza said to Erast, 'when you say "I love you, my friend!", when you press me to your heart, and look at me with your sweet eyes, oh then I am so happy, so happy that I forget myself, I forget everything except Erast. Is it not strange? Strange that I could live happily and in peace before I knew you. Now I hardly understand how, now I think that life without you is not life, but grief and longing. Without your eyes, the bright moon is dark, without your voice the singing nightingale sounds dreary, without your breath the breeze is not lovely to me.'

Erast was delighted with his 'shepherdess', for that is what he called Liza, and seeing how she loved him, he seemed himself to be worthier of love. All the glittering amusements of society appeared meaningless in comparison with the pleasure his heart felt at this passionate friendship with an innocent soul. He thought with disgust of the contemptible lust which had once gratified his senses. 'I will live with Liza as her brother,' he thought. 'I'll not abuse her love and I shall be happy always.' Impetuous young man! Do you know your heart? Can you answer for your every movement? Is reason the constant ruler of your feelings?

Liza asked Erast to visit her mother often.

'I love her,' she said, 'and I wish for the best for her, and I believe that the sight of you is a great happiness for anyone.' The old woman really did rejoice to see him. She loved to talk to him about her dead husband, and the days of her youth, how she met with her sweet Ivan for the first time, how he fell in love with her and lived with her in such love and harmony.

'O, we could never have our fill of the sight of one another—until the very hour when cruel death cut him down. He died in my arms.' Erast listened to her with unaffected pleasure. He bought Liza's work from her and always wanted to pay ten times the price she had set, but the old woman would never take any extra.

Several weeks passed in such a manner. One evening Erast waited a long time for his Liza. At last she came, but she was so unhappy that he was frightened—her eyes were red with crying.

'Liza, Liza what's happened to you?'

'Oh Erast, I have been crying.'

'Why? What's the matter?'

'I must tell you everything. A man has come courting me, the son of a rich peasant from the next village. My mother wants me to marry him.'

'And you've agreed?'

'O cruel man! How can you ask? I'm sorry for my mother. She cries and says that I don't want her to be at peace, that she will suffer even at death, if she hasn't found me a husband. Oh, my Mother doesn't know that I have such a sweet friend.' Erast kissed Liza and told her that her happiness was dearer to him than anything else in the world and when her mother died he would take her in and would live with her, by her side in the country and in the dreaming woods as in Paradise.

'But you may never be my husband,' said Liza with a quiet sigh.

'Why not?'

'I am a peasant.'

'You hurt me. The soul, the sensitive innocent soul is more important than anything for your friend—and Liza will always be closest to my heart.'

She threw herself into his embrace and from that moment their innocence was doomed. Erast felt an extraordinary agitation in his blood—Liza had never seemed so wonderful to him, her caresses had never touched him so, her kisses had never scorched him so. She knew nothing, she suspected nothing, she feared nothing—the darkness of the evening fed desire, not a single star shone in the sky, no ray of light illuminated the wrongdoing. Erast trembled, Liza too, not knowing why, not knowing what was happening to her... Liza, Liza, where is your guardian angel? Where is your innocence?

For only a minute they were lost. Liza, not understanding her feelings, was astonished, and she asked Erast. He was silent, he searched for words but could not find them.

'I'm scared,' said Liza, 'I'm scared of what has happened to us. I feel as if I am dying. As if my soul... I don't know how to say it. Erast, why are you silent? You sigh... Oh Lord. What is it?'

Thunder growled and lightning flashed. Liza trembled all over.

'Erast, Erast!' she said. 'I'm scared! I'm afraid the thunder will kill me, because I am a sinful woman.' A storm raged terribly, the rain poured down from black clouds, it was as if all nature lamented the passing of Liza's innocence. Erast tried to calm Liza and lead her back to her hut. The tears rolled from her eyes as they parted.

'Oh Erast, tell me that we shall be happy again as we once were.'

'We shall, Liza, we shall,' he answered.

'God willing. I can but believe your words, because I love you. Yet in my heart... But that's enough! Forgive me! Tomorrow, tomorrow we'll meet again.'

Their meetings continued, but how everything had changed! Erast could no longer content himself with his Liza's innocent caresses, her gazes, so full of love, the touch of her hand, her kiss, her pure embraces. He wanted more, more, and at last he had nothing left to desire, and he who knows his heart, who has considered the nature of his most tender pleasures, will naturally agree with me that the fulfilment of *all* desires is love's most dangerous trial. Liza was no longer that angel of innocence who had once lit up his imagination and delighted his soul. Platonic love had given way to feelings which he could not feel proud of, and which were not a novelty for him. As for Liza, now that she had given herself to him completely, she lived and breathed only for him and gave way to his will in everything like the lamb of innocence, and made his pleasure her happiness. She saw a change in him and often said to him,

'You were more joyful before, we were calmer and more contented before, and I didn't fear losing your love so much.'

Sometimes when they parted he would say,

'Tomorrow, Liza, I can't see you, I have important business,' and at these words Liza would sigh.

At last five days passed without seeing him and she was in a state of great distress. On the sixth day he came with a despondent face and said,

'Dear Liza, I must leave you for a while. You know we are at war, I am in the army and my regiment is going into battle.' Liza paled and nearly fainted.

Erast caressed her, said that he would always love sweet Liza and he hoped on his return never to be parted from her again. She was silent at length, then her eyes filled with bitter tears, she seized his hand and looking at him with all the tenderness of love, she asked,

'Can you stay behind?'

'I can.' He answered. 'But only with great disgrace, with a stain on my honour. Everyone will scorn me, despise me as a coward, a thankless son to my country.'

'Well if that is so,' said Liza, 'then go, go where God leads you. But you may be killed.'

'Death for one's country is nothing to be feared, dear Liza.'

'I will die, when you are no longer alive.'

'But why think that? I hope to remain alive, I hope to return to you, my friend.'

'By God's grace, God's grace. Every day, every hour I will pray for it. Oh, why can I not read or write? You could have let me know about everything that was happening to you and I could have written to you—about my tears!'

'No, Liza, look after yourself, look after yourself for the sake of your friend. I don't want you to cry without me there.'

'Cruel man! Do you wish to deprive me of that joy? No! Parted from you, I will only stop crying when my heart has dried up.'

'Think rather about that pleasant moment when we shall see each other again.'

'I shall think of it! I shall! If only it would come quickly. Dear, sweet Erast, remember, remember your poor Liza who loves you more than she loves herself.'

I cannot describe everything that was said then. The next day was to be their last meeting. Erast wanted to say goodbye to Liza's mother, who couldn't hold back her tears, when she heard that the 'dear kind gentleman' had to go to war. He made her take some money, saying,

'I don't want Liza to sell her work whilst I am not here, as we agreed it belongs to me.' The old woman covered him with her blessings.

'God grant,' she said, 'you return to us safe and sound, and that I see you once again in this life. And perhaps Liza will have found herself a suitable husband by this time. How I would thank God if you could be there at the wedding. And when Liza has children, you, sir, must be there to christen them. Oh, how I would love to live until that moment.' Liza stood by her mother and didn't dare look at her. The reader may well imagine how she felt at that moment.

But what did she feel when Erast, embracing her for the last time, for the last time pressing her to his heart, said, 'Forgive me, Liza!'? What a touching scene. The dawn, like a sea of crimson, spilled over the eastern sky. Erast stood under the branches of the tall oak, holding his poor, forlorn grieving friend, who in parting from him was parting from her own soul. All of nature was silent.

Liza sobbed, Erast cried, he left her and she fell, she dropped down to her knees, lifted her hand to the sky and watched Erast, who was leaving, going further and further, and at last he disappeared, the sun rose, and Liza, abandoned, poor Liza fell senseless.

She came to her senses and the light seemed dull and dreary. All nature's delights were gone for her, together with her heart's love.

'Why,' she thought, 'have I been left in this wilderness? What prevents me from flying after my Erast? War holds no terror for me, only being without my friend holds terror for me. I want to live with him, to die with him, or to save his precious life with my own. Wait, wait, my beloved! I am flying to you!' She wanted to run to Erast, but she was stopped by the thought of her mother. Liza sighed, she lowered her head and walked with quiet steps back to her hut. From now onwards her days were days of grief and yearning which she had to hide from her fond mother—her heart only suffered even more, and only felt relief when Liza, alone in the thick woods, could let her tears fall freely and moan over the parting from her sweet friend. Often the sad dove let its plaintive voice join in her moaning. But sometimes, if only very rarely, a golden ray of hope, a ray of consolation would light the darkness of her sorrow. 'When he returns to me, how happy I will be, how everything will change!' Her gaze brightened the roses in her cheeks bloomed anew, and Liza smiled like the May morning after a tempestuous night. So passed about two months.

One day Liza had to go to Moscow to buy the rosewater her mother used to treat her eyes. On one of the main streets she saw a magnificent coach, and in the coach she saw... Erast.

'Oh!' cried Liza and threw herself at the coach, but it drove past and turned into a yard. Erast got out and he had turned towards the porch of the big house, when he suddenly felt himself embraced by Liza. He paled. Then, without answering her exclamations, he took her by the hand, led her into his study, shut the door and said to her,

'Liza, my circumstances have changed. I am betrothed to another. You must leave me in peace, and for your own peace of mind you must forget me. I loved you and love you now, that is, I wish you the very best. Here's a hundred roubles. Take them,' he put the money in her pocket. 'Let me kiss you one last time, and go home.' Before Liza could come to her senses he had led her out of the study and had said to a servant,

'Escort this girl from the yard'.

My heart is filled with pain and compassion at this moment. I forget that Erast is human, I'm ready to curse him, but my tongue is still, I look at him and the tears roll down my face. Why, oh why am I writing not a novel but grievous reality?

So did Erast deceive Liza when he told her he had gone into the army? No, he really was in the army, but instead of fighting the enemy he played cards and lost nearly his entire estate. Soon peace was declared and Erast returned to Moscow, burdened with debts. He had only one way to change his fortunes and that was to marry a rich elderly widow who was in love with him. He decided on this course, and moved to her house to live, having heaved a sincere sigh at the thought of his Liza. But can all this justify him?

Liza found herself on the street and in a state which no pen may describe.

'He... he threw me out? He loves another? I am destroyed.' Those were her thoughts and her feelings. A terrible fainting fit interrupted them for a time. One kind woman who was walking on that street, stopped there, where Liza lay on the ground, and tried to bring her round. The unhappy girl opened her eyes and stood up with the help of the kind woman, thanked her and went on her way, without even knowing where she was bound.

'I shan't live,' thought Liza. 'I shan't... Oh if only the sky would fall on me. If only the earth would swallow up this poor girl... But the sky won't fall, the earth won't give way. Sorrow is mine.' She left the town and suddenly found herself on the edge of a deep pool in the shade of some ancient oaks, which had only a few weeks before been the silent witnesses of her raptures. These memories shook her to the depths of her soul, the terrible suffering of her heart was visible on her face. But after a moment or two she stood in deep thought—she looked around and saw the daughter of her neighbour (a fifteen-year-old girl), walking along the road. She called her, pulled out of her pocket the hundred roubles and giving them to her said,

'Dear Anyuta, dearest friend, please take this money to my mother, it isn't stolen. Tell her that Liza has done her wrong, that I hid from her my love for a very cruel man, for E—, well why know his name? Tell her that he betrayed me, and ask her to forgive me, God will help her, kiss her hand like this, as I kiss yours now, say that poor Liza told you to kiss her, say that I—' Then she threw herself into the water. Anyuta cried out and wept, but couldn't save her, she ran to the village and the people gathered and dragged Liza out, but she was already dead.

In such a way she brought the life of her lovely soul and body to an end. When we are both *there*, in the other life, I will see you, and I will know you, my sweet Liza.

They dug her grave by the pool under the gloomy oak, and placed a wooden cross on it. I often sit there in thought, leaning on the urn which holds her ashes. The pool's reflection ripples in my eyes, the leaves rustle above me.

Liza's mother heard the news of her daughter's terrible death and her blood ran cold in horror, her eyes were closed forever. The hut was left deserted. The wind moans through it and superstitious village people, listening to the noise at night, say,

'That is the moaning of the dead. That is poor Liza moaning.'

Erast was unhappy to the end of his days. When he heard of Liza's fate he was unable to find any consolation, he considered himself to be a murderer. I met him a year before his death. He told me this story and he brought me to Liza's grave. Perhaps now they are reconciled.

Scar

Evgeny Grishkovets

The Hotel Poima changed completely after its renovation. It wasn't even the look of the building—it went deeper than that—although outwardly it had been transformed, too. But it was the deep-down change which mattered.

What it had been like to stay there before the renovation, and what it was like now, Kostya couldn't say, because he had never once stayed in the hotel. And why would he? Kostya lived five minutes' walk away from Hotel Poima. Why would he want to stay in a hotel in his own town?

The town also boasted a Hotel Central, a Hotel Ivushka and a hotel that was considered the main one and was named after the town. The Central was a typical redbrick four-storey building: council workers from the region were put up there when they came to town on business; long-distance lorry drivers; and market traders, up from the South. Ivushka was way out in the sticks. Middle-ranking, and not-quite-middle-ranking, government people used the main hotel. Still Poima was the most beautiful hotel, the hotel on the riverbank.

There was also a railway hotel, a place by the airport and some recently opened insalubrious little joints with names like Northern Lights and Mon Plaisir, gracing the outskirts of the town. But none of these really counted.

At Poima the beauty of the design, of that period in architecture, could be felt. Kostya loved the building with its long high portico, stone steps and white painted pillars at the entrance. A balcony jutted out above the entrance and it had the same white painted balustrade.

At weekends in spring, summer and early autumn, the wedding parties celebrating in the hotel restaurant were photographed on the steps. Kostya had seen them as a little boy, when he'd been out cycling, or just dawdling along the embankment. And then the weddings took their noisy course behind the colonnade and the windows, and only very drunk men in already crumpled white shirts, unbuttoned to bare their chests, emerged onto the portico to smoke and recover a little.

Kostya had been to the restaurant with his parents. They had eaten there a few times. It had been boring for Kostya, but pleasant in the large, clean hall with its few sparse diners. It was a place you wanted to go back to.

And in front of the hotel, you would often see famous actors who were playing at the local theatre in the town. You could watch them, watch how they climbed the steps to the hotel unhurriedly, or strolled along the embankment by the theatre. You could look at them, and even feel something stirring inside you as you did.

But after the renovation everything changed. The steps and the colonnade remained, but became smoother, shinier. Coach lamps appeared on the walls, like the ones you see in old engravings. The heavy wooden doors with their white sign 'The restaurant is open' disappeared. They became glass sliding doors with a smoky-brown tint. The old doorman was replaced by two short security men carrying radios. And a car park appeared in front of the hotel, full of smart, clean cars.

But the biggest difference was that people began staying at the Hotel Poima. All sorts of people. Foreigners and people from Moscow, who were instantly recognizable. It was instantly clear that the foreigners were foreign, and that the visitors from Moscow were from Moscow. The actors still came, but they did not stick out in quite the same way anymore.

Kostya had been in Moscow a short time before that and had spent quite a long period there. He had been studying for three months and had spent further time working in a large technical library. He had taken himself to St Petersburg for a few days, just for the hell of it, to see the town and visit a new friend, one he had made in Moscow. He liked St Petersburg.

Three years before that he had graduated in engineering, but he had not followed his father into the car parts factory, although the factory had expected him to carry on the family tradition. He worked in a garage for a while, took a shot at setting up his own garage with a friend, but never carried it through, and even tried working at a dealer's, selling cars. Then he decided to go back to college in town, but to study economics. The college sent him to Moscow on a programme of some sort, and it was the first time he had been in the capital on his own, and for such a long time.

He wasn't really that taken with Moscow to start with, but when he came back home he felt sick to the teeth, walking on the embankment or around the rest of the town. And Kostya spent a fortune on phone calls to his new Moscow friends.

He noticed what was missing from his home town. And what was there annoyed him. People's behaviour, their dress, what they did, what they talked about, it all started to get up his nose. After a while Kostya realized that he wanted to go back to Moscow, that he was missing it, needing it.

In Moscow, Kostya had formed the habit of spending long hours with his new friends in a coffee shop not far from the library. He could spend half the day there, chatting, meeting new people, even reading in a distracted sort of way. He liked this life, he had developed a taste for it, and he felt keenly the lack of a cafe lifestyle in his own town. The cafes in the centre, on the most attractive street in town, the ice-cream cafe on the embankment—none of them was quite right, from the cups and saucers, the furniture, down to the customers and their children... And a good cup of coffee was out of the question.

But then all of a sudden Kostya discovered that there was a bar in the lobby of the Hotel Poima, open not just to residents, but to anyone who knew about it.

The discovery was unexpected. One of Kostya's Moscow friends sent a bundle of recent technical magazines. He gave them to a friend to pass on, someone who was flying to Kostya's town on business. Kostya and the man arranged to meet in the bar in the lobby of the hotel.

They met, had a coffee, a chat and Kostya basked in the same sensation he had had in Moscow, sitting for hours in a little cafe.

This bar had appeared during the renovation. A far corner of the foyer had been given over to a small cafe area, which was, as far as Kostya could judge, kitted out in an English style. Five little tables, chairs, a bar in some dark wood, dark green walls, and pictures of steam locomotives over the green walls. A large coffee machine with copper sides made a great din, and people sat at the tables reading papers; cigarettes smoked in the ashtrays and it smelt of good coffee and tobacco smoke.

Kostya then went back on his own, simply to have a coffee. He was a little anxious, he worried the security men would ask if he was meeting someone, or which room he was staying in. He was worried that perhaps the waiters wouldn't serve him, or something would be not quite right. He went back one afternoon and everything was splendid. There were two foreigners in the bar chatting and they even said hallo to Kostya, who was quite delighted by the whole experience. After that he went back almost every day.

It was nicest of all to go there early in the morning instead of going to lectures or doing other bits of business. In the mornings there were lots of people sitting in the lobby, but it had a morning feel: conversation was restrained, no one spoke loudly, or drank alcohol. Newspapers, coffee, cigarettes, quiet conversations: the guests were readying themselves for a day's business, enjoying the early morning pleasures of a hotel stay. And Kostya liked taking part in this ritual. He felt removed from the town, which irritated him so—the unsophisticated nature of the place. He liked pretending he wasn't local and acting in the way someone who wasn't local might act. And because he liked acting like this, he felt an affinity with a big city or even a European mentality and way of behaving.

He spent whole mornings in the bar, always ready to help any foreigner who didn't speak Russian, to offer advice, or to translate for the waiter. Apologizing all the while for his poor English he would engage in short pleasant conversations, even asking questions himself, like from which country the new acquaintance came? He enjoyed the compliments he received, about his English and so on. If he was chatting to someone from Moscow then he would be certain to mention that he often travelled to Moscow, and he would illustrate this with his knowledge of many Moscow streets and of Moscow spots, which were far from the tourist trail. This knowledge was always greeted with polite approval.

And there was good coffee there, elegant cups and saucers, the day's papers, lying on the bar, and the waiters had definitely not been trained locally.

Very soon Kostya held all his fairly infrequent business and other meetings in the lobby of the Poima. He felt there was a certain style in this. He decided to hold his meeting with Pasha, his elder brother, there, too. He desperately needed to meet Pasha, but Pasha didn't seem to feel the same urgency and cancelled one meeting after another.

It was simply that Kostya had decided to go to Moscow to find out whether he could transfer to a Moscow college and finish his studies there. So far the results of his enquiries about opportunities to do this had not been promising, and Kostya had made up his mind to fly to Moscow and find out for himself. Besides he was filled with an impatient desire to see the capital. He absolutely needed to go... But he had no money.

Kostya hadn't asked for anything from his father for a long while, apart from the car, and that only occasionally—if not very rarely. And he had definitely not asked for money. It was enough that he had to live with his parents, who were always categorically opposed to all of Kostya's life-choices, his means of existence, his wardrobe, etc., etc. He tried to go home as late as possible every night, and leave as early as possible in the morning, to avoid hearing his father's usual, 'Well? And what have we got to look so miserable about today? Eh?' or 'And when will you be home then?' His father had spent decades working as the senior engineer in the car parts factory and was always tired and irritable.

And Kostya's elder brother was very business-like. He was seven years older than Kostya, had recently celebrated his thirty-first birthday, and he had lived on his own for a long time. He earned a fair amount putting little bits of metal together at Kostya's father's factory and used all the opportunities the factory and his father's contacts offered him to work overtime.

Pasha had been married a good while, he had a son and had noticeably put on weight, and even lost half his hair. He looked like any successful industrious inhabitant of the town. His parents loved him and were pleased for him, but he rarely came round to see them. Kostya felt he always annoyed his brother, but that his brother still loved him.

So Kostya had decided to borrow some money from him. Kostya was also owed money for work he had done—he still did a bit of work for the garage, and he was always asked if they had some tricky technical problem. He usually agreed if the problem or the car itself interested him. He was owed a good bit, enough for the trip, but they couldn't give it to him right away and he couldn't wait.

The brothers agreed to meet in the bar at lunch time. Kostya arrived at one and waited a full fifty minutes for his brother. At last Pasha arrived.

'Well, you don't do thing by halves do you! Meeting in a place like this... Very nice!' Pasha began loudly, by way of a greeting. 'Anything happened? Have you been up to something?' he added, bearhugging Kostya, who had put down his paper and risen to his feet.

'Hallo, Pasha. Thank you for making the effort,' Kostya said quietly. He didn't like Pasha's loudness or that he wasn't behaving how people usually behaved in the place.

'Sit down, and I'll tell you all about it. Will you have a coffee? A strong one? A double espresso, please,' this last was called to the waiter.

'Oho. Well let's sit down and discuss matters, then,' said Pasha, with evident irony.

Kostya could see how Pasha didn't fit in there, with his jacket, exactly what a well-off successful local man would wear, and his shoes, even though they hadn't been polished a day or two. Pasha was altogether local. Kostya hated this because he loved Pasha and yet always found himself angry with him.

'So what's new?' Pasha asked, sitting down. Kostya, distracted, tried hard to speak calmly and to the point, and as a result explained in a confused and verbose way to his brother why he wanted to meet with him, what he needed, that he would never normally ask for money, that he had never done so in the past and wasn't about to start, but that just right now certain circumstances had arisen, still he would return the money very soon and there was nothing to worry about.

'You don't need to go on,' Pasha interrupted him. 'I get it. So you're another one who's off to Moscow. And there was me thinking you'd actually thought up something decent and you really needed some help.'

'Pasha, I just want to borrow some money, not for long, I really need it.' Kostya, who had been ready for

Pasha's reaction, replied. 'I'm trying to explain to you what I want to do and why I need the money and I'm asking...'

'It's just another one of your stupid ideas,' Pasha replied sharply, 'and I'm not going to help you with it. So you're going to Moscow, are you... Well that's original! And if that's not enough you want me to help you in your idiot scheme. So what's this big attraction with Moscow, then...?'

'Pasha, I told you. Why don't you listen to me? I want to go round all the universities, have a good look at them, make some decisions.'

'Decisions? In Moscow.' Pasha made a dismissive gesture as he said this. 'Oh, that's a good one... You can't make any decisions here, but in Moscow you're going to make some decisions, are you. I've heard it all before... Don't make me laugh, Kostya. You don't do anything here, so you're hardly going to start in Moscow.'

'Pasha! I asked you to loan me the money, and that means I'll pay it all back. I earn my own money, don't I? It's not like I'm dependent on anyone.'

'Oh, right, you're not dependent on anyone?' Pasha said, making a sour face. 'Oh I see. You live with the parents, eat their food, drink their drink, don't ask permission to go rooting in their fridge. And are you paying your way? Have you ever even expressed an interest in how the food appears in that same fridge? You're not a teenager any more, Kostya, you're an adult, but you're used to a free ride. That's it, you're a free-rider. And that's why you want to go to Moscow. Oh yeah, I see it all! That's where all the free-riders end up, from right around the country. That's the place for you, alright.'

'If you aren't going to lend me the money, then just say,' Kostya answered in a quiet voice. 'I've got no intention of sitting here whilst you preach to me in that voice... You said it yourself, I'm not a teenager any longer.' Kostya spoke, barely managing to restrain himself.

'Oh it's not the money I mind. If you'd decided to get married on the quiet or, I don't know, travel to the North Pole, you could have had as much as you like, I'd gladly give it. But Moscow... I'm sorry. I wouldn't do that to you, I'm not going to finance your shit plans. If you had some work going, then that would be a different matter... Work, understand that word? But I know what goes on in that Moscow of yours.'

'What do you know?'

'I know Moscow!' Pasha answered brusquely. You think they're all waiting for you there, that someone needs you? No one gives a shit about anyone in Moscow. They're all a load of free-riders. No one doing a decent day's work, all of them with their plotting and messing around. When I've been to that Moscow of yours I get back and I feel like I need a good wash, if I didn't have business partners there, you wouldn't catch me putting a foot near the place. And the business partners... Our partners in Moscow, they treat us like we're animals, don't they. So you don't need to tell me about Moscow.'

'I see,' Kostya answered very quietly. 'I'll sort it out for myself, do it all myself. I won't ask you for anything ever again.'

'No one else will give you anything, Kostya,' answered Pasha, putting his head on one side. 'So calm down. You're a talented guy, good with your hands, got the brains. There's loads you could be doing here. Just get yourself set up with something. Dad and I will help. We'll always help. You know that. If it's something sensible I'll always help out.'

'I asked you for help,' Kostya looked at the table in front of him, 'and did you help me? Never mind. You'll see.'

'See what?' Pasha said loudly and brought his hand down on the table, making the ash tray rattle. The people at the tables nearest to them looked up. 'Haven't you understood anything? We're not going to just sit and let you go to Moscow, there's nothing for you there!'

'Well, that's your decision, whether you're going to let me go or not, Pasha. That's it, this discussion is over,' Kostya said and began rising from the table.

'You stay right there!' Pasha almost shouted. 'If you haven't got brains enough for yourself, then others will have to do the thinking for you! Sit down, you son of a bitch!'

'So that's your Mother, too,' Kostya replied without sitting.

'What?' Pasha said, uncomprehendingly.

'You said "son of a bitch", so that must mean your Mother is a bitch, too.' Kostya spoke quietly and continued to stand. 'We've got the same Mother, you and I, so it must be your Mother who's a bitch, too.'

'Kostya, just for saying that, I could... Do you realize what you just said?'

'I do, unlike some of us. And you, Pasha, you can carry on using Dad, making out you're the hard worker. What are you without Dad? It's you who's nothing without him, you're the free-rider, you just remember that. You can just hang around getting fat and bald if you like, but don't you ever dare tell me what to do.'

'What?' Pasha breathed out, almost with a scream. He jumped to his feet and his chair fell back with a clatter. Everyone in the bar and in the whole hotel lobby immediately looked over. 'How dare you!'

'Pasha, keep the noise down. There's no need to scream like that here.' Kostya spoke proudly, feeling himself to be on home ground. 'Can we have the bill, please,' he asked the waiter with extreme politeness.

A week passed after this conversation between Kostya and his brother, a week that brought little in the way of good news. The weather took a turn for the worst, the autumn cooled and soured into a definite winter and it even sleeted on a few occasions. The day after the meeting with his brother Kostya met with his old friend, Yura, with whom he'd tried to start up a garage. Yura still worked with in the automobile industry and it was he who found Kostya work from time to time. It was also Yura who owed Kostya for the work he'd done.

The meeting was not a success, although this might well have been predicted. Yura said that he couldn't pay up, not until the next month, or in instalments. Kostya made demands, he got angry, he even threatened Yura. By the end of the meeting Kostya was almost hysterical and he left Yura without saying goodbye. Yura apologized, made gestures of helplessness, said there was nothing he could do about it.

Two days later they spoke again by phone and made it all up, they met again and Kostya took a little money from Yura, all that he could give him at that point.

The weather was terrible. Kostya was afraid to stay at home, and so he hung around town. He was afraid that

Pasha would tell their parents about their conversation, and then he'd have to sit through a whole lot of pointless, tedious lecturing. So Kostya simply hung around. He couldn't go to classes, or work or even read. He could take nothing in. He tried going to the cinema, but he couldn't concentrate on the film, he couldn't understand a word of what was going on. Moscow, the irritating lack of finances and, most of all, his hopeless situation pre-occupied him and he could think about little else.

Only the mornings which Kostya spent in the bar in the Poima hotel lobby brought him anything like relief. But he couldn't spend the whole day there, unfortunately. He didn't feel quite comfortable doing that, he had almost no money, and even if he'd had more, he couldn't have drunk coffee endlessly. Still he rushed over there in the mornings as early as possible, and these few hours were his favourite time of the day.

About a week after the difficult conversation with his brother, Kostya left home as usual at half past eight. He waited until his father had gone to work, so he didn't have to see him, and then he got up, washed quickly, dressed and left home.

It was sleeting heavily. Right by the entrance to the big Stalinist block, where most of the inhabitants were managers in local industries, stood their neighbour from the floor above. She was wearing a black leather coat and she held an umbrella in one hand and a lead in the other. At the end of the lead was Hektor, a massive Doberman, whom everyone feared, but no one was able to make his owners muzzle him.

Hektor, bent double, stood in a little flowerbed, covered in slushy snow, straining with all his might. The traces of his day's work lay on the snow, quite human in their proportions.

Kostya stared at all this. He stared his neighbour in the eye and tried to reduce her to a pile of ashes with a glance. He even felt like saying something. But all of a sudden he thought, 'Well, he could be shitting on her head for all I care...'

And he walked past, left the yard and hurried along the embankment to the hotel. The sleet was so thick that the other bank of the river was invisible. Kostya increased his speed so he could get there quicker—to the warmth and the ordered comfort, the scent of coffee and good cigarettes.

Wet, almost transparent snow stuck to his clothes and made his hair instantly wet. The passing cars gave off thick exhaust fumes and a freezing spray flew in all directions from under their wheels.

Kostya, his collar lifted and his back hunched, made his way towards the stone portico and white colonnade with long strides. He turned into the hotel and crossed the car park. There was no wet snow on the ground and the asphalt gleamed black. The cars which had stood in front of the hotel must have just gone, and the snow had not yet had a chance to cover the bare spaces.

Kostya crossed the car park, staring down at his feet, when he saw something on the wet asphalt... He saw, but in a sort of inertia, he stepped over it... and even took another half a step before a shiver ran through him and he stopped, looked back and stared at what it was he had stepped over.

On the wet asphalt, in fact in a puddle, lay a large black leather wallet. A car had clearly run it over, but it was still fat, and the edges of several wet notes stuck out of it. Kostya looked to either side, straightened up and looked around again unhurriedly. He quickly and carefully scanned the area around him. He did not want to be made a fool of, or to be laughed at, or deceived, and feelings of alarm, and danger and something else quite unbidden circled and hardened around Kostya. There was no one nearby. Even the security men at the entrance were not there. There was no one anywhere.

Kostya bent down and picked up the wallet, and without even shaking the water off it or wiping it, he shoved it in his pocket. He went quickly to the colonnade, took the stairs two at a time and went into the foyer. His heart beat terribly. He said 'hallo' to the women in reception and looked about, tensely. He shook out the sleeves of his coat and drops fell to the floor. Kostya stood there a few seconds and then went quickly into the toilet.

There was no one by the wash basins, he crossed and went into a cubicle. As he went he glanced in the mirror and saw himself: tousled, with wet hair and burning eyes.

He locked himself into the cubicle, put the toilet lid down and sat on it, and only then did he carefully take the wallet out of his pocket and open it.

It was a large, long wallet. In it, not even between the dividers, but between the covers, like in a book, there were two passports and some money, a lot of money. New notes in a torn plastic bag from a bank, slightly wet. Red notes of a large value, roubles, many, many roubles. The packet was probably almost full. Kostya looked at it and placed it on his knee. He found himself holding the passports, two of them, a passport for internal travel and a foreign travel passport. They were damp, too. Kostya opened the internal travel passport and looked at the photograph.

He saw a long thin face; the shoulders in a jacket; a shirt and tie. 'Skachkov. Vladimir Nikolaevich' he read. Born in Barabinsk, Novosibirsk region, passport issued in Moscow. Kostya then looked at the date of birth, his heart was beating so, he could hardly think, and with some difficulty he worked out that Skachkov was 34 years old. In the foreign travel passport the photograph was coloured and here Mr Skachkov was wearing a white jumper and smiling.

In this passport there were some visas and dozens of stamps. Kostya took the passports and stuffed them into his pockets. He felt himself sweating all over.

Someone came into the toilets, passed by the washbasins, moved towards Kostya's cubicle and rattled the handle. Kostya coughed loudly and flushed the toilet.

'Oh, sorry.' Kostya heard outside the door. He sat quietly and waited until the invisible other person had gone into the next cubicle, there was a creak of bones, a streaming, the clapping of the seat, the buzzing of a zip. Then the other man washed his hands outside in the basin and dried them on the dryer. And then he went out.

Kostya opened the wallet and looked through it. In the largest section he found a few roubles, five hundred-dollar bills and a very creased return plane ticket to Moscow which was folded in half.

In the little pockets there were credit cards and business cards. Kostya didn't touch them. In another section, under a cellophane protector there was a picture of a woman and two little girls, aged around six and three. The woman was blond, she was smiling, and the little girls were smartly dressed, the youngest had a princess crown on her head. Behind them a room with a window and a decorated Christmas tree. There were a few other bits and pieces in the wallet: receipts, scraps of paper, a chewing gum wrapper.

For no clear reason Kostya stared at this wrapper for a long time, put it back, then looked back at the photograph of the woman and the children. Then he got both passports back out of the wallet and looked at the registration of residency for some reason. There was the address: Moscow, Letchik Babushkin Street. The street name meant nothing to Kostya, but an inexplicable wry smile appeared on his face. It was not even as if his thoughts took any particular direction all this time, in fact he could feel nothing but the pounding of his own heart.

Kostya put the packet of money back, the passports too, he stuffed the wallet into his pocket, flushed the toilet again for some reason and left the cubicle. He washed his hands for a long time in the warm water and squirted rose-scented soap on his hands twice. He splashed his face with water, snorted and laughed. Then he took a packet of paper hankies out of his pocket and wiped his face and hands. He threw away the wet tissue and left the toilet, crossing the foyer in a diagonal line towards the reception.

'Good morning,' he said to the woman in glasses who sat at the reception desk.

'Morning,' she answered.

'Would you mind telling me what room Vladimir Skachkov from Moscow is...', here Kostya hesitated for a second, choosing his words, '... staying in?'

'One moment,' answered the woman, tapping on the keys of her computer. 'Skachkov... Room 316.' She answered quickly.

'Could you tell me if he's in his room right now?' Kostya asked.

'Olia, can you check room 316. Is the guest there or not?' the woman called across to a girl behind a long counter.

'The key's out, so he's probably in his room,' answered Olia.

'Can I go up?' Kostya asked the woman in glasses.

'Does he know you're coming?'

'Yes... Yes, he does,' answered Kostya.

'Because I can always ring up.'

'No, no, I'll go up myself.'

'The lift is straight ahead. Second floor.'

'Thank you. I should find it,' Kostya said, already on his way to the lift.

He entered the main part of the hotel for the first time. The lift was new and all mirrored inside. Sofas lined the lobby space on the second floor and corridors departed in two different directions. Kostya followed the sign and turned left. Green and brown runners along the corridors muffled the sound of his steps. A chambermaid was bustling about at the far end of the corridor.

A 'Do not disturb' sign hung on the door handle of room 316. From inside came the sound of a TV and some other noise.

Kostya stood by the door listening, his heart beating with renewed force. He stood there about thirty seconds, and then, at last, he knocked. It was a timid sort of knock. Kostya listened again. His knocking had had absolutely no effect. So then he knocked louder. Nothing again. Then he knocked very loudly, using his whole fist to beat the door. Nothing happened. Kostya even grinned to himself, sensing the complete absurdity of the situation, as if he needed something from this person, who refused to respond to his knocking.

Kostya began knocking even harder and knocked for a long time. He heard some activity behind the door and a voice, clearly a woman's voice, behind the door. She was saying something, but Kostya couldn't make out what it was. At last he heard a man's voice.

'Who is it?' someone shouted from behind the door. The voice came from within the room, the speaker had not come over to the door.

'Excuse me... I... Open the door, please.' Kostya said, more resolutely, blushing all over.

'You fucking know how to get on a guy's nerves in this shitty hotel...' Kostya heard an approaching voice say.

Then he heard steps, a lock turning, the jangling of the door chain and at last the door opened. It opened only a chink. Kostya saw some greasy blond hair sticking out in all directions, and a long puffy face with little red eyes.

'Well. What is it then?' The scent of stale alcohol blew over Kostya. The television was louder now, and the other noise in the room he recognized as the sound of water running from a tap or in the shower.

'Are you Vladimir Nikolaevich Skachkov?' asked Kostya.

'That's right. Skachkov. And who are you?'

'Won't you let me come in?' Kostya said, not at all sure what he should do.

'Oh, for Christ's sake... What the hell do you want?' the puffy face continued.

'It's just... Well... Oh it's just... This,' said Kostya, pulling the wallet out of his coat and showing it to the man. 'Is this yours?'

The door opened wide. The puffy faced man was wearing a towelling dressing gown and nothing else besides. He was barefoot and holding the dressing gown across him with one hand because it wasn't belted.

To the right of the door was the bathroom door. It was open and the noise of water came from in there. Behind the man in the dressing gown was a small corridor opening into the room. By his foot lay a woman's high heeled boot and a pair of pointy-toed men's shoes.

'Hang on,' said the man in the dressing gown. 'That's my wallet!'

'Can I come in now,' asked Kostya.

'Alright,' the man replied.

Kostya entered. The door shut behind him. Kostya took a step and found himself instantly in a stale and smoke-filled room. The television was turned up loud. The smell of a bout of heavy drinking hung around the room.

'Yana, switch off the television, how many times have I got to ask...' the man in the dressing gown shouted hoarsely, without taking his eyes off Kostya or the wallet.

'If it's yours then take it,' Kostya said.

'Where did you get it?' asked the man.

'I found it by the entrance to the hotel. It was lying on the ground. Your passports are in it. Your ID. That's how I knew it was yours...'

'Really? Would you believe it! Must have dropped it when I got out of the taxi.' He took the wallet from Kostya with these words, and opened it. 'Turn off that telly I said!'

A girl with coal-black wet hair coal came sniffling past, behind him. She was wrapped in a large towel and she stalked past on her tiptoes. The television was quiet.

'Would you believe it. I don't remember anything.' Skachkov checked through the contents of the wallet. 'Wasn't feeling my best, if you know what I mean,' he said winking at Kostya. 'Shouldn't drink, should I, eh, look what happens when I do...' He looked carefully at the packet of rouble notes and the remains of the plastic packet. 'So it was just lying there, and you found it?'

'That's right.'

'Well I see you took what you needed,' Skachkov said, holding the opened packet of money, 'Still, all the same, thanks mate. Thanks for the passports. Done me a good turn. And now get going.'

He opened the door to Kostya and almost threw him out into the corridor.

Kostya went out and the door slammed. He stood there, quiet still and didn't move a muscle for a few seconds.

'Guess what, I went and lost my wallet yesterday,' Kostya heard a loud hoarse voice say behind the door. 'Dropped it. And it had everything in it. That strange bloke found it. Look, he took himself some money and then came along here so I could say thank you to him. What d'you think of that, eh?'

Kostya didn't stay to hear any more. He walked fast, he nearly ran back to the lift. Soon he was walking along the embankment, uttering every obscenity he could think of to himself. The wet snow fell into his face and his eyes. It made his eyes fill with tears.

Kostya spent a long time just walking, he turned onto another street and walked and walked, until he was quite wet, and frozen. Then he caught an almost empty trolley-bus, with steamed up windows. He felt sick, he muttered to himself and ran his fingers over the steamed-up glass.

He got out of the bus near his university, went into the main building and spent a while hanging around in the empty foyer and the corridors. There was nowhere else to go. Then a bell rang and the building filled with sleepy students emerging from the lecture halls.

Kostya called Yura and told him he needed to see him. Yura replied that he didn't yet have the money, and Kostya said that he just needed to talk. Yura was busy at work and he said he could only meet Kostya after work.

So then Kostya rang his old girlfriend. She didn't answer straightaway. Sveta, for that was her name, had studied medicine and was doing her house training at the town hospital. Kostya chatted to her, told her a couple of jokes, she laughed and said she couldn't talk for very long, but she was glad he was well, and it was nice of him to call.

Kostya felt no better, he hardly knew how he got through the day. It was a horrible day.

In the evening he met up with Yura in Cafe Vostok. It was only sitting at the cafe table that he realized how tired and hungry he was.

'What's wrong, Kostya?' asked Yura, when he saw him.

Kostya didn't explain. Instead he ordered vodka and pelmeni and said if Yura wouldn't have a drink with him, then that would be the last straw...

Yura didn't resist. He was an old school friend, a strong man, with large hands and a large head, a round face and yet his shoulders were narrow. However hard he tried he couldn't find clothes to suit him. He wore glasses too, and the glasses absolutely didn't suit him.

They had a drink, ate pelmeni. Yura was saying it was like the first snowfall had sent everyone raving mad.

'It suddenly hits them. It's winter all of a sudden, and as usual it's completely unexpected,' he said, 'and so they all come rushing in to get their winter tyres fitted. And then they get cross because they have to wait their turn. No question of coming in earlier...'

They drank a little more and chatted and then Kostya decided to relate his morning's adventure. He told the story in great detail. Yura listened carefully. He heard the whole story and then he looked very serious, he said nothing and he appeared to be deep in thought.

'You found all that money and you gave it back?' He said suddenly. 'Why?' and this he asked in a serious, and even an angry voice. 'I've never ever found so much money, and you won't ever again. Why on earth did you give it back?' Yura got even angrier. 'Who do you think you are, doing stuff like that? You think you're so important, like you're in charge of the whole world, like you're some God or something... Eh? Someone up there takes the money off the other bloke and gives it to you, and you say, 'No way... I know how's best to do things, I'm giving it back. You're a bloody fool! Well you got what you deserved. How could you dare to do something like that!' Yura spoke in increasing rage and conviction.

'Yura, if there hadn't been any ID in there I would hardly have taken it to the Police Station...', Kostya began explaining, '... but there were the passports and it was clear that the owner was probably staying in the hotel...'

'Passports? You could have handed those in at reception and he would have been delighted. And thankful,' Yura interrupted him. 'But you know what I would have done? I'd have taken that wallet, gone as far as I could from the hotel and chucked the wallet and the passports, and kept the money for myself. And I'd have had no qualms about doing it. Don't you believe me? Well that's what I would have done. And I'd have reckoned I'd done the right thing, and that I was a good person, because I'd found that money. And you know why I found it? Because someone up there took the money off him and gave it to me. And who am I to argue with that?'

'Yura, what is all this? Someone up there, taking off him, giving it to you...', Kostya attempted.

'That's right! That's it.' Yura almost shouted, nodding his head. 'That is it. And I am really really pissed off with you. Just what have you done?'

They carried on arguing and drinking for a long while. And later they even laughed at length about it, went on somewhere else, met some girls they knew, laughed some more, drank some more. Yura paid for everything.

In the morning Kostya couldn't get up. He woke up late, and felt unwell. Happily there was no one at home. He lay in bed for a long time. Then he got up and had a long drink of water straight from the kettle's spout, before soaking for a while in the bath. He shaved, dressed and got ready to go out.

He left the house at midday. There had been a frost overnight and it was slippery, but it hadn't snowed any more and the cool air was pleasant, transparent and soothing. Kostya went onto the embankment and stopped. He couldn't go back to the hotel bar. He realized he couldn't make himself. It wasn't even the fear of meeting Skachkov, it was very simply that he was revolted by the thought of going back into that place where he had felt so uncomfortable, where in the toilet cubicle his heart had beaten so, and sweat had dripped down his back. He saw clearly in his head the five hundred-dollar bills, the gum wrapper, the photo of the children and the Christmas tree... He could hear the hoarse voice, see the white towelling gown, the skinny dark-haired girl... But most of all the money had etched itself in his mind.

Kostya stood there, and as on the day before, he didn't know where to turn. He didn't know whom he might or should ring, to whom he should speak... Nor did he know how to forget about the money, or how to stop regretting its loss...

He stood on the embankment, and had the bitter realization that he didn't know what to do, he didn't know how to deal with it all, and what's more, he saw very clearly, that this knowledge would not come any time soon.

Lady with a Little Dog

Anton Chekhov

I

There was talk of a newcomer who had appeared on the seafront—a lady with a little dog. Dmitry Dmitrich Gurov, who had been in Yalta two weeks and already felt at home there, had, like everyone else, begun to take an interest in newcomers. Sitting in the Verné Patisserie's pavilion he watched a young woman walking along the front, a blonde woman, not tall, wearing a beret. A white Pomeranian ran along behind her.

And then he began to see her in the town gardens and on the square several times a day. She was out walking on her own, in the same beret, with the white Pomeranian. No one knew who she was and so they called her very simply the lady with the little dog.

'If she's here without a husband or any acquaintances,' Gurov considered to himself, 'then it might be worth my while to make her acquaintance myself.'

He was not yet forty, but he already had a daughter of twelve and two sons at high school. His marriage had been arranged for him when he was still in his second year at university, and now his wife looked almost twice his age. She was a tall woman with dark brows, a forthright woman, imposing, full of self-worth and, as she put it herself, a thinking woman. She read a great deal, prided herself on her use of the modern spelling, always called her husband Dimitry in the old-fashioned way, and he privately considered her limited, set in her ways and lacking in refinement. He was afraid of her and he didn't like being at home. He had not been faithful to her for a long time, he had frequent affairs and probably because of this he almost always expressed a low opinion of women—when they were discussed in his presence he called them 'the lesser race'.

It seemed to him that he was well enough schooled in misery and disappointment to call them what he liked, but all the same he wouldn't have survived two days without *the lesser race.* He was bored in male company, he felt out of sorts. With men he was taciturn, cold, but when he was with women he felt completely at ease, he knew what to talk about, and how to behave, even staying silent was not hard with them. In his appearance, his character, in all his nature there was something appealing, something hard to define, which made women like him, and attracted them to him. He knew this, and he too was drawn to them as if by some force.

Over and over again his experience, his bitter disappointments, had taught him that any liaison in polite society, however pleasantly distracting to begin with, however delightful a little adventure, always ended up being hard work and unbelievably complicated—especially in Moscow where people were slow to react and indecisive—and the whole thing eventually became a burden. But this knowledge somehow slipped out of his mind whenever he met an attractive new woman; life became worth living again and everything seemed so easy and so much fun.

And then one late afternoon he was having dinner in the gardens and the lady in the beret came unhurriedly over to take the table next to him. Her expression, how she walked, her dress and hair all told him that she was from polite society, married, in Yalta for the first time and on her own, and that she was bored here. There was not much truth in the tales of loose local morals and he despised them, knowing that they were invented by people who would have loved to stray from the straight and narrow, if only they'd known how, but when the lady sat down at the next table, three paces away, he remembered those tales of easy conquests and trips into the mountains, and he was consumed by the idea of a brief and fleeting encounter, an affair with a stranger whose very name was unknown to him.

He beckoned the little Pomeranian over gently and when it had come to him he wagged his finger at it. The Pomeranian growled. Gurov wagged his finger again.

The lady glanced at him and immediately lowered her eyes.

'He doesn't bite,' she said, and blushed.

'Can I give him a bone?' and when she nodded, he asked by way of a greeting, 'Have you been in Yalta long, forgive me for asking?'

'About five days'

'I've held out nearly two weeks.'

They were both silent for a while.

'The time passes quickly enough, but it is actually very dull,' she said without looking at him.

'That's just what you're supposed to say, that it's boring here. Your average small-town inhabitant arrives here from the back-of-beyond and they're not bored there, oh no, but as soon as they arrive here all they can say is "Look at that dust! I can't tell you how bored I am!" You'd think they'd come from Granada!'

She laughed. And then they both carried on eating as if they'd never spoken. But after the meal they left side by side, and their conversation was the easy banter of people who are free, contented, who don't care where they go, or what they talk about. They strolled and spoke about the strange light on the sea, the water a lilac colour, warm and soft, with a golden stripe of moonbeam running across it. They spoke about the closeness of the evening after a hot day. Gurov told her that he was from Moscow, educated as a linguist, but that he worked in a bank. He had once trained to sing in a private opera company but he had given that up, and he had two houses in Moscow... And he learnt that she had grown up in St Petersburg, but had married in S., where she had been living for two years now, that she would spend another month in Yalta and her husband might come down, as he too wanted a break, to bring her home. She couldn't for the life of her tell him where her husband worked, whether it was in the governor's office or in the local council, and she found that funny herself. And Gurov learnt too that her name was Anna Sergeevna.

Then, when he got back to his room he thought about her, and about the fact that he would probably see her tomorrow. Yes, most likely they would meet. And when he was lying down to sleep he recalled that she had been a schoolgirl not long before, much like his daughter now, he remembered how awkward and timid her laughter, her conversation with a stranger, had sounded. It must surely be the first time she had been on her own, in a place where men looked at her, followed her, spoke to her, and all with the same hidden motive, one she could hardly fail to guess. Her thin, vulnerable neck, her beautiful grey eyes came to his mind.

'There is something rather touching about her,' he thought as he was dropping off.

II

A week had passed since they first met. It was a festival day. Inside it felt stuffy and close, and on the streets the dust was carried on fierce eddies of air, hats were torn from heads. It was a day on which everyone felt constantly thirsty, and Gurov made frequent visits to the pavilion, bringing Anna Sergeevna eau de sirop and ice cream. You couldn't move in town.

In the evening when things had quietened down a little they walked along the harbour wall to watch the steamer come in. There were plenty of people out strolling by the port; they had come to meet people from the boat and they carried bunches of flowers. And here the two distinctive traits of the fashionably dressed Yalta crowd could be clearly observed—the old women were dressed like young women, and generals were two a penny.

The steamer arrived late, after sunset, because of the rough seas, and spent a long while turning before it moored against the harbour wall. Anna Sergeevna looked at the steamer and its passengers through a lorgnette, as if searching for people she knew, and when she turned to Gurov her eyes were shining. She talked a great deal, and asked fitful questions immediately forgetting herself what she had asked. Then she lost her lorgnette in the crowd.

The elegant crowds dispersed, it became too dark to see faces, the wind had dropped completely, and Gurov and Anna Sergeevna stood there as if waiting for a last passenger to alight from the steamer. Anna Sergeevna was now silent, and she sniffed the scent of the flowers without looking at Gurov.

'The weather's much better now it's evening,' he said. 'Where shall we go? Shall we take a ride somewhere?'

She didn't answer.

And then he looked at her intently and all of a sudden he put his arms around her and kissed her lips and he was overcome by the scent and moistness of the flowers, and he immediately looked around nervously—had they been seen by anyone?

'Let's go to your room,' he murmured.

And they both went quickly.

It was stuffy in her room and it smelt of the perfume she had bought in the Japanese shop. Gurov, glancing at her now, thought 'Well here's a turn-up for the books.'

He remembered from his own past carefree, warm-hearted women, full of joy at their love, grateful to him even for short-lived happiness; and then there were those, like his wife, whose love was insincere, full of pointless conversation and hysterical, affected behaviour, whose faces seemed to say this was not love, nor passion, but something far more significant; and then one or two others, very beautiful, but cold, across whose faces a predatory expression would suddenly flit, the unyielding desire to take, to seize more from life than it could give. And these women were no longer young, they were spoilt, unreasoning, tyrannical, empty-headed women, and when Gurov's feelings cooled towards them, their beauty aroused his hatred, and the lace on their slips looked to him then much like scales.

And now this: the same awkward, timid look of inexperience and youth, a feeling of discomfort, and the impression of someone caught at odds, as if there had suddenly been a knock at the door. Anna Sergeevna, this 'lady with the little dog', seemed to feel quite differently about what had happened, very seriously, as if she had genuinely fallen—that was how it seemed, and it was strange and ill-timed. Her face had dropped, her features crumpled, and her long hair hung sadly to either side. She looked dejected, distracted by her thoughts, like a fallen woman in an old picture.

'It's no good,' she said. 'You won't have any respect for me.'

There was a watermelon on the table in the room. Gurov cut himself a piece and began eating unhurriedly. A half hour at least passed in silence.

Anna Sergeevna was a touching soul, she had the chaste air of an uncomplicated, honest woman who had not seen much of the world. The single candle burning on the table barely lit her face, but you could see that she was troubled.

'What would make me stop having respect for you?' asked Gurov. 'You don't know what you're saying.'

'May God forgive me!' she said and her eyes filled with tears. 'It's awful.'

'You don't have to justify yourself.'

'How could I? I'm a bad sinful woman, and I despise myself. I couldn't begin to justify it... It wasn't my husband I deceived, I deceived myself. And not just now, I've been doing it for a long time. My husband... he may be an honest, good man, but I tell you he's a lackey! I've no idea what he does, the job he has, but I do know that he's a lackey. And I when I married him I was twenty, I was overcome by curiosity, I wanted something better in life, there must be a different life, I said to myself. I wanted to live! To live... And the curiosity was burning me up... You can't understand all this, but I swear to God I couldn't control myself any more, something happened to me, I couldn't stop myself, I told my husband that I was unwell, and I came here... And I walked about here like a mad-woman, in the grip of a passion... And now I'm a cheap tawdry woman, beneath anyone's contempt.'

Gurov was tiring of listening by now, her naïve voice irritated him, the unexpected contrition, so uncalled for. If it hadn't been for the tears in her eyes he might have thought that she was acting a part, or playing a game.

'I don't understand,' he said quietly. 'What do you want?'

She hid her face on his chest and pressed herself against him.

'Please, please, I'm begging you, please believe me...' she said. 'I want an honest, virtuous life, sin disgusts me, I don't myself know what I'm doing. You know how old women say "the devil led someone astray", well that's what I feel has happened to me now, that has the devil has led me astray.'

'Don't, don't,' he muttered.

He looked into her fixed and frightened eyes, and he kissed her and spoke gently, softly to her, and gradually she calmed down and her lightheartedness returned; they both began smiling and laughing.

Later, when they both went out, there wasn't a soul on the front, the town with its cypress trees looked dead, but the sea still roared and threw itself on the shore. A single launch rolled on the waves and upon it the faint glimmering of a little lamp.

They found a cab and drove out to Oreanda.

'I found out your surname in the hall downstairs just now. It said Von Dideritz on the board,' said Gurov. 'Is your husband German?'

'No, I think his grandfather might have been, but he's Russian orthodox.'

In Oreanda they sat on a bench not far from the church and looked down at the sea in silence. Yalta was barely visible through the morning mist, motionless white clouds hung about the peaks of the mountains. The leaves on the trees were still, the cicadas sang and the monotonous dulled noise of the sea was carried up from below. It spoke of the peace, the unending rest which awaits us. The same noise had risen from below, before the existence of either Yalta or Oreanda, and the same dull, indifferent roar will continue to rise when we no longer exist. And in this constancy, this complete indifference to the life and death of any of us, the proof of our eternal salvation may lie concealed, the unceasing movement of life on earth, its unceasing perfection. Sitting next to a young woman who looked so very beautiful in the dawn light, and himself calmed and overawed by his sublime surroundings, the sea, the mountains, the clouds, the wide sky, Gurov thought how actually, when you thought about it, everything in the world was wonderful—everything except what we ourselves think and do when we forget about the higher goals of our existence and our dignity as human beings.

Someone came over—a guard probably—looked at them and then went away again. And this too struck them as mysterious and beautiful. The steam ferry from Feodosya could be seen arriving, lit up by the dawn breaking, its own lights no longer illuminated.

'There's dew on the grass,' said Anna Sergeevna, after a silence.

'Yes, it's time to go home.'

They went back to the town.

And then every day at noon they met on the front, breakfasted together, lunched, strolled, admired the sea. She fretted that she was sleeping badly, that she had palpitations, she asked the same questions over and over, agitated sometimes by jealousy, sometimes by the fear that he didn't respect her enough. And often on the square or in the gardens when there was no one near, he would suddenly draw her close and kiss her passionately. It was as if he had found a new lease of life in the complete idleness; these kisses in broad daylight, accompanied by fear and surreptitious glances around, hoping no one had seen; the heat, the smell of the sea and the constant flickering past of idle, well-dressed, well-fed people. He kept telling Anna Sergeevna how wonderful she was, how seductive, he was impatient in his passion, constantly by her side, whereas she would often fall into thought and ask him to admit that he had no respect for her, did not love her, saw her only as a cheap woman. Late in the evening almost every day they drove out of the town somewhere, Oreanda or the waterfall, and the trip was always a success. Every time they were left with the impression of something wonderful and majestic.

They were waiting for her husband to arrive. But a letter from him came, informing his wife that he had been suffering from a problem with his eyes and begging her to come home to him as quickly as possible. Anna Sergeevna made great haste to be away.

'It's good I'm going,' she told Gurov. 'This is fate deciding.'

She left by carriage, and he accompanied her. They travelled the whole day. When she had settled herself on the express train and the second bell had sounded, she began speaking:

'Let me just look at you again... One more time... There.' She didn't cry, but she was upset, she looked unwell, and her face trembled. She spoke some more.

'I will think about you often... remember you... Farewell. Don't think badly of me. This is our last parting. It must be so, because we should never have met in the first place. Farewell.'

The train was quickly gone, its lights soon disappeared, and after a minute it couldn't even be heard. It was as if everything had conspired to bring a rapid end to this sweet oblivion, this madness. And alone on the platform and looking into the far darkness, Gurov heard the crickets and the humming of the telegraph wires with the sensation of having just woken up. And he thought about how he'd had another adventure, another exploit in his life, and now that was finished too, and all that was left were memories... He was moved, and wistful, he felt a faint sense of regret: after all the young woman, whom he would never see again, had not been happy with him. He had been kind to her, and warm, but his relations with her, his tone, his caresses had been touched by the merest shadow of a sneer: the crass arrogance of a happy man, who was also almost twice her age. She had always called him a good man, an unusual, noble man, so he can't have appeared to her in his true light—he must have unwittingly deceived her...

There on the station it smelt of autumn already, and the evening was cool.

'High time I went back north, too,' thought Gurov, leaving the platform. 'High time.'

III

Back at home in Moscow winter was not far off, the stoves were being lit, it was dark in the mornings when the children were drinking their tea and getting ready for school, and nanny had long begun lighting the lamp. There was a frost. When the first snows fall, on the first day when the sledges come out, the white ground and the white roofs look lovely, the air is soft, wonderful to breathe, and it is then that we remember our childhood. The old hoar-white linden trees and birches have a kindly aspect, they are dearer to the heart than cypresses and palm trees, and when they are nearby the desire to think about sea and mountains vanishes.

Gurov was from Moscow, he arrived back in Moscow on a splendid, frosty day and once he had put on his fur coat and warm gloves and had taken a stroll along Petrovka, and once he had heard the ringing of church bells on Saturday evening, his recent trip and the places he had visited lost all their charm for him. Little by little he threw himself back into his Moscow life, devouring three newspapers a day, and yet claiming never to read Moscow papers *on principle*. He was quickly drawn to the clubs and restaurants, dinners and parties, and he felt flattered once more that well-known lawyers and theatre people came to visit, and that he played cards with a Professor at the Doctors' Club. And he could eat his meat straight from the pan once more...

It seemed to him that a month or so would pass and Anna Sergeevna would fade from memory and only rarely appear in his dreams, with her touching smile, as others had appeared. But more than a month passed and deep winter had come and still it all lived on in his memory, as if he had parted from her only the day before. And the memories rose up in him ever more strongly. He only had to hear the voices of the children preparing their lessons carrying into the evening silence of his study, music or a ballad sung in a restaurant, or even the howl of a blizzard echoing down the chimney, and immediately it was all resurrected in his memory: the harbour wall, the early morning mist on the mountains, the ferry from Feodosya and the kisses. And then he would pace about his room for a good while, remembering and smiling, and his memories soon became dreams, and in his imagination the past mingled with what would come to be. And then Anna Sergeevna was no longer in his dreams, she walked behind him, following him everywhere like a shadow. Closing his eyes, he saw her as if she were real, and she looked younger, softer, more beautiful than she had been, and he seemed better to himself than he had been in Yalta. She looked at him in the evenings from the bookshelf, the fireplace, the corner. He heard her breathing, the caressing rustle of her skirts. He followed women on the street with his gaze, searching for one who looked like her.

And he ached with the strong desire to tell someone about his memories. But he couldn't mention his love at home, and outside the home there was no one he could tell. He couldn't talk to his tenants after all, nor to anyone in the bank. And what would he say? Had he really been in love? Was there really anything beautiful, poetical or even instructive or just interesting about his relationship with Anna Sergeevna? And so he was compelled to talk generally about love and women, and no one guessed the matter, and only his wife twitched her dark brows and said,

'Dmitry, really, the role of Don Juan doesn't suit you in the least.'

Once, at night, as he was leaving the Doctors' Club with his partner for cards, a civil servant, he could not stop himself and he said,

'If only you knew what a charming woman I met in Yalta!'

The civil servant climbed into his sledge and drove off, but suddenly he turned and called back,

'Dmitry Dmitrich!'

'What?'

'You were right back then. The sturgeon was not up to scratch.'

These words, so very unremarkable, upset Gurov suddenly for some reason—they seemed humiliating, debased. What a despicable way of being! What despicable sorts they were! And the wasted nights, the meaningless passing of days! The furious gaming, eating and drinking till one split, the endless conversations about the same thing. And the pointless occupations and the conversations about the same thing took up the best part of one's time and energies, and at the end of the day, all that was left was a diminished, lopped off sort of life, a nonsense of a life, and you couldn't escape, run away, you were as trapped as a patient in an asylum, or a prisoner sentenced to hard labour.

Gurov didn't sleep that night, he lay there in dismay, and then spent the next day with a headache. And he slept badly the following nights, spent them sitting upright in bed thinking, or pacing from one corner of his room to the other. He was fed up with the children, the bank, he didn't much want to go anywhere or talk to anyone.

In December during the holidays he decided to go away. He told his wife that he was going to St Petersburg to busy himself on behalf of a young acquaintance, and he left for S. Why? He hardly knew himself. He wanted to see

Anna Sergeevna, to talk to her, to be with her a while if possible.

He arrived in S. in the morning and took the best room in the hotel. A grey military felt covered the floor of the room and there was an inkwell, grey with dust: a rider on a horse, his hand outstretched and holding a hat, his head knocked clean off. A doorman gave him the information he needed, Von Dideritz lived on Staro-Goncharnaya Street in a private house. It wasn't far from the hotel. He lived well, had wealth, his own horses, everyone knew him in the town. The doorman pronounced his name thickly, *Drydyritz*.

Gurov made his way unhurriedly to Staro-Goncharnaya and found the house. He saw there was a fence outside, a long grey fence of nailed boards.

'The sort of fence you'd run a mile from,' thought Gurov, looking now at the windows, now at the fence.

He considered. Today was a holiday and her husband was probably home. And besides it would have been inconsiderate to enter her house and cause her embarrassment. If he sent a note then that might fall into her husband's hands and spoil the whole thing. Best to rely on chance. So he walked up and down the street and hung about near the fence, waiting for this chance to come. He saw how a beggar went in through the gates and was attacked by the dogs, and then, an hour later, he heard someone playing on a piano, and the sound carried, faint and unclear. It must have been Anna Sergeevna playing. The front door suddenly opened and an old woman came out, and behind her ran the familiar white Pomeranian. Gurov thought of calling the dog, but his heart suddenly began beating loudly and in his confusion he couldn't remember the name of the Pomeranian.

He walked back and forth, hating the grey fence more and more, and he began thinking crossly that Anna Sergeevna had forgotten him and was probably already having fun with another man, which would be a natural state of affairs for a young woman forced to look out day and night at this cursed fence. He went back to his hotel room and sat for a long while on the divan, not knowing what to do, and then after eating lunch he slept for a long time.

'This is all so ridiculous and unsettling,' he thought, waking up and looking at the dark windows, for it was already evening. 'And now I've gone and overslept. How on earth will I get to sleep tonight?'

He sat on the bed, which was covered in a cheap grey blanket, just like a hospital blanket, and mocked himself irritably:

'You had enough of your lady with the little dog yet? How's this for a romantic adventure, then... Well, now you can just sit here and stew.'

At the station that morning a theatre bill covered in very large letters had caught his attention: the first night of *Geisha*. It came to mind then, and he took a cab to the theatre.

'It's very possible that she goes to first nights,' he thought.

The theatre was full. And here, as in all provincial theatres, the fog reached higher than the chandeliers, the gallery was noisy and restless; the local men of fashion stood in the first row before the show began, their hands behind their backs; and here, in the governor's box the governor's daughter sat in pride of place, wearing a boa, the governor himself tucked modestly behind the drapes so only his hands were visible. The curtain shook; the orchestra took its time tuning up. All the while, as the audience were coming in and taking their places, Gurov's eyes searched hungrily.

And Anna Sergeevna came in. She sat in the third row and when Gurov looked at her his heart constricted and he knew then without any doubt there was no person dearer to him, closer to him, more important to him in all the world: her, caught up in the provincial crowd, this little woman, in no way extraordinary, with her vulgar lorgnette in her hand—she filled his whole life, she was his despair, his joy, she was the only happiness he now desired for himself. And to the sound of a poor orchestra and feeble amateurish violins, he thought how fine she was. He thought and he dreamed.

A young man with small sideburns had entered the theatre alongside Anna Sergeevna, a very tall man, stooped; he wagged his head with every step he took, and appeared to be constantly bowing. This was likely to be the husband that she had once, in a sudden bitter outburst in Yalta, called a lackey. And actually, in his long person, the sideburns, the small bald patch, there was something of the humble lackey about him; he had an insipid smile, and some badge of learning glinted in his buttonhole like a lackey's number.

In the first interval her husband went out for a smoke and left her in her seat. Gurov, who was also sitting in the stalls, went over to her and said, in a trembling voice, and with a forced smile,

'Hallo'

She looked at him, and paled, and then she looked again in horror, unable to believe her eyes, and clutched her fan and her lorgnette tight in her hands, clearly making great efforts not to faint. They were both silent. She sat there, he stood, frightened by her confusion, hardly daring to sit down next to her. The violins tuned up and the flute rang out, suddenly it seemed terrifying, as if all the boxes were looking at them. But then she got up and went quickly to the exit, and he followed, and the two

of them walked the corridors and staircases without direction, now up, now down, and before their eyes flashed
people in their greatcoats, soldiers, students, court officials, all covered in badges, and women flashed past, fur
coats hanging on coat hangers, and a draught of wind,
carrying the scent of spent tobacco. And Gurov, whose
heart was beating hard, thought,

'Lord, these people, that orchestra, what's it all for...'
and at that moment he remembered the evening on the
station when he had seen off Anna Sergeevna, and how
he had said to himself that it was over, that they'd never
see each other again. But the end was nowhere near in
sight!

She stopped finally, on a dark narrow staircase with a
sign: 'To the Upper Circle'.

'How you scared me,' she said, breathing heavily, still
pale and shocked. 'Oh, how you scared me! I nearly died.
Why did you come? Why?'

'Anna, but just listen, listen...' he said in a low voice,
hurriedly, 'I beg you, just hear me out...'

She looked at him in fear, in love, pleadingly, she stared
at him, to fix better his features in her memory.

'I'm miserable,' she continued, not listening to him.
'All I thought about was you, the whole time, my whole
life was thinking about you. And I wanted to put it all out
of my mind, to forget, but why, why did you come here?'

Higher up on the landing two schoolboys were smoking and looking down, but Gurov didn't care, he pulled Anna Sergeevna towards him and kissed her face, her cheeks, her hands.

'What are you doing? What are you doing?' she said in horror, pushing him away. 'We've both lost our senses! Leave today, leave right now... I beg you, I implore you... There's someone coming!'

Someone was coming up the stairs.

'You have to leave...' Anna Sergeevna continued in a whisper. 'Do you hear Dmitry Dmitrich? I'll come to you in Moscow. I've never been happy. I'm unhappy now, and I will never, never be happy. Never! Don't make me even more miserable! I swear I'll come to Moscow. But we must part now. My dear, sweet, kind man, we must part.'

She shook his hand and went quickly down the stairs, looking back at him the whole time, and it was clear from her eyes that she was genuinely unhappy. Gurov stood there a little while, listening, and when everything had quietened down he found his coat and left the theatre.

IV

And Anna Sergeevna began coming to Moscow to see him. Once every two or three months she would leave S. and tell her husband that she was going to seek the advice of a consultant about her women's health problems. And her husband believed her, and didn't believe her. In Moscow she stayed in the Slavyansky Bazar Hotel, and always sent a bellboy immediately for Gurov. Gurov came to her, and not a single person in Moscow knew about it.

Once, on a winter morning, he was going to visit her in this manner (the message had reached him the night before when he had been out). His daughter was with him, he was walking her to school as it was on his way. Large damp snowflakes were falling.

'It's three degrees, and the snow is still falling,' said Gurov to his daughter. 'But actually this warmth is only on the Earth's surface, the temperature is quite different in the upper atmosphere.'

'Daddy, why is there no thunder in winter?'

He explained this too. And as he spoke he thought that there he was going to meet her, and no living soul knew, and probably no living soul would ever know. He had two lives. One open life, which anyone who needed to could see and know about, with the truths and deceptions peculiar to it, absolutely identical to the lives of his friends and acquaintances, and another life which flowed its secret course. And by some strange confluence of circumstances, perhaps itself chance, everything that was interesting, important, essential to him, everything he felt sincerely about, without self-deception, everything which was at the very heart of his life, happened in secret, without others knowing. But everything that was a lie, an outward shell under which he hid so as to hide the truth, like his work in the bank, the debates at his club, his 'lesser race', going to parties with his wife—all of this was lived openly. And he judged others by his own life and did not believe what he saw, supposing everyone to be leading a real proper life under secret cover, as if under cover of night. Secrecy lies at the heart of every individual existence, and perhaps this is, at least in part, why any educated person makes such nervous efforts to have their personal privacy respected.

Once he had walked his daughter to school Gurov set off for Slavyansky Bazar. He took off his fur coat downstairs, went upstairs and knocked very quietly at the door. Anna Sergeevna, wearing the grey dress he loved best and worn out by the journey and her expectation, had been waiting for him since the night before. She was pale. She looked at him and she didn't smile, and he had hardly entered the room before she fell into his arms. They kissed for such a long time it was as if they hadn't seen each other for several years.

'So how are you then?' he asked. 'Any news?'

'One moment, I'll tell you in a bit... I can't bear it...'

She couldn't speak she was crying so. She turned away from him and pressed a handkerchief to her eyes.

'Let her have her cry, and I'll sit down for a bit,' he thought, and sat in an armchair.

Then he rang and asked for tea to be brought, and even when he had drunk his tea, she still stood, turned towards the window. She was weeping with her troubles, feeling sorrow in the awareness that their life together was full of grief; they could only meet in secret, they hid from people like thieves! Wasn't this all proof that their lives were destroyed?

'Come on, stop it,' he said.

To him it was clear that their love was far from over, had no foreseeable end. Anna Sergeevna was binding herself to him closer and closer, she adored him and it was unthinkable he should tell her that one day they must call an end to it all; she would never have believed him if he had, anyway!

He went over to her and took her by the shoulders to comfort her, tease her a little, and at this moment he caught sight of himself in the mirror.

He had already begun to go grey. And it seemed strange to him that he had aged so much these last years, aged and lost his looks. The shoulders he had placed his hands on were warm and trembling. He felt compassion for this life, still so warm and beautiful, but close enough to the time when it would begin to fade and wither, like his own life. Why did she love him so? Women never saw him for himself, nor did they love him for himself, but found in him something they had created in their own imaginations, something for which they were searching desperately in their own lives; and then when they realized their mistake they carried on loving him anyway. And not one of them was happy with him. Time passed, he met new women, had affairs, parted from them, but never once loved; there was plenty of everything else, but no love.

And only now, already greying, had he fallen in love, truly, properly—for the first time in his life.

He and Anna Sergeevna loved each other like kindred spirits, like man and wife, like close friends, they felt as if fate had intended them for each other, and it seemed incomprehensible that they were married to other people, they were like a pair of wild birds, caught in flight and forced to live in separate cages. They forgave each other everything each of them was ashamed of in his or her past, forgave everything that happened now, and they felt as if their love had changed them both.

In the past when sadness had come upon him, he had calmed himself with all the rational thoughts he could muster, but he was beyond rational thought now, he felt deep compassion, he wanted to be tender and sincere...

'Don't, my sweet girl,' he said. 'Don't cry now, there we are... Let's have a talk, we'll think of something.'

Then they talked for a long time, discussed how they would free themselves from the need to hide, to deceive, to live in different towns and have such rare meetings. How to rid themselves of these unbearable bonds.

'How? How?' he asked, clutching at his head. 'How?'

And it seemed as if there was only a little way to go, and a solution would be found, and then a wonderful new life would begin; and both of them knew that the end was very, very far away and the most complicated, the most difficult part was just beginning.

Moscow

Igor Sutyagin

Whenever I hear someone saying 'How I dislike Moscow,' I nod my head in understanding. Yes, they're right, it's a huge, busy, agitated sort of city. And of course I have some sympathy with the speaker's irritation, but I always think to myself at the same time, 'You probably just haven't found your own Moscow yet.' Find it, find your own Moscow, that unique and irreplaceable Moscow of YOURS, and I don't believe you'll be able to resist loving it. That's how it happened to me.

I was born in Moscow, in fact. In the model Maternity Hospital No. 25, behind The Central Soviet Trade Union Council, set a little way back from Leninsky Prospect. And the very first few months of my life were spent in the main building of the Moscow State University, Zone V, on the seventeenth floor. It must be for this reason that the University became my first and dearest love in Moscow. Even on the train from Obninsk, when I reached the Moscow suburbs of Matveevskoe I would always have to look out on the right, over to where the silhouette of the university building towered above the other buildings. And then I entered the university too, and in my final years as a physics student I lived in the very same main building, and even in Zone V. And then I learnt how very fond one could become of the quiet parks on the Lenin Hills, islands of unhurried peace, so close to the busy avenues of the city.

But fourteen years after leaving these secluded meadows in the university parks, I got to know another Moscow. And just like the university parks it was well hidden from view, from those who weren't meant to see it—a little part of the world known in Russia as 'Through-the-prison-wall'. It is indeed as strange as Alice's Looking Glass world, and it deserves this name. Moscow's 'Through-the-prison-wall' began for me (I was held in the Kaluga Region first) in the Federal Security Service's Remand Isolation Prison Lefortovo.

This Moscow is actually distinctively reminiscent of St Petersburg—like St Petersburg because of its straight lines and its strict organization. None of the winding alleys of Zamoskvorechye, the old town in Moscow, but the unwavering straightness of Vasilyevsky Island. The unusual seriousness of Lefortovo against the background of typical Moscow slovenliness leaves one in a state of deep surprise for the first few minutes. The armoured gates (over an inch thick) through which you enter the prison yard, those alone, there's nothing quite like them. And the reinforced shutters at the prison governor's windows onto the yard, each with a slit for shooting through in case of trouble. Those are serious windows indeed!

Yes, the mere sight of those shutters completely captures the imagination. You can't help but feel that *in this place*, more than anywhere else in Moscow, they are prepared for possible trouble. And the two-inch thick doors ready to close at a moment's notice in the corridor leading to the governor's offices—even these are no longer a surprise. If you stand with your face against the thick glass—glass which even *looks* bullet-proof—of the remand cells' office, then on the left, behind another armoured door there is a corridor. There are seven rooms on this corridor. These tiny rooms with their high ceilings and the little windows right up high are for lawyers' meetings with defendants. But what is interesting about them is this: over the door on the little landing which faces the corridor with the seven rooms, right over the whole door opening there is an armoured shield. This shield is mighty convenient for machine gunners if they happened to be shooting down the corridor with its meeting rooms. It's slightly bent, to hide the machine gunner more comfortably, this two-metre high shield with its business-like, ridged edges. And these ridges have been rounded off nicely, so the sniper doesn't get caught on the metal edges. This rust-red painted piece of armour was the final touch. Although to be honest it didn't add much to the impression of Lefortovo, but it did make it an indelible and lasting image in the mind. Welcome to this quiet world, hidden from ordinary eyes and serious beyond anything possible in Moscow, a place where Moscow's careless, wanton ways hold no sway. Welcome to a Moscow you don't yet know. A precise and pitiless Moscow, like a well-oiled and terrible machine.

But the terrifying nature of this machine has nothing to do with unimaginable horrors. It is the inhuman, unassailable focus and organization of the place, the antithesis of Moscow life, which makes it so strange.

Would you like to know how many lost buttons you own, squirrelled away for better times? Visit Lefortovo! There, during the many hours of the initial search they pull everything out of your bags and count absolutely everything. I learnt, for example, that after a few years of prison in Kaluga I had brought with me thirteen spare buttons, 133 blank postcards (for writing short letters to my family every day), and, for some unknown reason, seventeen shoelaces. Everything is counted, scrupulously recorded in an unending list of personal effects, to the extent that the bath (as unavoidable as the welcome) is a great relief, because it brings to an end the tiresome counting of everything down to staples, folds of paper and carefully kept letters from loved ones.

And then, once you've received your meagre mattress, sheets and thin army blankets you enter Accommodation Block No. 5. More than anything it resembles a peculiar hybrid of cathedral, grain silo and hive. The walls of the corridors rise up and up, with no floors between them, and the cell doors are evenly spaced, like cells in a beehive, four floors of them, cut into the wall, as high as it goes. And light, pouring in from somewhere above... And silence. Only this silence isn't echoing, as it is in a cathedral, its stifling and close, like a pillow stuffed with feathers. Carpet runners along all the corridors? Not for interior design reasons or for comfort, but to hide the sound of steps. Tales of prison guards in soft felt slippers belong in the nineteenth century—now they wear ordinary shoes, but they walk on carpet runners and are absolutely noiseless. And you are reminded gently, but very, very insistently to 'Step back onto the runner!' if you make a polite step to the side to allow a Lefortovo prison guard to pass by.

Apart from the guards, and the other prison staff, you see *no one* in the corridors of Lefortovo. No one at all. The whole life of this remand isolation centre is so structured as to cut you off from any possible contact with any of the other prisoners. When you are taken to see your lawyers or the investigator the corridors are completely empty—the man in charge of Block No. 5 takes care to ensure that there is no chance of even two prisoners coming out of their cells at the same time. And if a meeting like this is unavoidable (if someone is returning to their cell, say) then for such moments kiosks are placed along the corridor—rather like telephone kiosks, only wooden and windowless. You are pushed politely, but firmly into one of these two-metre high closed-in vertical boxes, if the characteristic sound of a finger click is heard from around the bend in a corridor. When one of these special guards is accompanied by a prisoner he clicks his fingers constantly. And when he approaches a closed door he bangs a key on the metal handle. These sounds: the rhythmic finger click-ing and the ringing clang of a huge prison key warn of the possibility of forbidden contact. And the guard caught in a corridor with a prisoner takes measures when he hears these sounds—if there is no kiosk nearby then he leads you into the first free cell on your path (these days Lefortovo is two-thirds empty). But on no account may you see your fellow-in-misfortune walking towards you.

Even the lift which you take to your exercise (an hour a day) in little concreted spaces on the roof (a lift in a prison! A lift for prisoners! It's beyond imagining!), even this lift was not put in for comfort, but with the same goal—to isolate you completely. To prevent the prisoner from knowing if there is anyone else in the building. Yes, this Lefortovo is a desolate place, and you walk its carpet runners never once seeing anyone who resembles yourself. (I write this because after a few years in prison you begin subconsciously to distinguish yourself from those who keep you locked away.) Only you, guards, you and the long carpets.

Slightly narrower carpets and two and a half foot wide metal galleries characterize the upper storeys of the Lefortovo Prison. These are attached to the walls along the rows of cell doors which are cut straight into the wall. Metal nets between the galleries prevent leaps from life, throwing yourself headfirst into the space between, escaping as Boris Savinkov 'escaped' from the Chekists in the 1920s. But this is interesting: the whole metal structure along the walls of a three-storey building should by ordinary reckoning ring out with the sound of footsteps, and yet it keeps that same Lefortovo suffocating silence. So that a senior prison warden looking out suddenly from an upper gallery, seems, if not quite an angel of death, then certainly exactly like some peculiar diurnal bat. This building with all its carpets and built in the shape of the letter K, appears well-kept, but is hardly for living in. Most of all

Accommodation Block No. 5 looks much like what it is: a prison. Not like the prison colonies in Kaluga, or Kazan' or Izhevsk, or even the Moscow prison Matrosskaya Tishina: Lefortovo looks like a real prison. That is, the sort of place which is fundamentally inimical to humans. Because whatever people say, prison life is unnatural for human beings.

The silence in Lefortovo is in fact one of the ordeals which awaits you in an special FSB prison. When I was transferred to an ordinary remand isolation prison, while the Supreme Court of the Russian Federation made its decision, the first impression I had was one of *freedom*. The hum of voices, the chatter from the yard or from behind cell doors, how unlike all this the Lefortovo corridors are, filled with a tight silence. In Matrosskaya Tishina a stream of life trickled out from under all the doors. And life is, in essence, freedom! Lefortovo never seemed corpse-like, but if life did exist there, then it was in a very peculiar form, quite at odds with usual noisy Moscow living.

Perhaps it is because of this that the former military prison Lefortovo, built in 1881 in Moscow's former German area of the same name, remains so firmly in the memory. After all it is our way to remember what is in complete contrast with ordinary life. Especially when this contrast is so stark—and the contrasts in the FSB isolation remand prison were sometimes very stark. As when the stifling silence of the Lefortovo cells was filled to bursting with the roar of an aeroplane engine, being tested quite literally over the fence in the next building's yard. Then you felt absolutely certain that nearby and all around was the *living world.* Enormous, fascinating, powerful (as a plane engine)—because what could be more fascinating than aviation for someone who has been shut away in a cell for many years. Aeroplanes fly in the air, where there are no walls, and they fascinate anyone who has lived in this world, which is hemmed in on five sides by walls, and is called for that reason 'Through-the-Prison-Wall'.

They should probably have stopped them building the Aviation Motor Institute just on the other side of the Lefortovo wall. It destroys the stifling silence so carefully wrought by Chekist interrogators. A failure, a weakness! Although how good it is to know that they are not yet able to eradicate all signs of the living world. I'm sure they wanted to—after all there is a playful sign in almost all the interrogation rooms which reads: 'If you're still free then that is our failing, not your strength.' But they haven't managed it yet. And in this lies Russia's hope, or so it seems to me.

For better or worse Lefortovo was the gate to another life, very different from my former existence. I was brought from Kholmogor in the Far North (and they nearly managed to lose us in a prison van in the Archangelsk forests).

From Lefortovo I was taken and put in a YaK-42, which landed in Vienna to hand me over to an American Boeing, which then landed in Britain. So it happened that my last home in Russia was a small piece of prison Moscow—Lefortovo. And for better or for worse I can't forget it. So I remember two Moscows now: university Moscow, and prison Moscow, Moscow State University and Lefortovo. And memory, which never lets go, makes its presence felt every day—and that is a sort of love, isn't it?

But it's a strange thread that connects me with my hometown. Prison is no subject for sweet dreams. But it is still *Moscow*—try to remember that, hardly alluring, but real life, at least. And remember the Russian proverb 'love us when we're black, for when we're white anyone may love us'.

So when I hear someone saying, 'How I dislike Moscow!' I nod my head in understanding. But I always think, you just haven't found your Moscow. And you haven't realized how impossible it is not to remember it. Find it, and you will fall in love with it. Believe me. You will love it for the rest of your life. Yes, that's how it is.

From Lefortovo to Khamovniki

Vladimir Gilyarovsky

The day after my arrival in Moscow I had to go from Lefortovo to Tyoply Pereulok in Khamovniki. The money in my pocket was running short, two ten-kopeck pieces and a handful of copper coins. And the weather would have ripped my boots apart: ice on the unswept pavements, and snow water standing on the huge cobblestones. Winter had not yet arrived in full force.

On the corner of Gorokhovaya Street was a single cabdriver: an old man in a long felt coat tied with ends of broken reins, and a red sheepskin hat decorated with a bit of tow sticking out like a feather. The shaggy potbellied pony was harnessed to a sleigh—a low wide sleigh of bark, with a low seat for passengers and a little board sticking out at the front of the sleigh for the driver. The reins and harness were of rope. He had a whip stuck in his belt.

'To Khamovniki!'

'Where in Khamovniki?'

'Tyoply Pereulok'

'Twenty kopecks.'

I thought this was very expensive.

'Ten.'

He thought this was very cheap.

I started walking. He drove after me.

'Fifteen kopecks, and that's my last word on it. I've not got anywhere to go at the moment...'

After about ten paces he repeated,

'My last word, twelve kopecks...'

'Alright.'

The cab driver whipped the horse on. We slid as easily over the snow as we did over the clear wet cobbles because of the wide unmetalled runners made for the countryside. They slid along without cutting through the ice as the town sleighs did. But on any hills or little humps in the winding streets the sleigh swung about in wide arcs pulling the horse sideways and knocking against the wooden bollards. I had to hold on to the back to stop myself being thrown out.

Suddenly the driver turned and looked at me,

'You're not going to do a runner are you? It sometimes happens, you're driving along, and your man hops out and into a yard—and gone.'

'Where would I run to? This is my first day in Moscow.'

'I'm only saying.'

He complained about the roads.

'I wanted to take out the master's guitar today, but up round the Kremlin the roads are completely bare...'

'What?' I asked, 'A guitar?

'Yes, you know, a *koliber* like that over there, look.'

A strange contraption turned out of a side road, pulled by a shaggy little pony like ours. It really did look like a guitar on wheels. There was a seat for the driver in front. And on this 'guitar' sat a merchant's wife in a fur-lined cape and marten fur collar, her face and legs turned to the left, and an official, wearing a cap with a badge and carrying a briefcase, quite turned towards the right, his face looking in our direction.

This was my first glimpse of a *koliber*, which had already been mostly replaced by the *drozhky* with their lifted chassis and rocking body that rested on high springs in a semicircle at the back. Later these *drozhky* were made with flat springs and they began to be called, as they are called now, four-wheelers.

We travelled along Nemetsky Street. The cabdriver warmed up a bit,

'This horse is going out to the country tomorrow. I bought a Kirghiz mare for forty roubles at the Ilyushin horse market... Good-natured thing. Four years old. Plenty of life in her... A convoy came up from the Volga with fish last week. So the traders bought up all their horses and then double the prices for us. Still it's on credit, I pay three roubles every Monday. Hard life, eh? That's how all the cab drivers get their horses. The Siberians bring their wares into Moscow and sell half the horses...'

We crossed Sadovaya. By Zemlyanoy Val there was sudden commotion. On all the streets the cab drivers, coachmen and cart drivers were whipping their horses over to press up against the pavements. My conveyance stopped on the corner of Sadovaya.

Bells rang in the distance. The cabdriver turned to me and whispered, frightened,

'Couriers! Look!'

The bells rang out closer, and cries and beating hooves could be heard.

Along Sadovaya from Sukharyovka two beautiful and identical ginger troikas raced past at high speed, one after the other, pulling identical new open carriages. Both were driven by jaunty coachmen, in little hats adorned with peacock feathers, waving their whips and whistling and calling. In each carriage sat two identical pairs, on the left a *gendarme* in a grey greatcoat, on the right a young man in civilian clothing.

The troikas flashed past at full tilt and the street resumed its usual appearance.

'Who was that?' I asked.

'Gendarmes. Taking them from Petersburg to Siberia. Must be important ones. Novikov's son himself was riding on the first. That's his best troika. Courier troika. I was standing next to Novikov in a yard and I took a good look at it.'

A gendarme, with whiskers to his ears
And beside him some pale boy
Of no more than nineteen years...

I remembered Nekrasov, looking at this living illustration of his lines.

'It's anyone who's against the Tsar, they take them out to Siberia to do hard labour,' the old man explained in a half-whisper, turning and bending down towards me.

At the Ilinsky Gates he pointed to the wide square. On it stood dozens of charabancs with large mangy horses. The ragged coachmen and charabanc owners were bustling about. Some were bargaining with hirers, some were seating passengers to take them out to Ostankino, beyond the Krestovsky Turnpike, or Petrovsky Park, to where there was a regular service. A choir of deacons occupied one charabanc and the singers could be heard from right across the square, arguing in bass and descant.

'They're off to a wedding or a funeral,' my driver explained, and added, 'At Lubyanka now I'll give the horse a drink. Give us a kopeck. Passenger always pays for the horse's water.'

I did as he asked.

'It's a sorry business. If you're not one of them then they won't let you near the *funtin*, you pay a guard in a little kiosk. And he splits it with the bosses.'

Lubyanka Square was one of the city's central points. Opposite the Mosolov Building, on the corner of Bolshaya Lubyanka, there was a place where you could hire carriages of an antidiluvian design to serve as hearses and carry the dead. And there too waited some smarter carriages for wealthy men and men of business to hire for visits if they didn't have their own means. And cabs were crowded all along the pavement from Myasnitskaya to Lubyanka opposite the Gusenkovsky Inn, the cabbies' inn, with the horses' heads facing the square and cabs against the pavement. The horses' heads had sacks pulled up over them, or string bags with straw poking out hung from the shafts of the carriages. The horses fed whilst their drivers drank tea. Thousands of sparrows and pigeons darted fearlessly about under their feet, pecking up oats.

The cab drivers were running out of the inn to the fountain in their unbuttoned blue jackets, carrying buckets. Once they'd paid their kopeck to the guard, they scooped water up into their dirty buckets and watered their horses. Others were accosting passersby to offer their services, each of them praising their horses and judging the passer-by's rank by his clothes—'Your Worship', 'Your Health!', 'Your Lordship' or 'Sir!'

The noise, the hum of voices, the cursing became one general roar, topped by the thunder rolls of passing carriages, carts, wagons and waterbarrels over the cobbled street.

The water carriers stood in lines around the fountain awaiting their turn, and waving their shovel-like buckets on long poles above the bronze figures of Vitali's sculpture, they scooped water and filled their barrels.

Opposite the Prolomny Gates dozens of goods cart drivers were either sitting like stone idols or rushing all of a sudden, as if at a command, to surround some or other customer who had come to hire a cart. There was shouting and cursing. At last a price was fixed which all could agree on, even though only one of the drivers was needed and in one direction only. But the business wasn't yet done and the hirer couldn't just take the driver who offered the right price. All the drivers would gather into a circle and each would throw a marked copper coin into someone's hat. The hirer then drew out the 'lucky' coin and drove off with the coin's owner.

By the time my driver had queued for water, I had had long enough taking it all in, astonished by the bustle, noise and sheer chaos of the busiest square in Moscow at the time... The busiest and the smelliest too, with all the horses waiting there.

We went down the road towards Teatralnaya Square, and circled round the perimeter of the square, then we drove past Okhotny, Mokhovaya and climbed towards Vozdvizhenka. At the Arbat a coach on high springs came rumbling past, with a coat of arms on the door. A grey-haired lady sat inside. On the box next to the coach-man sat a footman with sideburns, wearing a top hat with braid on it and livery with large bright buttons. Two clean-shaven footmen rode at the back wearing long livery and braided top hats.

Behind the carriage rode a rather dandified official on a trotter, wearing a greatcoat with beaver trim and a plumed three-cornered hat, barely able to lodge his solid form on the narrow one-person fly, which was known back then as an *egoist*.

My Pushkin

Marina Tsvetaeva

It all begins like a chapter from *Jane Eyre*, the novel our mothers and grandmothers kept on their bedside tables. *The Secret of the Red Room*. And in the red room there was a secret cupboard.

But even before the secret cupboard there was something else, there was a picture in my Mother's bedroom: *The Duel*.

Snow, the black branches of little trees, two black figures dragging a third figure towards a sleigh, supporting him under the arms. And someone else, another figure, walking away with his back turned. The one being dragged away is Pushkin, and the one walking away is D'Anthès. D'Anthès challenged Pushkin to a duel, he lured him onto the snow, and there, amongst the bare black trees, he killed him.

The first thing I found out about Pushkin was that he was killed. Then I found out that Pushkin was a poet and D'Anthès was a Frenchman. D'Anthès took against Pushkin because he couldn't write poems himself, and he challenged Pushkin to a duel: he lured him onto the snow and there he killed him with a bullet right in his belly. And so, from the age of three, I knew for sure that a poet has a belly. And I was most worked up about this poet's belly, where Pushkin was shot, and which was (remembering here all the poets I have ever met) so very often empty. Yes, it agitated me every bit as much as the poet's soul. A 'sister' was born to me when I first saw Pushkin's duel. I'd even say that there's something sacred in the word 'belly' for me. Even a simple 'I've got a belly ache' fills me with a rush of trembling sympathy, puts me quite out of humour. That bullet wounded every one of us in the belly.

There was no mention of Goncharova, I found out about her only when I was grown up. A whole life later I send my mother thanks and praise for this omission. That bourgeois tragedy has acquired the proportions of a myth. And really there was no third presence at the duel. There were only two: Him, and Another. In other words, the perpetual cast list of all Pushkin's poetry: The Poet and the Crowd. The Crowd, dressed on this occasion in a single cavalry officer's greatcoat, killed the Poet. And you can always find a Goncharova for the purpose, or even a Nikolai I, for that matter.

'No, but you just try and imagine it!' said my Mother, who couldn't imagine the 'you' she was addressing for a moment. 'He's lying there in the snow, mortally wounded, and he still takes his shot. He aims, he hits, and he even says to himself "*bravo*"!' All this in such an admiring tone, and her a Christian, whose words should surely have been: 'Mortally wounded, covered in blood, and he forgives his enemy! He throws his pistol aside, stretches out his hand.' And, in so saying, she and all of us returned Pushkin to his native Africa, continent of vengeance and passion, and hardly suspecting what a lesson (if not vengeance, then surely passion) she was teaching me, aged four, and barely able to read.

My Mother's room, black and white with not even a patch of colour, the black and white window: snow and the branches of those trees, the black and white picture, *The Duel*, where a black deed was committed on the snow's whiteness: the deed which is forever black, the murder of a Poet by the Crowd. Pushkin was my first poet, and my first poet was killed.

And ever since then, ever since Pushkin was killed right in front of me, in Naumov's picture, daily, hourly, over and over, right through my earliest years, my childhood, my youth, I have divided the world into the poet and all the others, and I have chosen the poet, I have chosen to defend the poet against all the rest, however this 'all the rest' is dressed and whatever it happens to be called.

But even before Naumov's duel, because every memory has its pre-memory, its ancestor-memory, its great-great-great memory, just like a fire escape ladder which you climb down, never knowing whether there will be another rung—and there always is—or the sudden night sky, opening up ever higher and more distant stars to you—but before Naumov's *The Duel* there was a different Pushkin, a Pushkin when I didn't even know that Pushkin was Pushkin. Pushkin not as a memory, but as a state of being, Pushkin forever and forevermore, before Naumov's *The Duel* there was a morning light and rising out of it, and disappearing into it, was a figure, cutting with its shoulders through the light as a swimmer cuts through a river, a black figure, higher than everyone else, and blacker than everyone else, with his head bowed, and a hat in his hand.

The Pushkin Memorial was not the Memorial-to-Pushkin, but simply the *Pushkinmemorial*, all one word, and the separate concepts of Pushkin and memorial were equally incomprehensible, and did not even exist without each other. And there it was, standing there always, eternally—in rain or snow, oh how I can see those shoulders heaped with snow, heaped with the snow of all the Russias, those strong African shoulders—with its shoulders facing into the sunrise or the snowstorm, whether I am going towards it or leaving it, running from it, or running up to it, there it is, with its eternal hat in its eternal hand: the Pushkin Memorial.

The Pushkin Memorial was the limit and the extent of our walks: from the Pushkin Memorial, to the Pushkin Memorial; the Pushkin Memorial was also the finishing line of our races: who could run fastest to the Pushkin Memorial. But Asya's nanny sometimes shortened it for simplicity's sake: 'we'll have a sit-down by Pushkin', and that always drew my pedantic correction: 'Not by Pushkin, by the Pushkin Memorial'.

The Pushkin Memorial was also my first measure of distance: it was a verst from the Nikitskiye Gates to the Pushkin Memorial, that very same constant Pushkin-verst, the verst of Demons and the verst of A Winter's Journey, the milestone of all life in Pushkin, and of our children's anthologies, striped and sticking up at the side of the road, taken for granted, yet enigmatic.

The Pushkin Memorial was part of everyday life, as much a character of childhood life as the grand piano, or the watchman Ignat'ev outside, who stood almost as immutable, if not as tall. The Pushkin Memorial was one of two (there was no third) inevitable daily walks: to the Patriarch's Ponds, or to the Pushkin Memorial. And I preferred the Pushkin Memorial, because I liked to run to it, pulling, and even ripping open as I ran, my grand-father's white Karlsbad jacket, and once I'd reached it, to run around it, and then to stand, my head lifted, and to look up at the black-faced and black-handed giant, who did not look back at me, and was unlike anything or anyone in my life. And sometimes I simply hopped around it. And despite Andryusha's long limbs and Asya's weightlessness, despite my own plumpness, it was I who ran better than them, better than everyone, simply because my honour was at stake: get there first, and then collapse panting. It pleases me that it was at the Pushkin Memorial I won my first races.

There was another different game at the Pushkin Memorial, my own game, and it was this: placing a tiny white china figure, no bigger than a child's little finger—they were sold in china shops, anyone who grew up at the end of the last century in Moscow will know: gnomes under mushrooms, children under umbrellas—against the giant's pedestal and then slowly travel my gaze from the bottom to the top of the granite mass, until my head almost fell off, comparing the sizes.

The Pushkin Memorial was my first encounter with black and white: how black! How white! And because black was the giant, and white was the tiny comic figure, and because I definitely had to choose, I chose then, once and for all, the black, and not the white, blackness and not whiteness: black thoughts, and black possessions, and a black life.

The Pushkin Memorial was also my first encounter with numbers: how many little figures would it take, placed one on top of another, until you had a whole Pushkin Memorial. And the answer was already the same answer as it is now: you could never have enough—still in my modest pride I always added, 'But if you had one hundred of *me*, then *maybe*, because I'm still growing...' And at the same time: 'But what if you put a hundred tiny figures one on top of the other, would that be me?' And the answer: 'No, because I'm big, and because I'm alive and they're just china.'

So the Pushkin Memorial was also my first encounter with materials: iron, china, granite and my own.

The Pushkin Memorial, with me under it, and with the tiny figure under me, was my first proper lesson in hierarchy, too. I was a giant next to the china figure, but next to Pushkin, I was—myself. A little girl. But one who would grow bigger. And I was the same for the tiny figure as the Pushkin Memorial was for me. But then what was the Pushkin Memorial for the tiny figure? And after some hard thinking it suddenly dawned upon me: the memorial was so enormous that the figure simply couldn't see it. It thought it was a big house, or a rumble of thunder. And the china figure was so tiny that the Pushkin Memorial couldn't see it either. It thought it was just a flea. But it saw me! Because I was big and plump. And I would soon grow bigger.

My first lesson in numbers, my first lesson in scale and materials, my first lesson in hierarchy, my first lesson in thinking and, most importantly, a proper underpinning of all my later experience: that even if you had a thousand figures, even if they were piled one on top of the other, you couldn't make Pushkin.

Because I liked walking away from him, down the sandy or the snowy avenue, and walking back to him, along the sandy or snowy avenue, towards his back and his hand, towards his hand behind his back, because he always stood with his back to me as I walked away from him, or as I walked towards him, his back to everyone and everything, and we always walked behind his back, because the boulevard itself with its three avenues approached him from behind his back, and the walk was always so long that every time we forgot, from the boulevard, what sort of a face he had, and every time his face was different, but just as black. (I think with sadness that those last few trees never knew what sort of a face he had.)

I loved the Pushkin Memorial for its blackness—the opposite of the white of all our household gods. Their eyes were completely white, but the Pushkin Memorial's were quite black and quite round. The Pushkin Memorial was completely black, like a dog, blacker even than a dog, because even the blackest dog has something yellowish above the eyes, or something whitish about the neck. The Pushkin Memorial was as black as a grand piano. And even if they'd never told me that Pushkin was a black man, I'd have known anyway that Pushkin was black.

From the Pushkin Memorial I also have my intense love of black people, which I have carried with me through all my life, and even now, my whole being feels a sense of honour when, quite by chance, in a tram, or some other place, I find myself standing by a black man. My profane whiteness side to side with his divine blackness. In every black man I see and I love Pushkin, the black Pushkin Memorial of my, and all Russia's, unschooled early childhood.

Because I liked it that we walked towards him and away from him, but he was always there. In the snow, the flying leaves, the sunrise, the deep blue, the opaque milk of winter—he was always there.

Sometimes, although rarely, our Gods were moved about. And at Christmas or Easter they were flicked with a duster. But he was washed by the rains and dried by the sun. He was always there.

The Pushkin Memorial was my first vision of the immutable, the inviolable.

'Shall we go to Patriarch's Ponds today, or...?'

'The Pushkin Memorial!'

There were no patriarchs on the Patriarch's Ponds.

What a strange and wonderful idea—to place a giant amongst children. A black giant, amongst white children. A strange and wonderful idea—to bring down on white children their black kinship.

Those who grew up in the shadow of the Pushkin Memorial will hardly prefer the white race, and I, so very clearly, prefer the black race. The Pushkin Memorial, anticipating what is to come, is a memorial against racism, to the equality of all races, to the supremacy of any race that might bring forth a genius. The Pushkin Memorial is a memorial to black blood poured into white blood, a memorial to the intermingling of bloods, just as rivers intermingle, a living memorial to the intermingling of bloods, and a commingling of the most remote and the apparently most disjointed spirits of nations. The Pushkin Memorial is living proof of the base and moribund nature of racial theory, living proof of the opposite. Pushkin is the 'fact' which confounds all theory. Even before its own conception racism was thrown aside by Pushkin at the moment of his birth. No—even earlier than that—on the day of the marriage between the son of the Negro of Peter the Great, Osip Abramovich Gannibal, and Maria Alekseevna Pushkina. No, no, even earlier than that: on the unknown day, at the unknown hour when Peter turned his black, pale, joyous, terrible gaze on Ibragim, the Abyssinian boy. That gaze was a command to Pushkin to exist. So children growing up in the shadow of the Petersburg Bronze Horseman were also growing up in the shadow of a memorial against racism—and to genius.

What a strange and wonderful idea it was to make Ibragim's great-grandson black. To cast him in iron as nature had cast his great-grandfather in black flesh. Black Pushkin is a symbol. It was a strange and wonderful idea to give Moscow, in the blackness of a statue, a scrap of Abyssinian sky. Because the Pushkin Memorial stands for certain 'under the skies of my Africa'. What a strange and wonderful idea to give Moscow the sea under the feet of the poet, with his head bent, one foot forward, the hat removed from his head and held behind his back in a bow. For Pushkin stands not above the sandy boulevard, but above the Black Sea. Above a sea of unfettered natural force. Pushkin's unfettered natural force.

What a dark idea it was to place the giant in the midst of chains. For Pushkin is among chains, his pedestal is surrounded ('fenced') by rocks and chains: a rock, a chain, a rock, a chain, and all of it together made a circle. A circle of Nikolai's hands, which never embraced the poet and yet never let him go. A circle begun by the words 'You're no longer just Pushkin, you're my Pushkin' and only undone by the shot from D'Anthès's gun.

I, and all of Moscow's children of the past, present and future, swung on those chains, never once suspecting what we were swinging on. They made very low swings, very hard, very iron swings.

'Empire style?' 'Empire style.' *Ampir.* The empire of Nikolai I.

But with the stones and the chains it made a strange and wonderful memorial. A memorial to freedom, to fetters, to the forces of life, to fate and to the final victory of genius: to Pushkin, rising from his chains. This we can proclaim now, now they have replaced Zhukovsky's personally shameful and poetically talentless substitution:

And I will be remembered by the people with love
Whose better feelings my lyre called forth
That my quick verse usefully I gave...

With its un-Pushkinian, anti-Pushkinian introduction of the concept of *usefulness* into poetry, a substitution which has shamed Zhukovsky and Nikolai I for almost a century and will go on shaming them for the centuries to come, soiling Pushkin's own pedestal since 1884, since its very erection. At last it has been replaced by the words on *Pushkin's* Memorial:

And I will be remembered with love by the people
Whose better feelings my lyre called forth

In this cruel age I sang of freedom
And begged their pity for the fallen.

And if I haven't yet mentioned the sculptor Opekushin, it's only because there is great honour in anonymity. Who in Moscow knows that it is Opekushin's Pushkin? But Opekushin's Pushkin has never been forgotten. Our apparent ingratitude is a gift of gratitude to the sculptor.

And I am happy that I was able to give shape to his black offspring in one of my youthful poems, too:

And there in the fields beyond the imagination
Serving his heavenly Tsar
Ibragim's iron grandson
Set the dawn on fire.

Now this is how the Pushkin Memorial once came to our house to visit. I was playing in our cold white hall. Playing meant either sitting under the piano with the small of my neck at the level of the barrel holding the philodendron, or running wordlessly between the trunk and the shelf under the mirror, my forehead at the level of the shelf.

There was a ring at the door and a man came across the hall and went into the drawing room, and my mother immediately came out of the drawing room and whispered to me, 'Musya! Did you see that man?' 'Yes' 'That was Pushkin's son. You know the Pushkin memorial, don't you? Well that's his son. An actual Privy Counsellor. Stay there and don't make a noise, and watch out for when he comes back through. He looks very like his father. You know his father, don't you?'

Some time passed. The man did not come back out. I sat there, and made no noise and watched. I sat on the bent wood chair, on my own in the cold hall, hardly daring to get up in case he suddenly came through.

He came through, and it was sudden—not on his own, but with my mother and father, and I didn't know where to look, so I looked at my mother, and she angrily took my gaze and tossed it towards the man, and I managed to notice that he was wearing a star on his breast.

'Well, Musya, did you see your Pushkin?' 'I saw him.' 'And what was he like?' 'He had a star on his breast.' 'A star! Did you see nothing else! You've got a special talent for never looking at the right thing or in the right place...'

'Musya, listen to me,' continued my Father. 'Remember this, that you, aged four, saw Pushkin's son. You can tell your own grandchildren.'

I told the grandchildren straightaway. Not my own, but the only grandson I knew: nanny's grandson, Vanya, who worked at the tinworks and once brought me as a present a silver dove he made himself. This Vanya, who used to visit on Sundays and as a reward for his cleanliness, his meekness and his respect for the high rank of nanny, was allowed up to the nursery, where he spent a long while drinking tea and eating bagels, and in my love for him and his bird I never once left his side, I sat wordlessly, gulping at the same time as him.

'Vanya, the Pushkinmemorial's son was here.'

'What, Miss?'

'The Pushkinmemorial's son was here and Papa told me to tell you.'

'Well I suppose he must have needed something from your Dad then, if he was round here...', Vanya replied vaguely.

'He didn't need anything, he was just paying a call,' interjected nanny. 'He's a general or some such. You know Pushkin on Tverskoy, don't you?'

'Course.'

'Well it's his son, isn't it. Getting on a bit now, beard's all grey, combed into two, it is. His Highest Excellency.'

My mother's slip of the tongue, my nanny's prattle, and my parents' order to sit and take note, which I connected in my head only with objects: the white bear in the arcade, the black man high above the fountain, Minin and Pozharsky, and so on, and not ever with a person, after all weren't the Tsar, and St John of Kronstadt (whom I was lifted high above the crowd to see) sacred objects rather than people? All of this left me with only one certainty: the son of the Pushkin Memorial came to visit us. And in time the son's vague features faded too: the

Pushkin Memorial's son became the Pushkin Memorial itself. The Pushkin Memorial came to pay us a visit.

And the older I got, the more it was in me, my awareness grew stronger. It was the memorial that became what was once the son of Pushkin. A double memorial to his glory and his blood. A living memorial. So now, a whole life later, I can say with perfect presence of mind that on one cold white morning at the end of the century he came to our house on Trekhprudny Pereulok: the Pushkin Memorial.

And even before Pushkin, before *Don Juan* I had my own *Il Commendatore.*

Yes I had my own *Commendatore.*

And the son of Pushkin reached us by walking, or, most likely, riding past the Goncharovs' house, where the future artist Natal'ya Goncharova, the great-niece of Pushkin's Natal'ya Goncharova, was born and grew up.

The son of Pushkin passing under the window of the great-niece of Natal'ya Goncharova, who perhaps, without knowing, or realizing, or even suspecting, looked out of her window at him at that very moment.

My house and Goncharova's were near to each other—I only found this out in Paris in 1928—our house was number eight, and she didn't remember what number her house was.

But what was the secret of the red room? Oh the whole house was secret, the whole house was one big secret.

The forbidden cupboard, the forbidden fruit. This fruit was a huge lilac-blue book with a gold inscription across it at an angle: *The Collected Works of A. C. Pushkin.*

Pushkin lived in my eldest sister Valeria's cupboard: Pushkin—that very same black man with the curls and the whites of his eyes shining. And there was a different shining, even before you got to the whites of his eyes: my own green eyes shining in the glass, because the cupboard was hidden, behind mirrors, and in both mirror-flaps— me, and if I stood in exactly the right place, with my nose against the parting of its glassy waters then I had neither two noses, nor even one, but something unrecognizable.

I read this fat Pushkin in the cupboard, nose in the book and against the shelf, almost in darkness and in the flesh, and even a little suffocated by the weight, which was pressed right against my throat, and almost blinded by the nearness of the tiny letters. I read Pushkin straight into my breast and straight into my brain.

My first Pushkin was *The Gypsies.* I had never heard names like those: Aleko, Zemfira and the Old Man. I only knew one old man, Osip, with a shriveled arm, from the Tarusa poorhouse, whose arm had withered because he killed his brother with a cucumber. Because my grandfather A. D. Mein, was not an old man, because old men were strangers and they lived on the streets.

I had never seen any real gypsies, but from my earliest days I had heard about one gypsy woman, my wet nurse, who had loved gold so much that when she was given a gift of some earrings and she realized they weren't gold she ripped them and the flesh from her ears, and stamped them into the parquet right there.

And here is a completely new word—love. When it's all hot in your chest, right in the little hole in your chest (everyone knows the hole!) and you tell no one—that's love. I was always hot in my chest, but I didn't realize it was love. I thought everyone was the same, always felt the same. Then I found out only gypsies felt like that. Aleko was in love with Zemfira.

And I was in love with the gypsies: with Aleko, and with Zemfira, and Mariula, and the other gypsy and the bear, and the tomb, and with all the strange words in which the story was told. And I can't tell a word of this to anyone. Not to the adults because it was stolen, and not to children because I despise them, and most of all because it's a secret. My secret from the red room. My secret in the lilac-blue book, my secret, right from the little hole in my chest.

But to love, and not to speak that love—that would blow you apart in the end. And I found a listener, and even two, in the shape of Asya's nanny Alexandra Mukhina, and her friend, a seamstress who used to come and visit her, when they knew my mother was out at a concert, and Asya sleeping peacefully.

'Our Musenka is a clever girl', she can read, said nanny, who didn't like me, but when conversation about the master and mistress had run dry and the tea had been drunk, she would use the occasion to boast about me. 'Go on then Musenka, tell us the story of the wolf and the lamb. Or the one about the drummer boy.'

(Lord, how our fate is arranged for us! By the age of five I was already someone's spiritual resource. I say this not with pride, but with pain.)

And then once, screwing up my courage, my heart almost stopped, with a deep gulp:

'I can tell you about the gypsies.'

'Gypsies?' nanny replied distrustfully. 'What gypsies is that, then? Who's going to write about those beggars, with their thieving hands in your pockets?'

'These ones aren't like that. They're different. This is a gypsy camp.'

'Well those ones have a camp too. They're always camped out in front of the house, and then they come round to tell fortunes... One little devil comes to the door and says, please let me read your fortune, miss... And the old girl with her has the washing off the line, or the diamond brooch off mistress's dressing table...'

'Not gypsies like that. These gypsies are different.'

'Go on, go on, let her tell us,' says nanny's friend, hearing the tears in my voice. 'Maybe these ones really are different... Let her tell us, and we'll listen, won't we?'

'Well, there was a man. No, there was an old man and he had a daughter. No I'd better tell you the poem. "*Once a noisy throng of gypsies—in Bessarabia roamed—One night by a river, they set their tattered homes—joyful was their rest...*"' And so on, in one breath and without any pauses right up to: '"*The noise of...*"'

'Doesn't she speak nicely! Didn't she do well!' exclaimed the seamstress, who secretly liked me but hardly dared to, as nanny was Asya's nanny.

'"A bear..."' pronounced nanny disapprovingly, repeating the only word which had entered her consciousness. 'And that's right, a bear. When I was a little girl the old men used to say that those gypsies always used to lead a bear around. Hup, Misha, dance, they used to say. And off he'd go.'

'And what happened next? What's after that?' (the seamstress.)

'And, well, the old man's daughter comes to him and tell him that the young man's name is Aleko.'

Nanny: 'What?'

'Aleko!'

'Fine thing to call someone! That isn't a name. What did you say his name was?'

'Aleko.'

'Aleka-and-his-pecker!'

'You're being silly. Not Aleka. Aleko.'

'That's what I said. Aleka.'

'Yes, you said Aleka, but I said Aleko. ALEK-OOOO.'

'Alright, alright, Aleko then.'

'We'd say Alyosha nowadays' (the seamstress, placatingly). 'Why don't you let her speak, and stop being silly. She's the one telling the story, not you. Don't you get cross with her, Musenka. She's a silly woman, she's never been to school, and you have, you can read. You'd know.'

'Well his daughter's name was Zemfira' (this loudly and sternly). 'And Zemfira, this daughter, tells the old man that Aleko is going to live with them because she found him in the wilderness.'

I found him in the wilderness
And brought him to our camp to rest.

'And the old man is pleased and he says, "We'll all travel in one cart. Tum-ti-tum-ti, tum-ti-tum-ti... and travel around villages with the bear."'

'With the bear', echoes nanny.

'So off they go, and they all lived very happily, and the donkeys carried the children in baskets...'

'How was that then? In baskets?'

'Well: the donkeys carried the little children, in panniers they played, and men and brothers, women, girls, followed on the road. Shouts and noise and gypsy songs, and the bear's scraping chains.'

Nanny: 'At last, a bit about the bear. So what happened to the old man?'

'Nothing happened to the old man. He had a young wife, Mariula, who left him to go off with a gypsy, and so did Zemfira. First of all she sang: "Old husband, fearful husband, I'm not scared of you." She sang that about him, about her father, and then she went off and sat on the tomb with a gypsy, and Aleko was asleep and he was snoring terribly, and then he got up and he went to the tomb and then he stabbed the gypsy with the knife, and Zemfira fell down and she died too.'

Both of them with one voice: 'Oh-oh-oh, the wicked murderer! He stabbed him? And what about the old man?'

'The old man was alright. He just said: "Leave us, proud man." And he rode off, and the whole camp rode away, and Aleko was left all on his own.'

Both of them, with one voice: 'Serves him right. Couldn't beat him, so he killed him. We had one in our village who stabbed his wife, close your ears, Musenka' (in a loud whisper) 'caught her with her lover. And he does for him, like that. Sent off to do hard labour. Vasily his name was. Well... No shortage of sorrows in this life, is there... And all down to love.'

Pushkin infected me with love. With the word love. After all they're different things, aren't they: something that has no name, and something which has a name like *that*. When the maid passed a ginger cat sitting and yawning on someone's window light and brought it with her, and it spent three days under the palms in our hall, before disappearing forever—that's love. When Avgusta Ivanovna says that she's leaving us and going to Riga and never coming back—that's love. When the drummer boy went off to war and then never came back—that's love. When in Spring the pink gauzy naphthalene dolls were shaken out and put away again, and I stand and I watch and I know that I won't ever see them again—that's love. I mean *it* burns just the same and in the same place, from the ginger cat, Avgusta Ivanovna, the drummer boy and the dolls, as it does from Zemfira, Aleko, Mariula and the tomb.

And the wolf and the lamb isn't love. Even though my mother tries to convince me that it is very sad. Such an innocent white lamb, no trouble to anyone... But the wolf is good *too*!

The problem was that I was born to love the wolf, and not the lamb, and I wasn't allowed to love the wolf in this situation, because he had *eaten* the lamb, and I couldn't love the lamb, however white and eaten he was, I couldn't—love just didn't come, just as nothing has ever come of lambs for me.

... he said and he dragged the lamb into the forest.

I said a wolf, but I called him a leader. I said a leader, but I called him Pugachev: the wolf, who spared the lamb on this occasion, the wolf, who dragged the lamb into the dark forest, to love it.

But I will tell you somewhere else about me and the leader and about Pushkin and Pugachev, because the leader will lead us far away, and maybe even further than Lieutenant Grinev, right into the debris of good and evil, that place of debris where both are twisted into one indivisible whole, and in their twisting make up living life.

But for the moment I will tell you that I loved the leader more than family, more than strangers, more than all the dogs I loved, more than all the balls that had rolled into the cellar and lost penknives and more than all my secret red cupboard, where he was the biggest secret. More than the gypsies, because he was blacker than a gypsy, *darker* than a gypsy.

And if I could have shouted it out then that Pushkin lived in the secret cupboard, now I can only whisper—that in the secret cupboard lived... the leader.

It was natural that after all this endless stolen reading my vocabulary grew larger.

'Which doll do you like best? The one auntie brought from Nuremberg, or the one my godson brought from Paris?'

'The Paris one.'

'Why?'

'Because her eyes are full of desire.'

My mother, in a terrible voice: 'What?!'

I, stammering, 'That is...' I wanted to say '... her eyes are full of fire.'

My mother, in an even more threatening voice: 'Well then.'

My mother didn't understand, my mother heard only the sense, and maybe she was right to feel indignant. But she didn't understand. It wasn't her eyes that were full of desire, but the feeling of desire, which those eyes lit in me (and the pink gauze, the naphthalene, the word Paris, and the matter of the trunk, and how the dolls were out of my grasp), which I ascribed to the eyes. And not just me. All poets (and then they shoot themselves—when the doll isn't full of desire, after all). All poets, and Pushkin was the first.

A little while later—I was six and it was my first year of studying music—at the Zograf-Plaksina Music School on Merzlyakovsky Street, there was what was then called a Christmas public concert. A scene from *Rusalka*, followed by *Rogneda* and then:

And now let's fly across to the garden
Where they met: Tatiana, Onegin

A bench. And on the bench—Tatiana. Then Onegin comes, but he doesn't sit down, *she* stands. They both stand there. But only he speaks, the whole time, a long time. And she says not a word. And then I understand that the ginger cat, Avgusta Ivanovna, the dolls—*none* of that was love. That *this* is love: a bench, and she's sitting on the bench, and he comes, and he speaks the whole time, and she says not a word.

'Well, Musya, what did you like best?' said my mother at the end.

'Tatiana and Onegin.'

'What? Not Rusalka, with the mill, and the prince, and the wood sprite? Or Rogneda?'

'Tatiana and Onegin.'

'But how can that be? You didn't understand a word of it, did you? What could you have understood there?'

I am silent.

My mother, gloating: 'See. You didn't understand any of it, just as I thought. A six-year-old! What could a six-year-old find to like in that?'

'Tatiana and Onegin.'

'Well you're a very silly girl and as stubborn as a mule.' (Turning to the director of the school Alexander Zograf who had come over) 'I know what she's like. The whole way back home in the cab whatever I say she'll answer: "Tatiana and Onegin." I'm sorry that I even brought her. There's not a child in the world who would have preferred Tatiana and Onegin to everything else they'd seen, they'd all have chosen Rusalka because it's a fairytale, and simple. I just don't know what to do with her!'

'But why Tatiana and Onegin, Musenka?' This is the director in a very kind voice.

(I was silent, full of words: Because of... love.)

'She's in seventh heaven,' says Nadezhda Yakovlevna Bryusova coming over (the poet Valery Briusov's sister— M.T.), our oldest and best student. And so I learn for the first time that there is a seventh heaven, and it is a measure of the depth of feeling.

'What's this, then, Musya?' says the director, pulling out a mandarin from my muff where he had hidden it, and then putting it back again slyly (I see you), then pulling it back out, then putting it back in again...

But I was quite dazed and dumbstruck by then, and none of his and Bryusova's mandarin smiles or my Mother's terrible gazes could tease a smile of gratitude from my lips. On the way home—the quiet, late, sledge-ride home—my Mother scolded: 'Disgraced! Didn't say thank you for the mandarin! Little fool, six years old and in love with Onegin!'

My mother was wrong. I wasn't in love with Onegin, but with Onegin and Tatiana (and perhaps even with Tatiana a little more than Onegin), with both of them together, with love itself. And nothing of my own was written after that without me falling in love with two at the same time (with her a little more), not with them both, but their love. With love itself.

The bench they *didn't* sit on determined my fate. I've never liked it, not back then, nor afterwards, nor ever, when two people kiss, I like it always when they part. I've never liked it when they both sit down, but I like it always when they go their separate ways. My first love scene was an un-love scene: he *didn't* love her (I realized that) and that is why he didn't sit down, *she* was in love and that's why she stood up, they were not together, not for a moment, they did nothing together, each did the complete opposite of the other: he talked, she was silent, he didn't love, she loved, he left, she remained, so that if you were to lift the curtain on the stage, she would be standing along, or perhaps sitting again, as she only stood because *he* was standing and then she collapsed, and so she will sit for all eternity. Tatiana will sit for all eternity on that bench.

This, my first love scene determined all my following love scenes, all the passion of my unhappy, unreciprocated, impossible love. From that moment I desired no happiness and so condemned myself to *un-love.*

And that is what all this is about: he didn't love her, and that is why she loved him so very much, and that is why she loved *him*, and chose no one else for her love, because she *knew* in her heart that he couldn't love her. (I say that now, but I *knew* it back then, I knew it then, but now I have learnt how to say it.) People with this dreadful gift for unhappy, one-sided love, taken-all-upon-oneself love, are just genius at finding inappropriate objects.

But Evgeny Onegin decided something more for me, not one thing, but many other things. If I have always until now been the first to write, to stretch out my hand, and my hands, never fearing judgement, then this is only because at the dawn of my life Tatiana in a book, lying with her hair tousled and falling in a braid across her breast, did this right before my eyes. And if afterwards when they left (they always left) if I not only never stretched out a hand after them, but never even turned my head, then this is only because long before, in a garden, Tatiana stood motionless as a statue.

A lesson in bravery. In pride. In faithfulness. In fate. A lesson in loneliness.

What other country has a heroine in love like her: brave and dignified, in love and unchanging, prophetic, and loving?

There is no trace of vengeance in Tatiana's response. That's why retribution is absolute, why Onegin stands there like a man 'struck by thunder'.

All the cards were hers to play: she could have pointed this out, driven him mad, she held all the cards, she could have humiliated him, trampled him into the ground beneath that bench, brought him down to the level of the parquet in that hall, and yet all this she rejected with one utterance: 'I love you (there's no point in lying).'

No point in lying? What about to triumph over him? Still, where's the point in triumphing? But to this question, there really is no answer for Tatiana—no clear answer, and so she stands again, in the enchanted circle of the hall, just as she stood before in the enchanted circle of the garden, in the enchanted circle of her loneliness in love—back then she was unwanted, now she is feted, and then and now she loves, and yet cannot be loved.

All the cards were in her hands, but she wouldn't play.

So girls, first confess your love, and listen to his response, and then get married to some respectable veteran with battle-wounds, and then later hear out confessions of love without returning them—and you'll be a thousand times happier than the other sort of heroine, who has her every desire fulfilled and all that is left to her to do is to lie down on a railway line.

I made the choice between being full of desire and having that desire fulfilled, between my fill of suffering and empty happiness at my birth, even before I was born.

Because Tatiana had her effect on my mother, even before me. When my grandfather A. D. Mein made her choose between her beloved and himself, she chose her father, and not her beloved, and then married later, even outdoing Tatiana, as 'for poor Tanya all lots were equal', whereas my mother picked the very hardest lot of all—a widower twice her age with two children and still in love with his dead wife. She married someone else's grief and offspring, loving and continuing to love another man, a man she never tried to meet, a man she met unexpectedly, long after, at one of her husband's lectures, and in answer to whose question on life, happiness etc., etc., she said,

'My daughter is a year old, she's a very big baby, and clever, and I am perfectly happy...' (Lord, how she must have hated me at that moment because I was not *his* daughter.)

So Tatiana did not just affect my whole life, but even the fact of my existence: if it hadn't been for Pushkin's Tatiana, I wouldn't have existed.

For that is how women read poets—in that way, and no other.

Still it says something that my mother didn't call me Tatiana—she must have pitied her little girl after all.

Very Proper Nouns

Marina Boroditskaya

Old Lizaveta on 3rd Yamskaya Street never had the slightest problem with any household appliances.

And do you know why?

Because she called every labour-saving device by its own proper name. The washing machine she called Katya, the Hoover was Kip and the electric stove was Ella. The German whisking-mixing machine, a gift from her grand-children, she referred to respectfully as Herr Teodor. The fridge even had its own surname: Comrade Papanin.

When Lizaveta brought her basket of washing over to the machine she would say,

'Good morning, Katya-Katerina, my lovely! Time for you to fill yourself with water and do my little bit of washing! And you, Ella, my heated little friend, be patient, don't go burning yourself out with excitement, it's still a while till lunch...'

The other old ladies would sit on the benches outside and grumble. Someone's iron had fused, someone else's television was fuzzy. And Lizaveta would instruct them,

'Really, what can you expect if you haven't given them names! When I lived in the country, I remember my mother used to give all the animals names, even the chickens, she called them by their names, all of them she spoke to like friends. Cows now, they love to be chatted to. Why don't I have a little word with your iron, what's his name, he's a Garik I'd say...'

And she would talk to the iron. And it would do the trick! Not always, of course, but often. And slowly, slowly, little by little, word spread throughout the area about Lizaveta, who, it was said, put a spell on electronic goods, took the curse off them, restored their wellbeing, and all sorts of other nonsense.

The people came from far and wide: someone with a fan, someone with a floor polisher. And then one day, to crown it all, her neighbour Kolka from the stationery shop came running.

'Auntie Liza, give us a hand! My car won't start!'

Liza was quite astonished. She waved Kolka off, saying,

'What do I know about cars! Honestly what do you take me for—a garage mechanic?'

But Kolka pleaded and pleaded, and dragged the old lady out to the street, and she got into the car and cupped her chin in her hand.

'Are you feeling the cold,' she said, 'little Ladushka? Is it a bit chilly, my sweet? But you know there's nothing for it, you've got to go. Your owner'll be late for work otherwise...'

And what do you think happened?

You're right.

After this Lizaveta had no peace from car drivers or car lovers. And then one day her phone rang.

'Elizaveta Prokofyevna?' said a very official-sounding man's voice. 'This is Orlov. Air Chief Marshall Orlov. We are currently testing a new model of jet fighter—'

'She's not here!' squeaked Lizaveta, her voice even surprising herself. 'This is her niece here. She's gone to the country... To... er... to regain her powers of... wellbeing...'

The old lady pulled the telephone wire out of its socket and for a whole week she didn't go out of the house, and she wouldn't open the door to anyone. If she didn't fade away entirely then it was only thanks to Comrade Papanin.

But things were soon settled for the best. Lizaveta was invited to the Moscow Energy Institute and every week since then she has read a lecture there.

Her subject? 'Treating electrical goods nicely'. The students adore the old lady, and she's very pleased with it all herself. A nice little addition to the pension, a few fresh faces to talk to.

And Kolka takes her to work in his car.

Clean Monday

Ivan Shmelyov

The harsh light in the room wakes me: a bare sort of light, cold, dreary. Yes, today is the first day of Lent. The pink curtains with their hunters and ducks were taken down whilst I still slept, and that is why it is so bare and dreary in the room. Today is Clean Monday, and everything in the house is cleaned. Grey weather today, a thaw. Outside the sound of dripping, like tears. Our old carpenter and joiner Gorkin said yesterday that once *Maslenitsa* was over there would be tears. And it is crying: *drip... drip... drip...* There! I gaze at the torn paper flowers, at the gilded *Maslenitsa* gingerbread—the toy brought back from the bathhouse yesterday: no little cut-out bears, no little sugar hills—the joy of it all gone. But a new joy nestles in my heart: how different it all is, how changed! Now 'the soul is waking itself up'—Gorkin told me yesterday that the soul 'needed preparing'. Going to communion, fasting, preparing for the Holy Day.

'Call Kosoy to me!' I hear my father's angry shout.

My father has stayed at home today. It is a special day today, a day of strict observance. My father doesn't shout much. Something serious must have happened. But hadn't he forgiven Kosoy his drunkenness, absolved him of his sins? Yesterday was the day of forgiveness. And Vasil-Vasilich had forgiven all of us, hadn't he said so, on his knees in the dining room, 'I forgive you all!' So why was father shouting?

The door opens and Gorkin enters with a shining copper tub. Smoking out *Maslenitsa*! In the tub is a hot brick and some mint, and vinegar is poured over. My old nanny Domnushka walks behind Gorkin and pours on the vinegar, and the bitter steam rises, the holy steam. I can smell it even now, down through the long years. Holy— that's what Gorkin calls it. He walks to each corner and quietly shakes the tub. And he shakes it over me.

'Get up, my boy, no time to lie abed,' he says gently, and holds the tub up under the bed curtain. 'Where's that *Maslenitsa* spirit, what's fattened itself? We'll chase it out, won't we? *Woe betide the wolf at Lenten Tide...* We're off to the Lenten Market today. The Vasiliev Singers will be singing there: "my soul, my soul". You'll be carried away by it all.'

That unforgettable, holy smell. The smell of Lent. And Gorkin quite different, as if he were himself holy. He had been to the bathhouse even before dawn, had bathed in steam and put on clean clothes, for today was Clean Monday! Only his coat is old. Today everyone wears their oldest clothes, because that is how 'it must be done'. And it is a sin to laugh, and you must put oil on your head, like Gorkin. Now he will eat no oil with his food, but he must wear oil on his head because that is how it is done, 'for his praying'. A radiance comes forth from him, from his neat grey beard, shining quite silvery, his combed hair. I know that he is holy. Saints are such as he. And his face is pink, like a cherub's, pink with scrubbing. I know that he has dried for himself crusts of black bread with salt, and he will drink his tea with these ''stead of sugar'.

'Why is Papa cross... so cross with Vasil-Vasilich?

'Oh, sins...' says Gorkin with a sigh. 'It's never easy turning over a new leaf... now everything is strict, it's Lent. Well let them get cross. But you bear up there, you think about your soul. This is the time when it's most like the last days on earth... That's as it should be! You say the "O Lord and Master of my life" now. That'll cheer us up.'

And I begin reciting to myself the recently learned prayer of Lent.

It's quiet and empty in all the rooms, it smells of the holy smell. In the hall, before the very old red-tinted icon of the Crucifixion, which had belonged to my great-grandmother who had kept the old faith, the Lenten lamp burns, with bare glass, and it will burn now ceaselessly until Easter.

When my father lights the icon lamps—on Saturdays he lights them all himself—he chants in a sweetly melancholy tone 'We bow down before your cross, O Master', and I chant after him the wonderful,

'And we praise... Your Most Holy
Res-urr-ection!'

Something joyful lights up in me at these words and throbs in my soul so that it brings me close to tears. And I can see in my thoughts, at the end of the chain of Lenten days, the Holy Resurrection, all in flowers. This blissful little prayer illuminates all the sad days of Lent with its gentle light.

I begin to feel that now my former life is ending and I must prepare myself for the life to come, which will be... where? Somewhere in the sky. The soul must be cleansed of all its sins and that's why everything is different. And there is something peculiar close by to us, something invisible and fearful. Gorkin told me that at this time 'the soul is parted from the body, see'. And *they* keep watch—to catch hold of the soul—and the soul trembles and cries out 'O wretched me, o woe is me!' And that's what the *Efimony* is all about, at vespers this week.

'Because *they* know that their end is coming with the Resurrection of Christ! And that's why we fast, on account of it keeps us closer to church, waiting for the Holy Day. And not thinking, see... not giving any thought to the worldly matters. And the bells all ringing: all remember... all remem-ber!...' he says with his beautiful country 'o's sounding out as he speaks.

The top windows are all open at home, and the weeping, calling bells can be heard: 'all remem-ber... all remem-ber...' A pitiful ringing, a keening for the sinner's soul. Its name is the Lenten call to prayer. The curtains have been taken down from the windows and everything will be as in a poor house until Easter itself comes. The old covers have been put over the furniture in the drawing room, the lamps have been cocooned in material, and even the only picture *Beauty at a Feast* is covered with a sheet. The Priest advised it. He shook his head dismally and whispered,

'A sinful temptation of a picture.'

But my father likes it. It's smart. And the print is covered too, that my father calls the Pryanishnikov picture for some reason, with an old deacon dancing a jig and his old wife thwacking him with her broom. The Priest liked this picture a great deal, he even laughed.

Everyone at home looks very austere, in our poorest clothes with patches, and I was made to put on a jacket with holes in the elbows. The carpets are all taken up, and now you can skate ever so nicely on the parquet floor, only it's a bit frightening—Lenten Tide: if you were to get carried away by skating you'd surely break your leg. There's not a crumb left anywhere from *Maslenitsa*, its spirit has been driven out. Even the jellied sturgeon was sent back to the kitchen yesterday. Only the most everyday plates are left on the dresser with their greying spots and cracks—the Lenten ones. In the hall are bowls full of yellow salted cucumbers, with the umbrella heads of dill stuck into them, and chopped cabbage, sour and with aniseed thickly scattered on it—a wonderful dish. I take some in my fingers—how it crunches! And I give my word to myself that I will abstain from forbidden foods while it is Lent. Why bother with meat and dairy foods that corrupt the soul, when everything is so good without them? We'll have compote and potato cakes with prunes and dried apricots, and peas, and poppyseed bread with beautiful sugared poppyseed twists, and pink bread rings and cross-shaped biscuits on the Sunday of the Veneration of the Cross. Frozen cranberries with sugar, marinated nuts and sugar coated almonds, soaked peas and rings of bread and little rolls, raisins on the vine, and jellied rowanberry sweets and Lenten sugar, boiled up with lemon and raspberry essence, and with candied peel in it, and halva... and hot buckwheat porridge with onions and a glass of *kvas* to drink it down with! And Lenten pies with milk-caps and buckwheat pancakes with onion on Saturdays, and rice boiled with jellied fruit on the first Saturday of Lent, a sort of sweet rice pudding! And almond milk with a white floury kissel, and cranberry kissel with vanilla... and the long stuffed fish pie on the Feast of the Annunciation with sturgeon, and the sturgeon's dried cartilage! And fish soup, marvellous salty fish soup, with specks of blue-black caviar and marinated cucumbers... And soused apples on Sundays and warmed sweet sweet *Ryazan*... And little 'sinners'— buckwheat cakes with hemp oil, all crusty on the outside, and warm and hollow inside.

Surely *there*, where we all go when we leave this life, there'll be a Lenten Tide like this! So why does everyone look so dreary? Everything is new and changed after all, and there is so much, so much to rejoice in. Today they will bring in the first ice and begin packing the cellars, the whole yard will be filled. We're going to the Lenten Market where there's a noisy roar of voices, and the great mushroom market that I've never been to before... I begin leaping about in excitement, but I am stopped.

'Lent! don't you dare! You just wait, you'll break your leg.' I'm scared. I look at the crucifixion. The Son of God, his suffering! But why did God... why did He allow it?

I feel that in this lies the great mystery. *God.*

My father is in his study, shouting, banging with his fist and stamping. On a day like this! He's shouting at Vasil-Vasilich. And it was only yesterday he forgave him. I am afraid to go into his study, he'll chase me back out in his rage, and so I tuck myself behind the door. I see Vasil-Vasilich's broad back through the crack in the door, his flushed neck and the back of his head. The folds move on his neck like an accordion, his back sways and his great fists are flung backwards, as if he were warding something off—an evil spirit? He must even now be tipsy.

'Drunken oaf!' shouts my father, banging his fist down on the table, and the piles of money jump and jangle. 'And still drunk even now! On such a day as this? You sinning devils, and you make me a sinner alongside you... Lord, forgive me! A few people nearly killed at the slopes sledging? Where was that fool of a steward? A whole bag of money lost... three hundred!' Thank the Lord the old cab driver is a god-fearing man, and brought it back... Left the money at his feet, did you!? Get back to the country, you're sacked!...'

'I'm as fresh as a daisy, so don't you mind me, sir... I've been at the baths washing myself... On account of it's Clean Monday, sir, was up there five in the morning, sir, as it's proper to be...' Vasil-Vasilich reports, swaying, still warding something off behind him... 'You count it up sir, it's all there... Master's property... *Life it with my... guard...* sir... It's all in its place...'

'People near crippled! Drunkards out sledging? I've had a note from the constable in Presnya... I tell you what this looks like! So what was going on?'

'You count up your thousand there, sir. You'll see by the notes that it's all there. And this is what happened. I did come across the constable, aye indeed, I did wrong... but all in the name of my master... Towards nightfall some drunken lads leapt on a sledge, and it was all 'Come on, faster! Let's see Maslenitsa out! And they're off, sledging down the hill, and shouting "faster!", eight of them there were and Anton Kudryavy can't barely stand up on the runners, since dinner he's been off, knackered he was, what with the sledging, well... he'd had a little bit to drink as well...'

'What about you, are you sober?'

'Sober as a priest, I even gave the constable a little ride, he was all for having some fun... They took me captive! It was like this, see, sir. Some butcher's lads from Taganka turned up... came with their pancakes to the slopes, and their sacks... They were very pleased to see me...'

'Ay! Liked the look of your drunken face, no doubt! Go on then with your stories...'

'So they seized me, took me by force on the big sledge and Antoshka pushed us off... But they've got me on both sides, won't let me do anything, so they're flying down the hill and Lord, I sees that it'll be the death of us, so I shout out "Antoshka, brake, dig your heels in!" So he starts braking with his heels... but couldn't hold on, and fell under the sledge, and it turns over three times at full speed, and I got a bump the size of my fist you know where... And then the fools, without my knowing... they let another sledge go with the drunks on board. Petrushka Glukhoy was driving it... and, well, he was a bit the worse for wear seeing off Maslenitsa... And they went straight into us, eight people! There was a crash, but God kept us safe, they went into the bottom of our sledge and knocked it out, but luckily the people were just thrown out... And then a third sledge comes racing along, Vaska, not minding his own business, and half way down he sends everyone flying... Gets one foot caught, lucky he was in felt boots or it'd been broken. Would have hit all of us otherwise as we were lying there on the ice, right in the way... So the constable's clerk starts puffing and blowing, all set to write a crime report, but the constable stops him, after all no one was fatally killed, see! So I took the clerk off to an inn and this newspaper man is threatening to put your name in the papers... So I got them to serve him some soup and we had a drink together, sir. And all in my master's interests, sir. And then the constable shuts the slopes at nine, by law, because of Lent, so as to make everything quiet and orderly... so all the merrymaking was died down.'

'So Antoshka and Glukhoy, are they in bed?'

'They've been to the bathhouse, they're right as rain, Ivan Ivanych the apothecary came and had a look, told them to put some grated horseradish under their heads. No, they're already asking for some cabbage. I was about to get worried, on account of the two of them lying there yesterday clean out... concussed they were, sir! But I sorted the whole thing out, I went home, and I'd broken my own head on the sledge, had no idea what was going on... And I only forgot one sack of change, sir... and anyway that cabbie's almost part of the family, sir, hasn't he known your family for forty years!'

'Leave me,' my father says dispiritedly. 'You've upset me, and on a day like this... You try being a Christian with you lot around!... Stop... There aren't any orders for today, order in the snow from the stores, twenty cartloads of ice from the Moscow-River after lunch, special order, thirty kopecks a load. You rascals! Asked me for forgiveness yesterday and not a word about this sorry business! Get out of my sight.'

Vasil-Vasilich sees me, gives me a sleepy look and gestures with his hands as if to say, 'well that was all unnecessary, wasn't it?' I feel sorry for him and ashamed of my father—on such an important day, to sin like that!

I stand there for a long time, unable to make up my mind whether I should go in or not. I push the door and it squeaks. My father, in a grey dressing gown, down-hearted—I can see his furrowed brows—counting money. He counts quickly and piles the money up in columns. The whole table is covered in silver and copper and the window-sills are filled with the little columns. The abacus clicks, the brass coins clatter and the silver ones jingle against each other.

'What do you want?' he says severely. 'Don't get in my way. Take your prayer book and go and read it. The rascals... Don't hang around wasting time, go and say some prayers.'

He was so upset by the whole business he didn't even pinch my cheek.

In the workshop Pyotr Glukhoy and Anton Kudryavy are lying on piles of woodshavings right up by the stove. They've wrapped their heads in pickled cabbage leaves to sober themselves up. The carpenters who had been to the bathhouse are resting, repairing their sheepskins and felt coats. Gorkin is by the window reading the Gospel, shouting it, syllable by syllable to the whole workshop like the deacon in church.

They listen silently and without smoking: smoking is forbidden in Lent, Gorkin has forbidden it. They can go out to the yard. The kitchen woman, trying to listen and not make too much noise, is mixing up a soup of *kvas*, soaked bread and vegetables. There is a strong smell of cabbage and radish. Huge steaming round loaves lie in a pile. Buckets of *kvas* and pickled cucumbers stand around. The black clocks tick in a dreary way. Gorkin reads and keens,

'And... all... the... ho-ly... an-gels with Him.'

Anton's cropped head lifts itself, he looks at me with bleary eyes, looks at the bucket of cucumbers on the worktop, listens to the chanting of the holy words—and in a quiet, pitiful, pleading voice he says to the kitchen woman,

'Wouldn't mind a drop of *kvas*... or a cucumber...'

And Gorkin, wagging his finger, reads in a stern voice,

'Go from me... you cursed ones... into the eternal fire... which is ready for the Evil One and his angels!'

And the clocks ticking in the silence: tick... tick... tick...

I sit quietly and listen.

After a gloomy lunch in complete silence—my father is still upset—I wander glumly about the yard and poke at the snow. The mushroom market is tomorrow, and it's still too early to go to *Efimony* at vespers. Vasil-Vasilich is walking around gloomily too, miserable. He pokes at the snow a bit, stops and stands around. I heard that he hadn't been at lunch. He chops the wood a while, knocks the icicles down with a broom... and then stands there, breaking his nails. I feel very sorry for him. He sees me and takes up a spade, stares at it for a bit and puts it down. Not a word.

'Why did I get it in the neck then?' he says downheartedly to me, looking up at the roofs. 'He tells me to take my leave... after thirty years! I was in service to Ivan Ivanych, your grandfather, when I was a little boy. Others have bought houses, opened inns with your money, and here's me—given the sack. Well I'll take my leave, I'll go back to the country, I won't serve anybody any more. God forgive them...'

I feel choked by his words. Why? On a day like this? Everyone ought to be forgiven, and Vasil-Vasilich was forgiven along with everyone else yesterday.

'Vasil-Vasilich!' I hear my father's shout, and I see my father come quickly over to the store room where we are talking. 'What's all this about, according to the ticket stubs I should have received a thousand, but here's three hundred roubles more—what kind of miracle is this?'

'All the money there is yours, and there's no miracles about it.' Vasil-Vasilich says sternly, looking aside. 'As if I'd take your money. Me with a cross round my neck...'

'Now man, don't take on... You know me. I've got enough on my plate as it is.'

'Well there were crowds yesterday at the slopes, having a party, and they were eager as anything, didn't want to wait, threw the money in through the ticket office window and didn't even bother with tickets... We're not cheating you, they said. So we collected it all up... I shook it out of all the bags. You can trust our lads... Well, perhaps they spent a little on drink, no more than five, that would be it... But I... your property... Well here's your property!' Vasil-Vasilich is shouting by now and he stands and turns out the pockets of his jacket.

A bitten piece of black bread flies out of one pocket onto the ground, and out of the other a chewed stump of salted cucumber. Even Vasil-Vasilich can't have expected this. He bends down and collects it up in some confusion, and begins shovelling snow.

I look at my father. His face has lit up somehow, his eyes sparkle. He marches over to Vasil-Vasilich, takes him by the shoulders and shakes him hard, very hard. And Vasil-Vasilich, putting down his shovel, stands with his back to him and says nothing. And that's how it finished. Neither said a word. My father marches off. And Vasil-Vasilich, blinking a little, shouts as jaunty as ever,

'Come on, stop standing around! Hey, lads! Take up your spades, clear the snow... The ice'll be dropped off soon, and there won't be anywhere to put it.'

The carpenters, rested after their lunch, come out. Gorkin came out, Anton and Glukhoy came out, rubbing their heads with snow. The work started and went with a swing. And Vasil-Vasilich watched, and slowly, and very contentedly, chewed his cucumber and bread.

'You fasting, Vasya?' Gorkin says, chuckling, 'Come on then, let's see you with that spade... We'll work those pancakes off us in no time.'

I watch the snow flying about, and I watch how they carry it off to the garden in baskets. The shovels rasp on the snow, I hear the men roaring, there is a smell of bitter radish and cabbage... The bells begin their sad call to prayer: *o re-member, re-member...* for *Efimony* at vespers.

'Let's go to church, Vasiliev's choir is singing tonight,' Gorkin says to me.

He goes to get changed. I go, too. And I hear my father calling cheerfully out of the window from the hall,

'Vasil-Vasilich... Come over here a minute, my friend.'

When we leave the yard, to the calling of the bells, Gorkin says to me in excitement, his voice trembling,

'That's how you should do it, take a lesson from your father, never give people cause for upset. And 'specially when you should be looking to your own soul... He gave Vasil-Vasilich a twenty-five rouble note for Lent, and he gave me one, too, for no reason... The boys got five roubles apiece and the workers got a half rouble each, for the snow. That's how you should treat people. Our lads are good lads... they value that, they do...'

The twilight in the sky, the sticky melting snow, the calling bells... How long ago it was! A warm, almost spring breeze—even now I can feel it in my heart.

'Tsar or Prince, King or Queen, Bootmaker, Tailor, which will you be?'

Larisa Miller

Watching skills and trades die out
Is much like burying yourself in earth.
Arseny Tarkovsky

At the beginning of the 1950s a tall lumbering man, rather like a gypsy, with a mighty moustache and a gold tooth used to come to our house regularly. He bore himself with dignity, he wore a baggy coat and a wide brimmed hat. The people in our block called him 'our very own cobbler'. The gypsy would sit himself down on a chair and place his feet wide apart, putting down a travelling bag between them which smelt through and through of leather, glue and boot polish, and click open the metal catches, pulling out into the light our shining, rejuvenated shoes. Not shoes, but rather crystal slippers, so carefully did he place them down before us.

This wonderful cobbler sometimes brought shoes of his own making, his own handiwork, and this was the highlight of his visit. I was not a spoilt child but on one occasion I quite lost my head at the appearance of a pair of brown slip-ons with a bow and elegant heels. Remembering that modesty was my best quality (and highly valued by my mother), I was silent, but I didn't take my eyes off the shoes. It all ended with the cobbler making me a pair, a smaller pair, which I then never let out of my sight. I carried them more than I wore them. I put them on the ground when I was doing my lessons, and placed them on a chair next to my bed when I was asleep. As soon as my feet had grown a little, a new pair appeared, a copy of the first pair. The last pair I wore in 1956. Our very own cobbler was a magician. He could even pull a handkerchief from his pocket like a conjuror: he pulled and pulled and the handkerchief just kept coming. And he needed a hanky as capacious as that just to wipe his tanned expanse of bald head and his enormous brow.

We knew another cobbler who lived on the opposite side of the road on the ground floor of a low building typical of the Zamoskvorechye area. He sat by the window, which was always wide open in the summer, wearing a huge leather apron, mumbling away to himself, banging with his hammer, or wielding his awl, rubbing in ointments, or patching felt boots. As children we used to stand by his window and watch him. 'Only don't block out my light,' he used to say. All our street would go to him with pleas for help: 'Petrovich, help us out!' And he would help out.

Mother's dressmaker Nine Iosifovna lived close by: the same yard, on the first floor. The windows of her flat looked out onto the gable end of the next block and so she had to keep the lights on all the time—probably the pay off for not living in a communal flat and having her own place, even if it was tiny. Everything was fascinating: the foot-operated sewing machine, the spools and pins, the motley pieces of material, which I was allowed to collect, the fashion magazines on glossy paper. And I was fascinated watching her, with her mouth full of pins, crouching by my mother's legs, pinning something to my mother that glittered and rustled, and then, eyes half-closed, studying it all in the long mirror in the hall.

But the special attraction was her husband, Nikolai Ivanovich. When we arrived he would greet us and then immediately run away to his brightly lit corner to work, copying out music. He had plenty of work, he was always pushed, but he did it all carefully and in good time. I would peep over his shoulder, watching as the black and white garlands of notes, flats and sharps, dots and bar lines would appear with fantastical speed on the five little lines. Nina Iosifovna only made serious pieces: suits, evening dresses, and she only used expensive material, so my mother did not visit her very often, and wore what she had made for a long time.

If something easy and cheap, something for the summer was called for, then she would invite round Zheshka. Zheshka was about sixty, but everyone spoke of her merely as Zheshka. Asking Zheshka meant having her live with you while she sewed. She had nothing of her own, no family, or children or home. She was always staying at someone's, yet never bemoaned her lot, congratulating herself rather on an easy character, good taste and, this most of all, an amazing figure. Her elegant legs crossed, she sat cutting up mother's dressing gown and telling endless stories about her brief and long-distant career as a ballerina in the corps de ballet, about the sculptor, devoted to her, who had sculpted her legs a whole lifetime ago, about a new friend, 'such a stunner the men all die when they look at her'. But her favourite story was as ancient as the hills and eternally fresh: it was about another admirer who had followed her down the street entranced, until he managed to run ahead of her and look into her face. He took a good look, and fell back in horror and took to his heels.

Here Zheshka would begin to laugh, she laughed until she cried, she laughed until her stomach ached. She was fantastically ugly, but turned even this fact into a source of merriment. A week later, slightly dazed by Zheshka's chatter, we gazed in delight at mother's outfit in the mirror: floating, the lightest of touches, and yet natty, chic. No one would ever have guessed that it was sewn from old clothes.

Our 'very own hairdresser' was over the small Kamenny Bridge, by the 'Udarnik' cinema and mother often took me with her to keep her company and amuse her. I kept the whole salon amused, reading out poems and singing songs. Vertinsky's songs went down particularly well and there were always requests for encores. The audience was a demanding one. The hairdressers looked like lords, reserved, always entirely correct, they kissed their ladies' hands. One of them, a grey-haired and stately man, was the most lordly of all, and the best hairdresser. But all of them, despite their bulk, fluttered around their ladies like butterflies around flowers, in impeccable white coats, wielding tongs with extraordinary ease, heating them up, letting them cool, waving them in the air, pressing them for an instant to their lips, so that having brought them to exactly the right degree they could construct a prodigious wonder on their lady's head. Huge mirrors, spacious chambers, wide windows, and on the window sills, for some reason, the aged and cracked marble busts of women who might have been Roman matrons, or might have been goddesses. It could have been a palace hall, not a hairdresser's.

Our own hairdresser, our own cobbler, our own dress-maker—and yet mother and I barely made it to payday, especially while we lived together. But when we had enough we 'feasted', and bought two chocolate biscuit cakes from the patisserie on Stoleshnikov Street (and only there!), and a hundred grams of cheese from the cheese shop on Gorky Street. Goodness, what a spirit of cheese reigned in that shop! It seemed that even the shop assistants and the shop sign were made of butter and fresh cream.

Moscow at the end of the 1940s and during the 1950s was a town of a million temptations, a town created especially for my Mother and me out on our strolls. The Ermitazh Gardens alone were measureless pleasures. We sometimes spent the whole of Sunday there, wandering, reading, dozing on a bench, and in the evening we went to one of Raikin's shows. Thick overgrown patches made the gardens mysterious, but every shadowy tree-lined path always led to a little cafe, or a tent selling something delicious. It was quiet and uncrowded during the day, but at night it sparkled with fairy lights, and crowds of perfumed and well-dressed people appeared and a band began playing on the bandstand. Performances were staged in summer and winter theatres, and films in the cinema, and you hardly knew where to go first.

A furrier lived not far from the Ermitazh in one of the side streets, and when I heard this strange word for the first time, I was desperate to go there. To my disappointment the furrier turned out to be an ordinary elderly woman, whose only distinction was a blue mark on her lip. But there was nothing interesting about this—she had pricked herself with a pin, my mother explained. Her flat, however, quite exceeded my expectations. It was a den, rather than a flat, in which furs and hides lived their quiet, dark lives. They lay scattered on the wide divan, unrolled on the table, pinned up on the wooden mannequin, which spun round easily on one foot. But the real lair was an enormous mirrored wardrobe, in which black, ginger and silvery furs lay on countless shelves, and finished and unfinished fur coats and jackets hung on hangers. It seemed as if you could push these aside and enter into an endless forest of fur coats, from which there was no return. Many years later, reading *The Lion, The Witch and the Wardrobe* to my children, I remembered this deep and mysterious wardrobe. But what was mother doing at a furrier's, I wonder for the first time as I write these words. After all in those days she didn't have a fur coat. And suddenly I see very clearly the coat with the astrakhan collar and matching hat—mother's unchanging winter outfit for many years.

'Tsar or Prince, King or Queen, Bootmaker, Tailor, which will you be?' The counting rhyme of my childhood, which I spent in a postwar Moscow still in disarray, but all the same an incredibly homely city. It was people going about their ordinary everyday lives that made it a city fit for living in. I was too young to appreciate their labours, but in their very bearing, artistic and unfussy, their beautiful and confident movements there was dignity, gravity, goodness and a sort of rootedness. Even Zheshka, who, you might think, lived life in the same happy-go-lucky way she sewed clothes, even she had her own style, and her own inimitable magical stamp on things.

There was the watchmaker as well, a craftsman, whom you only heard about by word-of-mouth. Even before the war grandfather used to take all the family's clocks and watches to him. After the watchmaker died at the beginning of the seventies, grandfather took our ancient bronze clock to a workshop for mending, and brought it home completely dead. Doctor Beleny belonged to some high guild of craftsmen. He was a children's doctor and he visited me in my first year of life. Mother always said that he knew everything about babies, he didn't mind if they peed on him or pulled on his nose, and despite his great dimensions he had soft and incredibly sensitive hands— hands which had tapped and tested nearly all of newborn Moscow.

Tsar or Prince, King or Queen, Bootmaker, Tailor... Each of them was indeed a King in his or her own tiny state, ruled by a code of honour. Swindlers, frauds, poor workmen—none of these belonged there. Each of them was an inheritor of the 'cursed past', a relic whose very distinctiveness had been protected by some miracle from the state's repeated attempts to eliminate all identity.

And now these people have completely died out. Even the most crowded world is a desert without them. No— I'm not going to wallow and pretend it was 'better in the old days'—that's a tedious and thankless occupation. It's just when you live in a desert and you feel proper thirst you try to quench it in the only way you're able, by falling down to the old and dried up springs. Will they once more give you refreshment?

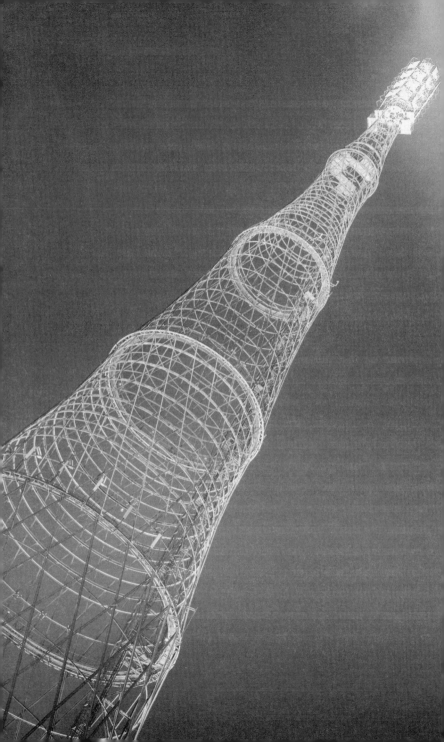

Underground Sea

Maria Galina

Artemy Mikhailovich found himself in a completely unfamiliar place.

At first sight there was nothing very odd about this, as he had fallen asleep on his way home. But a tram is not a car, and not even a bus, and cannot by its very nature leave the rails. And Artemy Mikhailovich had been travelling on this route for twenty years at least. He had seen the city change gradually, the old buildings fall apart, the new buildings rise, the branches of plane trees cut back to ugly stumps, then shooting out knots of green which soon became rigid rolled tubes, and then turned brown and dropped, the yellow leaves lying on the dark blue asphalt, and the delicate Shukov Radio Tower, either black against the light sky, or yellow, lit up in the dark night. The sweet shop outside the famous confectionery factory had been there since history began and was still there, but the 'Milk' shop on the corner had become a 'Mini-market', and after that the sign had read 'Intimate', until some of the illuminated letters had blown their bulbs, and then the sign itself disappeared and the door was crossed with boards.

In the evenings there were fewer and fewer lit up windows. Instead of the curtains and potted plants, re-plastered ceilings and LED lighting appeared in windows, then all the lighting went out, as if by command and it sometimes happened that the rumbling tram dragged itself past entirely dark blocks, with not a single light in a window, for several minutes at a time. And Artemy Mikhailovich had less and less opportunity to play his old game of imagining himself to be someone he had seen in a lit window. The people sometimes flickering in the gap between curtains seemed to be bright and wonderful, and so their lives must be just as bright and wonderful... Artemy Mikhailovich had never admitted to dreaming in this silly fashion, and would have been very surprised to know that all those who make a beeline for the window seat in a tram and not the exit, amuse themselves in exactly the same way.

It's worth adding that all those who sit by a tram door when there's space are energetic, forceful and preoccupied with matters at home, or, as surprising as it may sound, the opposite: incredibly shy—even the thought of disturbing someone whilst pushing their way from window seat to door upsets them. But those who prefer sitting by the window are prone to the detached observation of their surroundings and to a little dreaming. Often they barely notice who's sitting next to them, and only later, suddenly shaking off their trance, they discover that the attractive blonde in a tightly belted mink has been replaced by an enormous glum old lady wearing a fluffy grey shawl over a woollen grey coat with a moth-eaten goatskin collar. Where on earth did she come from?

For this very reason—the old ladies who had taken this tram route to their hearts for its proximity to a few churches and a hospital—Artemy Mikhailovich preferred to sit on the window seat in a bank of two. Far too often when he chose the single seats he would have to stand and give up his seat to another reproachful old bag, but hidden away like that no one ever saw him.

Artemy Mikhailovich probably had slight claustrophobia. Not perhaps bad enough for his blood pressure to go up in the metro or his heart to start pumping, or to be short of breath, but he was slightly uncomfortable, especially in the rush hour when the passageway to the circle line was full to bursting with people all involuntarily stepping in the same rhythm. Sometimes his imagination drew for him a picture of these people all compressed into a round pellet, with the same terrifying pellets of humanity pushing it along from behind and he could even hear within himself the hollow crack of bending ribs. A catastrophe of some sort, an explosion or just panic, and straightaway there are no individuals, just a quivering mass of humanity. He chased these thoughts off by remembering something he had seen on television or read recently, but the palms of his hands were wet, and ashamed of this, he wiped them surreptitiously on his trousers, although no one would have seen anyway. No one sees anyone in the metro.

In any case the tram was more convenient for him. He could travel home from the skin and venereology clinic, where he worked in the laboratory, without changing trams. And that is what he did, year in year out, except that the tram he took home was red and yellow to begin with and then became blue and white and acquired a stylish and almost angular profile, then it developed a complicated entry gate system, an electronic device against which Artemy pressed his flat square season ticket. These journeys were secret little holidays, a moment to catch breath, when he could simply sit (or at least stand) and think about nothing, just ride along through the familiar landscape which changed its seasonal colours only with reluctance and reserve.

But now he lifted his head and looked around bewildered. He must have sensed something out of place, even in his sleep, which had been troubled. It must be that the tram had turned off its usual route onto some service line which led to the depot (he knew that the tram depot was somewhere round here, not far away), and his subconscious, used to the routine, had registered the change. The tram was standing still, the rows of brown upholstered seats were empty, the conductor in her strikingly bright orange vest was standing in the aisle holding a crowbar. He had barely come to, and he shuddered in fear: she had a stern expression on her face.

'Get out,' she said, although not unkindly, 'we're here.'

'Where?' his half-asleep voice was both hoarse and thin, and he was ashamed of it.

'The depot,' said the conductor coldly. 'Didn't you hear? This tram's going to the depot. Leave the carriage please.'

And as if to make a point, she waved the crowbar, which was only ever used to change the points, but again she looked terrible and menacing.

He obeyed without thinking, as he always obeyed those who were in positions of power, even the receptionists in the clinic or the security guards at the door. The seat had been warmed by his body and warm air still flowed beneath the seat. It was that heat which must have made him uncomfortable. The woman in the orange vest had already climbed onto her driver's throne and was waiting there, her hands lifted, just like a pianist the moment before he descends on the keys, showing with all her person that she was only waiting for his departure.

Hurriedly he slid sideways off the last step, and as if it had been waiting for this, the bell jingled and the tram moved past, casting little scraps of light on the wet rails and wet asphalt: a warm little box, lit up from the inside. Artemy Mikhailovich breathed in the raw air which enfolded him like cold river water.

The rails divided in the twilight and swam into indistinctness just as when you press on the eyeball, the streetlamps shone through the damp mist. One light, right over Artemy Mikhailovich's head, suddenly went out, and then slowly winked back to life. For some reason it irritated him, and stopped him concentrating.

It got rapidly and utterly dark as it always does in October, the gaps in the dim layered clouds, indigo like porcelain and transparent, were extinguished, bleeding into the clouds, the mist became drizzle and home was the only place to be. But to get there he had to retrace his steps, find the right tramline and either catch a tram or walk home. Here Artemy Mikhailovich realized that he had no idea where he was, or how far from his home the tram had carried him. Now he looked around at his surroundings again, and this time more carefully.

The tramline curved, and throwing off a weak luminescence into the mist, it disappeared through a wide gateway, through which windowless box-like buildings could be seen against the darkness. But before it vanished a line broke off like a little shoot and bent round to the left into the dark hole of a side street. The surrounding space could not have been called a road: a veritable chaos of low buildings, dark, impenetrable fences with barbed wire over them, strange little lean-tos and cabins loomed on all sides.

The streetlamp winked again, bringing on a moment's dizziness. The puddles between the tram rails quivered, scattering splinters of light. The weird, derelict landscape was empty. The ugly phrase 'industrial zone' came floating to the top of his consciousness—the workday over, the place was as deserted as the moon's surface.

A shiver went through Artemy Mikhailovich. He suddenly felt like a child, like in the children's book when the children suddenly shrink and have to fight off a spider with the help of a sting they sawed from a dead wasp. This impression was heightened by the tramlines, gleaming under the street lamps like a snail's slimy trail.

The streetlamp went out again and sky was visible, dense and dark with a strip of glowing crimson across it, and white pillars of light struck up at this glow from below. It was probably always like this in the evenings, but Artemiy Mikhailovich rarely looked up at the sky. The glow was strongest a little way ahead and to the left, indicating where the centre of the city was. He supposed that he should go right, but on the right rose the stepped wall of the strange place into which the tram had crawled and where something was now moving with a squeaking and clanging. Suddenly and quite out of nowhere he remembered the children's book *Where the Tram Goes to Sleep*. The tram in that book had gone to a bright airy and comfortable hall with crystal ceilings, and it had slept in a huge bed for a tram, covered in a bright blanket—but this was quite different, real and black and frightening.

Well, he would just have to walk back up the line, that would be the most sensible. Although he didn't know how far the tram had come from the usual line, but surely it hadn't crossed the city? Tramlines are like rivers or streams, if you follow them you must always come out somewhere, to a familiar stop, or even, at the very least, to a metro station. He was suddenly aware that he wanted to be in a damp and trampled station vestibule, with its smell of a vegetable store, in an underground place, but one that was bright and peopled. What was the closest station: Shabolovskaya? Tulskaya?

But behind him there were more unexpected industrial zones, and beyond that monstrous cone-shaped cooling towers smoked like volcanoes. Going that way was pointless and frightening. So he followed the little growth of line which crawled off down a side street, where dim lights hung on wires and dark low buildings stood so close together it seemed as if there was nothing—not other streets, nor even yards—beyond them.

He lifted his head in search of a sign with a street name, but couldn't find one. Were there no signs at all, then? What was the local council doing?

The windows on the ground floors were entirely covered by shutters, the doors were locked—some with huge bolts and padlocks. Where there were signs it was not clear what they meant: 'Vesta Limited', or 'Tri-angle'. Even a normal word like 'Seabreeze' could have stood with equal success for a hairdresser's, a cafe or an accountant's.

And in addition he had worked out what had been alarming him all this time: not one window in any of the buildings was lit. Why were no windows lit?

Perhaps, he thought, the whole area had been bought by some company, and it had put its offices in all the buildings, on all the floors. If it hadn't been for this daft exploit he would have been home a long time ago by now, his tea brewed, sandwich ready, he would switch the television on and watch it until he could feel his eyes closing of their own accord. He imagined the little clean kitchen, the talking head on the TV on its wall bracket, the circle of light from the lamp on its one bent leg.

'Built enough bloody offices...' he said out loud, to cheer himself up, 'bloody capitalists.'

A wave of drizzle moved through the air and hit the wet walls.

Water quivered between the cobblestones.

He walked past a few more buildings. Then there was a fence with some sort of a building site, over which hung a gloomy crane. A metal sign hung on the fence with stencilled lettering. He almost ran to it rejoicing, because such signs usually have the address of the site alongside other information. The sign was rusty, drops of water caught in the peels of paint, but he still managed to read it:

'The building of an eight-storey block of flats on Ton Dyk Tkhang Avenue. Work carried out by SMU-305. Projected date of completion: May 1972'

Who the hell was Ton Dyk Tkhang? And why 'Avenue' when it was no more than a side street? Were they going to pull it down and build a big road? Very strange.

The unfinished eight-storey block stared at him with its holes of windows, its bristling metal struts. Clumps of tough grass escaped from under the fence.

Artemy Mikhailovich, with a sort of sob, drew in the damp air through several orifices, and wandered on further. The fence ended, there were some small single-storeyed buildings, then a factory of some kind, redbrick and squat, with a whole strip of faceted windows, then some more single-storeyed buildings with little porches at the side, and a streetlamp dancing above a porch illuminated a corrugated little roof with drops running along the edge, growing heavier and falling.

By the porch on the ground floor, light came from a tiny window with a slanting metal grate. The window was covered with cardboard on the inside and the light escaping from a crack was a sort of flat, impersonal light, as when a single bulb hangs from a wire, but Artemy Mikhailovich was glad even of this. For a short while he hesitated, because he was shy of strangers, and conversations with strangers, but then he bent his head and ran up the two steps, feeling a little stream of water running over the back of his shaven neck, and he pressed on the dirty square bell push.

The bell didn't work. He crooked his fingers and tentatively knocked. Then he knocked louder, no longer with his knuckles but with his whole fist, and he flinched when he heard shuffling footsteps on the other side of the door. He had already lost hope that anyone would answer him.

'Who is it?' a voice asked from beyond the door.

'Excuse me,' said Artemy Mikhailovich, 'I just want to ask something.'

There was silence behind the door, then the shuffling steps began again, only this time they were receding. Artemy Mikhailovich drummed on the door in desperation, now with his open palms,

'Wait!' he shouted. 'Wait, don't go away! I only want to ask! I want to know the way! Wait!'

The door opened slightly—to Artemy Mikhailovich standing outside, even a light like that seemed unbearably bright. A sharp old snout with pale eyes and spiderwebs of veins across its sharp cheekbones poked out from the crack.

'What way?' The old man was in a t-shirt and clumps of grey hair poked out from the neck. 'There's no way round here.'

'What do you mean, no way?' Artemy held onto the door just in case the other tried to slam it shut and suddenly noticed that blood gleamed dully on his knuckles. 'There must be a way. There must be some way.'

'Where to?' asked the old man. He smelt of damp rags.

'I don't know... Shabolovka, say. The way to Shabolovka?'

'Where?'

He was deaf as well.

'What's this street called?'

Christ, he thought fleetingly, why is this happening? What does it matter what it's called? But he carried on insistently.

'What's the address here? Where am I?'

'I'm not allowed to tell you,' said the old man and pulled the door behind him.

'Listen to me!'

'This is a site, you hear me? You stop this mucking around! I'm going to call the police on you! Cap and all!'

Artemy Mikhailovich wasn't wearing a cap, he was wearing a beret which had slid down to one side whilst he had been pulling at the door, and was completely wet through, but he was so bewildered that all he could say, quite without thinking, was,

'It's not a cap it's a beret.'

'What you at me about now!' squealed the guard, and making a last effort, pulled the door with such strength that it slammed shut. Artemy Mikhailovich was left outside and he nearly burst into tears because it was warm in there and the light was on, and there was probably a kettle on the old hob with its red hot coil, or maybe the kettle was electric, with a cord hanging from it, but whatever there was, that old man was in warmth and safety and he was in the frightening dark street, where the black trees shone dully in the dim streetlight.

'Let him ring the police,' he muttered. 'What does it matter?'

He suddenly had the desire to pick up a stone and toss it at the window, but when he looked closer he could see that the window was covered in cardboard for the very reason that a star-shaped hole already yawned in it.

He brought his injured hand close to his eyes, then took a handkerchief from his pocket and wiped the blood and dirt off. 'I'll probably get an infection as well,' he thought. He twisted his wrist so the light shone on it and looked at his watch. It was half past nine.

Usually by this time he was finishing dinner and watching some or other serial, although this he never admitted to his work colleagues as he knew himself how stupid those serials were.

'Ridiculous!' he said to himself. 'You just need to keep going.'

He climbed down from the porch (brown leaves were wedged under the ridged metal door mat) and he continued on down the street, singing nonsense songs to cheer himself up.

'Ataman Makhno... looks out the window... all's dark in the meadow...'

Everything really was all dark. He passed some enormous gates, locked with enormous bolts. Behind the gates a lonely tree swayed and creaked, its foliage still miraculously intact, a four-storey building as dark as all the others and something else, angular and mysterious. He carried on and sang a song about the dead, with their braids of hair, standing at the roadside, but then he stopped, because he didn't like singing this song in the darkness. The street-lights, hanging from wires had stopped without him notic-ing, and in the fading light of the last one he saw that the tramline had simply stopped. There were no more tram rails, and the cobbles had been replaced by a thin and lumpy strip of asphalt.

And that was all.

He stamped up and down distractedly, unsure what he should do next. Go back? There was no point. Go on? Probably. There was no tramline, but there was a street. A very dark street, it was true.

Now, without the streetlamps in the way, he saw a fearful dead sky above him, crimson-violet, crossed through with white pillars of light and smoke curling from the cooling towers. He thrust his frozen hands into his pockets, put his head back and looked around.

There had to be some kind of landmark—one of Stalin's skyscrapers, you could see those everywhere, or those new ones which had risen up in the most unex-pected places, the glass prisms of rooftop penthouses and the red signal lights flashing on top. He just had to find one and make a beeline for it.

He sighed in relief. The Shukhov Radio Tower.

It was as if he had forgotten its existence, although when he had first begun travelling on this route he would take furtive admiring glances at it: it was like a throwback to his childhood, the little blue lights, the reports from Baikonur, or that voice which had a deep down hypnotic effect 'Reporting from Moscow on a special day,' and sparklers, and his parents still alive... Not that supercilious Ostankino TV tower, but the homely, friendly radio tower with its lacy black silhouette in the many-coloured sky.

It should be clear from here—those horrible cooling towers were also always flickering on the horizon he remembered now—but the radio tower was always closer, like a friendly wave of the hand. When had he last followed it with his eyes, as he had ridden past indifferently?

But although he scanned the horizon from corner to corner the familiar shape was nowhere to be seen. It was as if the radio tower had suddenly taken offence at his lack of attention to it, and had stopped appearing to him.

Loneliness enveloped him, together with the rain and darkness.

And with the loneliness came the sudden understanding that he, Artemy Mikhailovich, was no more than a warm human body, separated from the surrounding world by dampish clothing and a heavy coat that was wet through. Not the complex system of communications and responsibilities, nor the flat which he wore like a second skin, or his most loved books or less loved television serials, not his workplace where he had spent twenty years of his life, but this protein structure standing in the rain in a frightening, strange, unfamiliar and deserted city.

'Is this me?' he asked himself in astonishment. 'Is this really me? This thing standing here on the road? Is this it? All my memories, my past, everything I like and dislike, is this it, standing here?'

But these were uneasy thoughts, and he suddenly remembered something, rummaged in an inside pocket and got out his mobile phone. The body of the phone was slightly warm, it fitted his hand comfortably and this made him feel calmer. The screen lit up in a friendly way, as if trying to tell him that somewhere life carried on as usual, and invisible but strong threads linked him to that life.

He went into the address book and wrinkling up his eyes he began looking at the names there. A mist of water covered the screen. What if it were to break?

'Anna Work'—oh yes, Anna, the lab assistant, very young still, he'd put in her number just in case, after all you never knew. Should he ring her then? What could he say to her? That he was standing in the darkness on an unknown street? Hardly.

'Varvara Leonidovna'—the Lab Director. Ringing her would be totally ridiculous.

'Veniamin Nik' Who was that? Nik—Nikolaevich? He couldn't remember. Clearly someone he'd found useful at some point.

'Passport Off' well that was clear, the passport office, his passport needed renewing and he'd noted it down just in case.

He felt frightened. The cursor jumped from name to name, and they were all the names of people who might have been important or unimportant to him, but they were all strangers, and there was no one to tell that he, Artemy Mikhailovich, was standing on a dark street in the rain, that he was lost and wanted to go home, that he was lonely and sad.

At this point something needs to be brought up. Artemy Mikhailovich was a bachelor. Not by conviction, but his mother had been too insistent in pairing him up with girls: ugly, awkward and absurd girls, the daughters and nieces of her aging friends. Or girls who were quite the opposite: forceful and self-satisfied, too certain that everything would go their way, and his mother would look into his room from time to time and nod in a meaningful way, and the girls talked and talked, and he, Artemy, would say something, and then, once, he brought home a girl, but his mother really didn't take a shine to her. So everything followed its usual course: at first it seems like you've got the whole of your life before you, and then time begins passing very fast. To begin with his mother was there, and then she wasn't, every morning he went to work, every evening he came home and at the weekend he did technical translations or went shopping, or tidied the flat, and only when all his jobs were done, and the TV programmes all watched, would he look around in astonishment, not knowing from where this misery, this sense of pointlessness sucking away at him had come. But Monday would arrive again and everything would begin once more, a lab assistant would drop a three litre bottle of Sulphuric acid, health and safety would carry out an inspection, a bacteriologist would go on maternity leave, a batch of slides would be a dud lot, and the agar would run out.

But the cursor's bright tick was still moving down the alphabetical list. When it reached 'Mitya' he sighed in relief. Mitya, a friend from childhood, a layabout and a ladies' man who had just got divorced and had remarried—a silly young woman from work—but he was still a proper friend, someone who remembered him as a little boy, and in this alone would seem to confirm his existence: that he really did exist, that he had been a child, had had a mother, that his mother had once slapped Mitya's face when he'd said something he shouldn't have in front of her...

Why did they see so little of each other? No time? That was an excuse, thought Artemy, it was fear: fear of changing the usual order of things, of finding oneself naked, exposed to the piercing winds of time without the protecting shell of routine.

He pressed the button with a freezing finger.

The ringtone. What was it that Mitya did, anyway?

The call ended itself. He pressed the button one more time—in the middle of the empty street.

Finally Mitya's voice answered.

'Artemy is that you?'

'Yes,' said Artemy Mikhailovich and coughed, his throat suddenly constricted.

'What is it, then?'

Mitya spoke as if he was waiting for Artemy Mikhailovich to spit it out and then get off the phone. Artemy Mikhailovich remembered that that was the reason why he had stopped phoning Mitya. Mitya always behaved as if everything that had happened in the past was not important, it was what was going on now in his life that was important, and as what was going on now kept changing, and Artemy Mikhailovich was used to a measured life, he found all this very tricky and strange. He liked quiet, intense conversations, openness and reminiscing, whereas Mitya was upbeat and energetic. It suddenly dawned on Artemy Mikhailovich, that he, Artemy Mikhailovich, took up very little space in Mitya's life, and the space he did take up was insignificant and marginal.

But still he said,

'Oh, just ringing. You'll never guess... Something funny's happened.'

'Yeah?' said Mitya, by his voice you could tell that he was doing something else at the same time, but Artemy Mikhailovich carried on all the same.

'This funny thing. I just came to this place by accident on the tram, and I don't know where it is and I'm just standing here and it's a completely empty street and I don't know—'

'Hang on,' Mitya interrupted with new interest. 'Have you been drinking?'

'No. Of course not. I'm coming home from work. I fell asleep and the tram landed me here and that's what happened.'

'Well I never,' said Mitya a long, long way away, in his warm flat. 'Happens.'

Artemy Mikhailovich thought that Mitya was only pretending to be sympathetic, his voice actually sounded indifferent and if he, Artemy Mikhailovich, really had been drunk, Mitya would have been more interested in his adventure, because in the long history of their friendship Artemy Mikhailovich had never once been really drunk.

Artemy Mikhailovich also thought that Mitya didn't think his adventure was important, or even a good enough reason for a conversation, *I mean, so he got on the wrong tram...* For a minute it even seemed to him that everything was fine, in no time at all he'd find a bright place with some people, and actually he'd just remembered an old friend and decided to find out how he was doing. So he asked:

'How are you doing?'

'Yeah fine,' said his friend irritably. 'Windows is down, and I can't get my work done. It's due in tomorrow. I mean, yesterday. Listen I can't talk right now, but it'd be great to see you. Why don't we get together at the weekend? Come round.'

The dank dark night began closing in on him again. Really Mitya couldn't do anything for him, even if he'd wanted to, because he didn't know the street name or where Artemy Mikhailovich was. It was extraordinary, after all nothing terrible had happened, just he couldn't ask for help from anyone in any way. No one could help, not the emergency services, not Chip 'n Dale. It turned out there were times when help was impossible to give, and really life was made up of such situations, however much we tried to convince ourselves of the opposite.

'OK,' he agreed. 'We'll definitely get together.' He turned off the phone. The screen was covered with a soft film of water and he wiped it with his hand before shutting the phone.

'Just got to keep walking,' said Artemy Mikhailovich. 'Keep walking.' It was ridiculous—all he had to do was stop a passing car and either the driver would give him a lift or explain where to go.

But there were no cars in sight, although there was the constant, fluctuating, almost slurred hum of a big city with its ceaseless life. Still he would probably come out to a place where there were cars. Whatever there might be, there would be cars. Even if there weren't people around.

His shoes were letting in the water and his feet were getting damp. He wiggled his toes inside the wet socks, his toes felt each other, they were wet and cold. His coat was weighed down, his shoulders hurt, the skin was sore and beginning to ache over a protruding vertebra in his neck, a bulging disc, the usual pain, which he almost never felt at home or work where he instinctively found the most comfortable position. He tried to straighten his shoulders, the weight of the coat was better distributed and it made him feel more confident.

He walked, and the surface water bubbled out from under his soles, the windowless buildings loomed black and angular, like children's building blocks, from behind them peeped black wet trees rubbing their branches in glee.

The street turned almost ninety degrees, he nearly banged into another set of locked gates, rusty and wet, across which was written in white paint 'Site No. 2' The paint was so fresh it almost seemed to shine in the darkness.

He turned obediently to follow the pavement, water gurgled down a gutter filled with fallen leaves... So why was he so scared anyway, at least there weren't any hoodies, it was a good area, not a residential area at all.

And then he heard behind him and from a long way off a regular pounding clattering beat like horses' hooves on asphalt.

He turned sharply: a black dog ran along the road. It seemed huge to Artemy Mikhailovich. It was the dog's claws making the sound, and this was odd as the claws of most stray dogs are worn to the quick.

Artemy Milhailovich stamped up and down on the spot distractedly. He knew that dogs are supposed to know when a person is scared, and that you should never try to run away. He went on standing there on the uneven edge of the pavement, and the dog passed him, giving off the thick smell of wet dog, and ran towards the gates and squeezed through the gap under them. To do this the dog had to flatten itself almost completely, its back end and tail stuck out briefly and were then dragged under the gate with a jerk.

The dog paid Artemy Mikhailovich no attention at all and this fact made him seriously doubt his own existence for the first time. It came to mind that a man exists whilst others see him, and as soon as he is alone he begins to fade out and eventually dissolve in the air. Perhaps normal life is for humans something like a cast into which their unstable essence is poured?

Artemy Mikhailovich remained standing there, his palm pressed to his chest. It was as if all his senses had become wrapped in some oily film over the last few years and had lost their acuity, their keenness. But now taking frequent irregular breaths he breathed in suddenly with the watery mist the smell of the fallen leaves, tar, rusting steel, the wet earth. He was defenceless and alone, as he had been in his childhood, and the surrounding world was huge and mysterious, just as in his childhood.

He remembered that when he was small he had often had the sudden feeling that some miracle was about to happen—usually at New Year when he went over to the window and looked out at the grey-tinged snowflakes falling slowly from the white sky, and the streetlamps slowly increasing their warm light, so they looked like large gilded mandarins.

When did all that end? He hadn't noticed.

But now, standing in the darkness under the huge sky, which was still slowly darkening, with the many lights turning off in windows, he threw his head back and licking the wetness on his lips he whispered something, inaudible even to himself.

Once again he heard the clattering on the asphalt. His heart beat louder, and then faster in joy: someone light and quick, in a light-coloured jacket and tight jeans tucked into narrow boots. When she saw him she half-stopped for a moment. He could almost see himself in her eyes, a dark, motionless, even threatening figure in an empty street.

What could he say so as not to frighten her?

But she spoke first.

'Have you seen a dog? A black one...'

'Yes,' he had to clear his throat to make his voice sound normal. Almost normal. 'It went under there. Under the gate.'

'Bloody dog,' the woman said with frankness.

She crouched down, sticking out her bottom in its tight denim amusingly, and she bent lower and tried to look through the gap between the ground and the rusty gate.

'Busya!' she called in a thin plaintive voice. 'Busya!'

A scruffy canvas lead was wrapped around her waist.

Busya was not coming out.

Artemy Milhailovich stood behind her stamping his feet.

'Love conquers all,' said the woman ruefully and she stood up and shook her legs out.

'What about climbing over the fence?' Artemy Mikhailovich recommended bravely.

'There's barbed wire along the top,' the woman said. 'But I know where there's a hole in the fence. Will you stay here, though? It's kind of scary on my own.'

'I'll go too,' said Artemy Mikhailovich decisively, his fears had left him, and he only wondered why this completely unknown young woman wasn't scared of him. 'What is there in there?'

'Bits of metal. And dogs. It's like a dog wedding in there. I let him off for a quick run, and he ran away. That's the third time.'

She walked alongside the fence purposefully and he hurried after her, deeply happy that everything had ended so well: people with dogs knew places well. A bit further along there really was a hole in the bumpy grey fence, wide enough for a grown person to squeeze through. And she did this, not even worrying about staining her white jacket—it must have been an old jacket, specially for dog walking. He slipped through after her, his bulky coat caught on something, he heard a tear, and when he felt down he realized that he had ripped the pocket.

The rain stopped. The crimson clouds tore in places and cold white stars appeared in the torn gaps.

The site was covered with some long dark hangars, concrete pillars stuck up in the air, and a metal structure fanned out. Hurrying after the woman Artemy Mikhailovich slipped and his foot went into a pothole filled with water, so one of his feet was now completely wet. Without hesitating the woman darted purposefully between some piles of building materials and her white jacket stood out in the darkness.

He went faster so he wouldn't be left behind, and got a stitch, but at least he wasn't feeling the cold any more.

'Busya,' the woman shouted from time to time, and whistled in some special way—he had never been able to whistle like that.

All of a sudden a barking dark ball rolled out of the dead grasses, and he jumped away in surprise. But the woman dived towards it, grabbed something in the ball and staggered, holding with one hand the collar of Busya, angry and bitten. With the other hand she hurriedly unwrapped the leash around her waist, clicked the catch on it and straightened up. The ball fell apart into several furry patches of dark, the dogs leaped about and barked desperately and their white teeth glittered in the darkness. Busya growled hoarsely and tried to escape from his collar. Artemy Mikhailovich stood motionless, afraid to move.

'Scare them off!' shouted the woman.

'How?'

'Well... Pretend you're picking up a stone. They know what a person with a stone means.'

Artemy Mikhailovich bent down and feeling totally ridiculous he pretended to be feeling around on the ground. His fingers actually came across a stone and he squeezed it in his dirty fist. With his elbow sticking out awkwardly, he drew back his arm to throw it. The dogs went immediately quiet and retreated. He gestured again to make sure. The dogs sat down on their furry backsides and waited silently, following the two of them with their eyes.

Dragging the resisting Busya they squeezed sideways through the hole in the fence and were back in the street, which seemed to Artemy Mikhailovich almost friendly after the terrifying metal dump.

'What on earth did he see in the bitch?' the woman shrugged. 'Nothing much to look at. A redhead, I suppose. Busya's a one for the redheads.'

'Could you...' Artemy Mikhailovich tried to catch his breath, 'could you tell me how to get to the metro from here? Or a tram stop?'

'Are you lost? People are always getting lost around here.' She patted Busya on the neck distractedly, trying to calm him. 'Come on, I'll show you.'

Artemy Mikhailovich's fear vanished, so abruptly, so quickly, that he gave a great sigh of relief so deep he felt almost a pain in his chest. He stood beneath the beautiful wet sky, the wet trunk of a beautiful black tree glittered, and beside him he could see the white face and white jacket of an unknown, young and probably attractive woman.

He suddenly felt himself to be slightly silly, awkward, as he had felt on occasion in his youth, and he made an effort, as he had once long ago made efforts, to sound light and casual.

'You saved my life,' he wanted it to sound over the top, and therefore ironic, but his voice broke and ended up a surprising falsetto.

'One good turn deserves another,' he could tell from her voice that she was smiling. 'You saved me from some mad dogs.'

He caught her tone:

'I do it all the time. Almost every evening.'

'Well I have to show someone the way almost every evening,' she answered seriously. 'Come on.'

They walked the length of the fence, she a little ahead, a resigned Busya dragging himself along behind her.

I should say something, he thought. It's a bit awkward otherwise.

'What's this street called?'

The woman shrugged.

'No idea. I come along here so often and I've never given it a second's thought. Funny, isn't it?'

'It's so deserted. Dark. There's no one to ask.'

'That's because of the factory,' the woman said. 'They bought up several blocks in the early 1990s and moved everybody out. They wanted to make those... those robot transformers. And then they didn't get the business. So everything was just left.

'Toys?' asked Artemy Mikhailovich, just to make sure.

'Toys? No. To guard the borders. It was a military contract. But you know there's open warfare over those military contracts? The director was shot down right outside his door, he lived in our block. He got out of his car, another car drove up, they shot him, didn't touch the driver, didn't touch his wife... I was actually just about to take Busya out, I'd put my coat on, and then these shots rang out...'

He shook his head in affected dismay.

'But they did manage to make a few transformer robots,' he said, joining in the game. 'And now they walk about at night destroying things.'

'Yep,' said the woman, nodding. 'So you've heard the rumours, too. Only they don't destroy anything. They just wander around. The military function was never activated.'

'And you can hear their heavy footsteps in the lonely streets,' he continued to play.

'They don't walk the streets much,' said the woman, 'more and more they're in the wastelands. The streets are too narrow for them. Hey, and there you are... Can you hear?'

A long way off there was a heavy crash, as if a stack of metal joists had collapsed. Busya sat down very suddenly on the wet road, lifted his head to the sky and howled.

'They haven't got any sense of direction. They're not even at the prototype stage. There's a lot of half-built ones. They walk around bumping into things.'

Artemy Mikhailovich realized something was sticking into the palm of his hand. He was still holding the stone he had used to threaten the dogs.

'Very strange area, yours,' he said as casually as he could muster.

She shrugged. Her shoulders seemed extremely broad in the shabby padded jacket. She tugged the lead and at the same time she whistled to Busya, who had stopped howling and was pressing himself against her leg nervously.

'Well there's a lot of... stuff... around here. Especially if you know where to look. Like, for example, on Tatishchev Street there's a mysterious house, and no one ever comes out of it and no one ever goes in, but there's light at all the windows. All night the lights are on. And what's in there? No one knows.'

'Secret meetings, probably. A Masonic lodge. With an underground passage leading in.'

'It's definitely not a Masonic Lodge. There's one of those in the next street along. Over there. I think it's the followers of Cthulhu. There's a drawing of him on the door. There's a metal door with a bolt, an enormous padlock, all rusty, and Cthulhu, almost as big as a person. Drawn in coloured chalk.'

'Who?'

He had been so absorbed by the conversation that he hadn't noticed how they had turned off the street into another, and then between blocks until they had emerged on a relatively lit bit of road. The buildings had lit-up bay windows and they looked harmless and lived-in, and in places lights shone in windows, despite the late hour.

'Cthulhu. The Ancient One. He sleeps at the bottom of the ocean and has dreams. Sometimes people have his dreams. And then they find each other and... He's like an octopus. One day he'll rise up from the water. We should be prepared.'

'Is he good?'

'Good!? He's evil incarnate. Him and the other ancient ones.'

'Well say this Cathul, or whatever you called him, say he did rise up out of the waters, Moscow's the last place he'd come to. It'd be hard to think of a place further from the sea.'

'Really!' she said. 'Didn't you know? There is an ancient underground sea under Moscow. A huge and terrible sea. A briny ocean. It's terrifying when you think about the sightless creatures living down there in the gloomy depths.'

'And having dreams?'

She smiled.

'Maybe. Sometimes, you know, when there's a mist, and it's quiet... You can hear it. The muffled noise, from under the earth. People think Cthulhu lives in distant warm seas. They're so stupid! He's an Ancient One. Since he fell asleep all the continents have changed shape. Don't you wonder why everyone in Moscow is unhappy? And lonely? It's because of him. His poisonous breath.'

A bit of an odd woman, he thought. You get these fantasy-obsessed types. Always trying to sound enigmatic.

'Which way is the metro?'

'We're walking towards it.'

'Is it far?'

She was striding along, slightly ahead of him. Busya was pulling on the lead and trying to go faster. Artemy Mihailovich looked at his watch surreptitiously. Ten to twelve. It wasn't too late, actually, it was only that at this hour he was usually in bed. And he'd never even given a thought to the fact that the city carried on even now in its own peculiar rhythm.

'No, not far at all. You know what?'

'What?' he asked cautiously.

'Why don't you come to my place? We could have a coffee. Or tea. You're frozen through.'

He hesitated, not knowing what to say.

'Or is someone waiting for you at home?'

'No,' he said. 'No one's waiting for me.'

Should he agree? Only half an hour ago he had looked hard at his measured, unhappy life, and had prayed to the heavens for a miracle. Perhaps if he were to turn her down now he would miss something wonderful, something life-changing? Perhaps he was being offered a last chance? How many times had he turned down doubtful under-takings, chance opportunities to change his work, busi-ness trips to odd or disagreeable places... The ruins of roads not taken... And she was a free woman, a single woman, and she was inviting an unknown man back to her home. Practically in the middle of the night. Perhaps that was what you did these days?

'Aren't you frightened? I could be a maniac or something.'

'No,' she said, and he could hear from her voice that she was smiling. 'Maniacs are scared of dogs. That's tried and tested.'

'Ah,' he said, although Busya, who was a pretty good size and was sniffing about in a businesslike way and pulling on the lead, really did arouse a cautious dislike in him. 'Ah... Dogs feeling what a person's like, you mean?'

'No,' she shook her head. 'I mean people feeling what a dog is like. What metro station is closest to you?'

'I'm at Tulskaya.'

'You could walk from here. It's about twenty minutes. Well, half an hour. You were probably frightened the metro would shut, weren't you?'

'Well I wasn't exactly frightened...'

Anyway he could always get a taxi. Probably. He hadn't spoiled himself like that for a very long time, but the service must still exist. He could ring directory enquiries. It used to be 09. Wonder what it is now. He could ask her. What was her name, anyway?

'Alright, let's go. I'll just ring.'

She got a mobile out of her pocket and easily, with one finger, dialled a number. The light from the screen lit up a soft cheek and a small ear with two earrings—that's how everyone wears them now, he thought, and moved away a little so as not to embarrass her, and to move out of reach of Busya who was now sniffing his coat and drooling over it. Who was she ringing? Home? Her mother? Her husband? How old was she anyway? She'd seemed very young

at first, then a grown woman, and now very young again...
You couldn't tell with women.

The telephone light went out. She put the mobile in
her pocket and turned to him.

'Alright... Let's go.'

'Er...' he wavered, and she understood.

'That was my friend. I said I'd ring her today and
forgot. She goes to bed early.'

So not her husband then. Was that a good thing? Well
yes, seeing as she probably wouldn't have invited him back
if her husband had been there. But why wasn't she scared?

Another turning, a walk across another dark yard and
they came out on a boulevard, bare trees swept the wet sky
from behind a low iron railing, an advertising column was
lit up at the crossroads: a handsome black-haired man,
smiling unnaturally, talking into a mobile phone, but the
top of the poster was sticking out from its glossy cover,
and this was vaguely troubling. A single car of foreign
make stood at the traffic lights, its engine turning over. It
left a ruby tinge on the wet asphalt, and a way off, over the
wet roofs, shining with a melancholy light against the low
clouds, was the radio tower.

'Well there you are.' The black haired mobile-man
blurred and quivered oddly. 'And I was lost!'

'You aren't the first,' she said.

He blinked back the shameful tears and stole a look at her, trying not to embarrass her by staring excessively. Her face was pale with a pointed nose and thin lips, she wasn't attractive at all, although he had imagined she was back then in the darkness. And there was something else... When he looked more closely he realized what it was: her upper lip almost imperceptibly twitched, like a nervous tick. Perhaps that was why she'd been so quick to invite him back, because she was ugly. And what did she mean by 'you aren't the first'?

He should probably just say no, and pretend he was in a hurry. Say that someone was waiting for him at home. But he'd just told her that no one was waiting for him. It was all horribly awkward. He slowed down very slightly, very very slightly, but she noticed and placed the hand that was not holding back the racing Busya on his elbow. Now, if he wanted to free himself he would have to pull out of her grasp, and that would be completely absurd. He suddenly realized that he was walking arm in arm with a woman for the first time in many years: anyone who saw them might well think them an old married couple having a stroll before bedtime.

'Is... is it far?'

He felt a sharp longing to go home now that his home was so close. To sit down in the kitchen, drink tea, watch the evening—no, the nighttime—news, climb into bed, pull the covers up, make everything as it should be: warm, no deserted dark streets, no unknown women, with whom he didn't know how to behave.

'We're here,' the woman still held his elbow with her palm. 'Nearly.'

He looked around. The dome of a market building, dimly lit on the inside: it looked like a flying saucer which had landed in the wrong place, and beside it a row of brightly-coloured kiosks, unusually deserted. But after his ridiculous and terrifying adventures everything around him seemed slightly wrong. As if whilst he had wandered lost on the dark streets, some strange and huge Cathul-thing with all his Ancients had rushed to wipe out all those roads and buildings he had known since childhood and just as quickly had replaced them with something similar, but a wax copy, a fake...

Ridiculous, he said to himself, it's just the market, they're just little shops, like that one with its appliqué jewels, mobile top-ups, smooth cases for phones, LED lights, glass and fake crystal glass. Or that pink one, 'Moscow Sausage', or the brightly painted factory cake shop.

He should make his excuses and go home.

'This way,' said the woman pressing slightly on his elbow.

Artemy Mikhailovich took an obedient step and realized that she was pushing him in the direction of a two storeyed building with little turrets set back from the road. From a little way away the building looked like a fairytale castle and he had often wondered what was inside.

'Do you live there?'

The secret castle was surrounded by thin bare trees and it appeared to be quite dark. There was the distinct smell of wet earth, and mushrooms for some reason. Ridiculous! Whoever heard of mushrooms growing in a city?

'Live there! No I work there. Did you think I was taking you home? I'm on nightwatch.'

'But... the dog?'

'Can't leave him at home all night. And the boss doesn't mind.'

She was quiet for a moment.

'And then it isn't so frightening. Although I don't live too far away, but walking through all those dark bits... I got him specially when I started work here.'

He relaxed slightly. She wasn't some nymphomaniac, then, just someone who was bored at work. That was completely different.

'What do you do?'

'It's kind of medical work.'

'Me, too.' He was pleased, and then immediately embarrassed because he was usually nervous about telling people he worked in a skin and venereology clinic. But if she was something in the medical line, too... well, that was a different matter. Strange that they allowed a dog at work if it was something medical.

They had arrived by now at the entrance porch, decorated with a lacy little metal hood, and she pressed the bell, letting go of his arm for a moment to do so, but still holding the dog's leash in her other hand.

'Is there... someone there then?'

'The guard.'

Was that a good thing, a guard? Or a bad thing? He'd spend ten minutes there, just to show willing and then he'd go. Perhaps he should ask for her number? What did people do in such situations? People did get together after all, why hadn't he...

He heard shuffling steps from behind the door and then it flew back—a huge man in a white coat, stained with something brown, something yellow, stood there on the doorstep, his face was yellow, disfigured, rubbery, and from the slot of a mouth on this dead, yellow face fell the word,

'Welcome!'

He staggered back, but the woman held him up from behind, squeezing his elbow tightly, and when he turned to her, maybe to push her away, or to ask her to let him go, he saw her eyes rolling, the whites of her eyes glistening in the dim lamplight, her lips drawn back to show her teeth, he saw the dog's eyes, lit in red, and the sign by the door: 'FORENSICS & MORGUE'

In despair he waved his free arm, the stone which he still clutched feverishly, like a talisman, came loose and hit the woman on the cheek. She gasped in surprise and let him go. Blood trickled along her cheekbone. The dog lunged on his leash and snarled, but he had already jumped from the porch and giving a short squeal like a hare, he ran from the terrible place, the building with its turrets, the dark sidestreet, the underground sea, where unknown sightless creatures sleep and have terrifying dreams, from vast humanoid transformers, wandering blindly through the deserted night.

'Idiot!' the woman shouted from behind, clutching her injured face. 'It was a joke! Stupid!'

But he didn't hear.

Six months later, in March, in a flat that wasn't his, with a fresh bunch of yellow flowers reflected in the kitchen worktop and an open bottle of champagne fizzing, Artemy Mikhailovich sat on the floor, his head buried against the knees of a woman we haven't yet met. He was crying. He had just asked her to marry him, and he was frightened and sad and happy all at once.

And the woman thought that, well, he wasn't handsome, and he was a pedant, but pedants made good husbands on the whole, even if they were boring, and time was passing, and he was a kind man, a pleasant man, and he didn't have any relatives which was a big plus, and they could rent out one of their flats, only they'd have to think which one, his or hers, and she stroked his head and said,

'There, there, everything will be OK... I love you... everything will be OK.'

Notes on the Stories

1. *Musa* by Ivan Bunin (1870–1953)

Musa is taken from a cycle of Bunin's later stories called *Dark Avenues*. Bunin wrote in a letter to the Russian writer Teffi that 'All the stories in this book are only about love, love's "dark" and often very grim and cruel avenues.' *Musa* was written in the late 1930s when Bunin was living in France and Europe was moving fast towards war. Bunin's wife later wrote that the cycle appeared as a way of retreating from war 'into another world where blood wasn't flowing and people weren't being burnt alive...'

'I lived on the Arbat near the Praga restaurant in a room in the Hotel Stolitsa': The Arbat is a fairly intact historical street in the centre of Moscow, with many literary connections. It is now pedestrianized and a major tourist destination (Metro: Arbatskaya). Bunin stayed in the Hotel Stolitsa a few times himself. The enormous Praga restaurant was built at the turn of the century at the end of the Arbat where it now joins the New Arbat. It remained

Praga through Soviet times (as an elite post-war restaurant for party officials and the high-placed).

'I saw you yesterday at the Shor concert': David Solomonovich Shor was a pianist, Conservatoire teacher and an acquaintance and travelling companion of Bunin.

a poor landowner who lived on his own about two versts from us: A verst is a pre-evolutionary unit of measurement, a little over a kilometre.

2. *A Couple in December* by Yury Kazakov (1927–1982)

This story first appeared in *Ogoniok* Magazine in August 1962. It opens with a typical weekend morning in winter in the Soviet Union, the suburban railway stations of Moscow a constant stream of cross-country skiers. The story also gives a sense of some of the 1960s post-war interest in life style and consumer goods.The suburban lines radiate out from Moscow, in some cases for hundreds of kilometres. The couple take one line in one direction and then ski across to another line to catch a train back.

'What bliss it had been, and might be again, if there was no war': This must surely hint at the mounting cold war tension at the beginning of the 1960s.

3. *Kashtanka* by Anton Chekhov (1860–1904)

Chekhov first mentions 'Kashtanka' in 1887, but the story as we know it was not published until 1892. Chekhov saw it originally as a children's story. It seems likely that an incident from Chekhov's native Tambov Region supplied the idea of a dog in the circus, but *Kashtanka* is set in the Moscow circus world. Chekhov wrote about Vladimir Durov, the famous clown and animal trainer in his 'Splinters of Moscow Life' (lit.) in 1885: the audience's favourite, Durov's performing pig 'danced, grunted on command, shot with a pistol, and, unlike other Moscow snorters, read the papers'. In the same year he described the performing goose in the Moscow Salomonsky Theatre. The cat Fyodor Timofeich lived a quieter life with the Chekhovs themselves. Chekhov was fond of animals and owned two dachshunds (Kashtanka is a dachshund). He named them 'Bromine' and 'Quinine'.

Kashtanka means 'chestnut'.

The sledge stopped by a large strange building, like an up-ended soup tureen: There was a rush of circus building in the 1880s. The Salamonsky Circus was first, with a custom-built circular theatre on Tsvetnoy Boulevard. But in 1886 competition appeared on the same street, when the Nikitin Brothers set up circus in the circular building which had formerly housed the Plevna Battle Panorama (this building is still there, although very changed, as the cinema *Mir*).

The Salamonsky Circus, now known as the Circus on Tsvetnoy, is still a famous circus. (Metro: Tsvetnoy Bulvar)

'Ha!' shouted their owner. 'Uncle Fedor Timofeich and dear Auntie Tyotka!': Tyotka in fact means 'Auntie' in Russian. Impossible to tell whether the owner has been planning this routine all along.

4. *The Red Gates* by Yury Koval (1938–1995)

The Red Gates was first published in 1984 as one of a collection of stories for children.

My brother Borya, my dear brother Borya and I, were rowing a boat down the Sestra river: The Sestra river is in the Moscow Region, about two hours from Moscow on a suburban train. It is still popular with fishermen.

All the inhabitants of our block at Krasniye Vorota knew: Krasniye Vorota, which means 'Red Gates' (Metro: Krasniye Vorota) is on the large circular road, the Sadovoye Kol'tso (lit. 'Garden Ring') which rings the central part of the city.

CDKA were playing a match against Dinamo: CDKA, Dinamo, Torpedo, and Spartak are all Moscow football teams.

Everyone in our family was occupied by what was happening just then in the world: It seems possible that this refers to the speech Khrushchev made on 25 February 1956 at the 20th Party Congress criticizing Stalin. The speech sent major shock waves through the Soviet Union.

If you were to walk for a long, long time: The narrator is describing the walk around the Garden Ring. Borya's new home is roughly diametrically opposite the Red Gates. The walk around the ring road is fifteen to sixteen kilometres.

'*The traitorous pupil fell from the bough like a fruit...*': The first line of a poem by Pushkin. Protopopov continues to quote this poem and then moves on to other classroom favourites, it is less important to know where these are from than to understand that he is using 'old stalwarts' to illustrate a point.

'*Not for those birds, not for the loons, was the excitement of life's battle...*': Another school curriculum favourite: Gorky's 'Stormy Petrel' (also know as 'Storm Herald'). A short revolutionary poem symbolizing the oncoming of the revolution as a storm over Antarctica.

'*Who are these judges? Since ancient times / Their hatred of freedom has been implacable*': From *Woe from Wit* (also known as *Chatsky*), Griboyedov's verse play.

'Teacher', teased Protopopov at that and he would pummel me on the chest with his fist. 'Let me humbly kneel at the sound of your name...': A quote from Nekrasov's drama *The Bear Hunt*.

'*Fly, blizzard / In your pink tricot!*' Protopopov quotes the twentieth century poet Vladimir Narbut.

' *... And the leaves rustled like a voice in a fever* / **The dawn glittered beyond the Kama's shore** / *Bluer than a mallard's feather*': A quote from a Pasternak poem ('On a Steamer').

the vaults of the Moscow State Pedagogical Institute: This important teacher training institute still exists.

Like, for example, take Yury Vizbor...: A number of the names he quotes here are genuinely famous (some are less famous, and some are friends). Vizbor and Kim were 'bards', cult Soviet singer songwriters. Fomenko was a well-known theatre director with a famous Moscow troupe.

'**Oh cover your pale legs!**' Famous Russian monostich by the turn-of-the-century poet Bryusov.

5. *The Transition* by Tatyana Shchepkina-Kupernik (1874–1952)

This story comes from a collection of short stories published in 1903 dedicated to Moscow theatre life. Shchepkina-Kupernik was the grand daughter of a famous actor, Mikhail Shchepkina, and she had acted herself for a season, before establishing herself as a playwright, poet and play translator. She was linked with both the Maly Theatre (Metro: Teatralnaya) and The Korsh Teatr (now the Teatr Natsy on Petrovsky Pereulok).

'And didn't the silly little girl come up trumps!' in *Tomboy*: *Tomboy* and *Secret* were genuine comedies of the time. *Tomboy* was written by the prolific and commercial playwright Viktor Krylov and staged in 1888.

6. *Poor Liza* by Nikolai Karamzin (1766–1826)

This is the earliest story in *Moscow Tales*. Nikolai Karamzin wrote *Poor Liza* in 1792. The story, an early example of Russian sentimentalism, was extremely popular and spawned many copies. The pool where Liza died became a place of pilgrimage for Moscow's young women. Karamzin was a reformer, he sought to introduce a literary style more French in style and syntax, which would allow for the transplanting of European Sentimentalism onto Russian soil.

Danilov Monastery: Still intact today, and fairly near the centre of contemporary Moscow. (Metro: Tul'skaya)

Sparrow Hills: These are the very visible hills upon which the Moscow State University stands. (Metro: Universitet)

Kolomenskoye: An area of royal palaces and churches, now completely reconstructed. (Metro: Kolomenskaya)

the gloomy gothic spires of the Simonov Monastery rise: The Simonov Monastery was founded in 1370 and moved to its spot on a hill overlooking the Moscow river in 1379. It had been an important and wealthy monastery, but by the 1770s, it was being used as a plague house, and the buildings weren't returned to the church until 1795.

It suffered a sad fate: the Bolsheviks blew up the monastery in 1930, leaving only the walls and wall towers, and replaced it with the Zil Automobile Factory. The handsome constructivist Zil Palace of Culture was built where the graveyard had once been. (Metro: Avtozavodskaya)

She left the town and suddenly found herself on the edge of a deep pool in the shade of some ancient oaks: Lisa's pool, according to most accounts, was filled in (with some difficulty as it was fed by springs) in the 1930s, and eventually became the site of the Dinamo (Electrical Goods) Factory's office block. It is thought to be the pool dug out by the founder of the Simonov Monastery. (Metro: Avtozavodskaya)

7. *Scar* by Evgeny Grishkovets (1967–)

Grishkovets came to fame as a playwright and actor who acted out his own monologues. *Scar* comes from his first collection of short stories, published in 2006.

The hotel Poima changed completely after its renovation: The word 'Poima' means flood plain, it derives from the Russian word 'to catch', which seems somehow to have poetic resonance for the story.

Instead he ordered vodka and pelmeni: 'Pelmeni' are made by wrapping balls of meat (beef and pork) in a thin pasta-like dough, freezing them and them boiling them in stock. They resemble small ravioli and are sometimes served in a broth and with sour cream.

8. *Lady with a Little Dog* by Anton Chekhov

Chekhov wrote *Lady with a Little Dog* in 1899, sending it to be published in Moscow from Yalta, where he was living in a house being finished around him. This period also marks the intensification of relations with Olga Knipper. In the summer of 1899 Knipper visited Chekhov in the Crimea and they left for Moscow together.

Sitting in the Verné Patisserie's pavilion: The Parisian Patisserie Verné was in a pavilion building on the seafront.

prided herself on her use of the modern spelling: Written Russian was constantly being reformed over the nineteenth century, but in 1873 a definitive guide to Russian Orthography was published by philologist Yakov Grot. Presumably Gurov's wife's adherence to modern spelling shows her pedantic, over-determining nature.

And then one late afternoon he was having dinner in the gardens: There was a restaurant in Yalta's public gardens at the time.

They found a cab and drove out to Oreanda: Oreanda was the location of a royal estate, a few kilometres outside Yalta. A high verdant cliff stands over the sea. At the time Chekhov wrote the story there were the ruins of a palace high on the cliff, and a waterfall, descending through a dramatic ravine to the sea. A bench stood beyond the waterfall.

and had taken a stroll along Petrovka: Petrovka was one of the main shopping streets of nineteenth-century Moscow. The Bolshoi Theatre is at one end, the boulevard ring at the other. It is still a beautiful street to stroll on. (Metro: Okhotny Ryad)

In Moscow she stayed in the Slavyansky Bazar Hotel: Slavyansky Bazar opened in the 1870s at 17 Nikolskaya Street. The hotel boasted large luxurious living apartments, and the first Russian restaurant. It was fashionable and expensive, Gilyarovsky writes that it was frequented by ministers and Siberian goldmine owners, but also by the arts and theatre world (in 1879 Stanislavsky and Nemirovich-Danchenko held long discussions here which led to the founding of the Moscow Arts Theatre). (Metro: Ploshchad Revolyutsy)

9. *Moscow* by Igor Sutyagin (1965–)

Igor Sutyagin wrote this account of life in Lefortovo for this collection. Sutyagin was convicted of treason in 2004, in a trial criticized by many as a miscarriage of justice, and sentenced to fifteen years. He was held in Lefortovo before being sent to the UK as part of a 'spy swap' in 2010. He has always maintained his innocence.

Lefortovo is a Federal Security Service (FSB) remand isolation prison, named after the area Lefortovo, where it is situated (Metro: Aviamotornaya). The prison was opened in 1881 and is notorious. During the purges in the 1930s interrogations and torture were carried out here, and as a KGB (the Soviet Committee of State Security that was superseded by the FSB in 2003) institution it later housed a number of prominent dissidents, including Solzhenitsyn.

how very fond one could become of the quiet parks on the Lenin Hills: 'Lenin Hills' is the Soviet name for the 'Sparrow Hills', mentioned by the narrator at the beginning of *Poor Liza*. As Sutyagin writes the university and its parks are on these hills.

escaping as Boris Savinkov 'escaped' from the Chekists: Savinkov was a Socialist Revolutionary, who was sentenced for opposing Soviet power. The official version is that he committed suicide but many, including Solzhenitsyn, believed he was thrown to his death in 1925.

or even the Moscow prison Matrosskaya Tishina: The other prisons Sutyagin names are 'ordinary' prisons, rather that isolation prisons, and not FSB prisons. In these prisons overcrowding, rather than isolation, is the norm.

10. *From Lefortovo to Khamovniki* by Vladimir Giliarovsky (1853–1935)

Giliarovsky, a writer and journalist, devoted his writing life to describing Moscow at the turn of the century, and his sketch-like accounts of different parts of the city together form his best known work: *Moscow and Muscovites*. In this short account his describes a cab ride right across Moscow on only his first day in the city. There are many bewildering street names in this sketch, but it is important to note Lubyanka Square, later the address of the KGB, but then the point for cab drivers to stop for water, with Vitali's statue at the centre (Metro: Lubyanka).

11. *My Pushkin* by Marina Tsvetaeva (1892–1941)

This is a part of the prose piece which Marina Tsvetaeva wrote in 1936–7 in emigration in Paris and published in an émigré Russian journal. I chose to present this fragment, rather than the whole, as later in the piece Tsvetaeva spends more time on the Pushkin poems of her childhood, and less on Moscow itself.

D'Anthès challenged Pushkin to a duel: The Russian poet Aleksandr Pushkin was famously mortally wounded in a duel with D'Anthès in early 1837 (exactly 100 years before this prose was written).

There was no mention of Goncharova: Pushkin's wife, Natalya Goncharova, on whose account Pushkin fought the duel.

The Poet and the Crowd: This famous phrase which Pushkin himself used to describe his isolation from the mass of people is sometimes translated as the poet and the masses, or the poet and the mob. The Russian word *Chern* comes from the word 'black' and might literally be translated as 'the indistinguishable masses'.

Pushkin to his native Africa, continent of vengeance and passion: Pushkin was the great grandson of Abragim Petrovich Gannibal, an African child slave who was bought by Peter the Great and brought to Russia. Pushkin was proud of his heritage, and wrote the biographical account *The Negro of Peter the Great.*

Naumov's picture: This famous late nineteenth-century painting can be seen at http://www.museum.ru/alb/image. asp?29871

The Pushkin Memorial: Opekushin's famous statue of Pushkin now stands on Pushkin Square (Metro: Pushkinskaya/Tverskaya).

So children growing up in the shadow of the Petersburg Bronze Horseman: The Bronze Horseman is a statue in St Petersburg depicting Peter the Great on a leaping steed. Pushkin wrote a narrative poem of the same name.

'under the skies of my Africa': A line from Pushkin's 'Eugene Onegin'.

The empire of Nikolai I: Tsar Nikolai I, during whose reign Pushkin died.

replaced Zhukovsky's personally shameful and poetically talentless substitution: The lines of poetry at the base were originally doctored because of their call to freedom.

An Actual Privy Counsellor: A high-ranking title in the extensive Tsarist Russian civil service.

'Musya, listen to me,' continued my Father: Marina Tsvetaeva's father was Ivan Tsvetaev, the creator and first director of the Pushkin Museum of Fine Arts (Metro: Kropotkinskaya).

Minin and Pozharsky: The statue in front of St Basil's on Red Square commemorating the victory of Minin and Pozharsky's army against the Poles in 1612.

St John of Kronstadt: John's emotional preaching and charitable works led to a pop-star status in late nineteenth-century Russia. Massive crowds would turn out to see him.

where the future artist Natalya Goncharova: Natalya Goncharova was a well-known avant-garde artist whose style encompassed many approaches, amongst them Cubism, Futurism, Rayism. She emigrated to Paris with her husband, the painter Mikhail Larionov in 1915.

My house and Goncharova's were near to each other: As a child Marina Tsvetaeva lived just off Pushkin Square on Tryokhprudny Pereulok (Metro: Tverskaya/Pushkinskaya). The house is no longer there.

My first Pushkin was 'The Gypsies': Pushkin's narrative poem, 'The Gypsies'. Tsvetaeva retells the story to the Nanny and the seamstress.

... he said and he dragged the lamb into the forest: This is a quote from the well-known *Fable of the Wolf and the Lamb*, written in 1808 by the Russian fabulist Ivan Krylov, in which a wolf, coming across a lamb, provides lots of reasons for the lamb's guilt, but concludes: '"You're guilty because I'm hungry," / he said and dragged the lamb into the dark wood.'

I said a leader, but I called him Pugachev: Pushkin's story 'The Captain's Daughter' is set in 1773–5 at the time of the Pugachev Rebellion, a popular uprising led by Emelyan Pugachev, who turns out to have a honourable heart in the Pushkin story. Lieutenant Grinev is the Captain's daughter's beloved.

Zograf-Plaksina Music School on Merzlyakovsky Street: Valentina Zograf-Plaksina was the founder and first director of the music school which is now the academy linked to the Moscow Conservatoire. Marina's mother desperately wanted her daughter to be a pianist and Tsvetaeva as a child practised music for many hours every day.

12. *Very Proper Nouns* by Marina Boroditskaya (1954–)

This short story comes from a collection of modern day 'telephone' fairytales published in 2001. Two single mothers, Marinda and Miranda, tell each other tall tales on the telephone when they're lonely.

Old Lizaveta on 3rd Yamskaya Street: A central Moscow street, just off Tverskaya.

The fridge even had its own surname: Comrade Papanin: Papanin was a Soviet Polar explorer.

13. *Clean Monday* by Ivan Shmelyov (1873–1950)

Shmelyov wrote *Clean Monday* in emigration in Paris during the 1930s as part of a cycle of stories based around the religious year, and filled with his memories of childhood in Moscow's Zamoskvorechye area, an area opposite the Kremlin on the other side of the river, which was a community of merchant families. To this day the area is relatively untouched and retains the feel of the old low-rise Moscow. (Metro: Tretyakovskaya)

The title of this story refers to the first day of Lent in the Russian Orthodox Calendar. Clean Monday is not an official religious name, it refers to the Russian practice of cleaning the house and bathing in order to rid oneself of the 'spirit' of *Maslenitsa*. *Maslenitsa* is the lively festival before Lent, roughly equating to Mardi Gras.

And that's what the *Efimony* is all about, at vespers this week: *Efimony* is the evening service during the first week of Lent.

my father calls the Pryanishnikov picture for some reason: Illarion Pryanishnikov was a nineteenth-century artist, well known for his genre paintings.

and a glass of *kvas* to drink it down with: *Kvas* is a fermented drink based on yeast and rye bread.

and warmed sweet sweet *Ryazan*: This list of Lenten foods has been analysed and described at length as one of the best sources of information about the Lenten diet in pre-revolutionary Russia. But so far no one seems to know what *Ryazan* is. Ryazan is a town in Russia, so presumably a recipe or a product associated with this town.

We're going to the Lenten Market: The Lenten market was a large and animated pre-revolutionary mushroom market. Rows of stalls lined the river between Ustinsky Bridge and Moskvaretsky Bridge.

'You count up your thousand there, sir': The narrator's father owned a sledging 'slope'. Such slopes were often artificially created for *Maslenitsa* by building a wooden platform, covering it with snow and then pouring water over it to freeze. Sledging on slopes was a typical festive *Maslenitsa* treat. Vasil-Vasilich had been sent to charge the festive sledge-riders and issue tickets.

14. *Tsar or Prince...* by Larisa Miller (1940–)

This account was first published in 1998.

Vertinsky's songs went down particularly well: Popular Soviet variety singer and actor who sang songs based on poems by Tsvetaeva, Blok as well as his own original material. He emigrated in 1920, but returned to Russia during the Second World War.

The Ermitazh Gardens alone were measureless pleasures: A small park set close to the boulevard ring, opened at the end of the nineteenth century and home to the Ermitazh Theatre. Here the premieres of Chekhov's *The Seagull* and *Uncle Vanya* took place. It is associated also with Rakhmaninov, Sarah Bernhardt, the Lumière Brothers amongst others. Here Miller saw Arkady Raikin, the famous Soviet actor performing. (Metro: Tverskaya/Chekhovskaya)

15. *Underground Sea* by Marina Galina (1958–)

Maria Galina's uncanny story was first published in the journal *Novy Mir* in 2010.

the delicate Shukov Radio Tower: The radio tower was designed by Shukov and was finished and began transmitting in 1922. (Metro: Shabolovskaya)

'Ataman Makhno... looks out the window... all's dark in the meadow...': A pop song from the late 1990s. Refers to a Civil War fighter and leader of the Cossacks, Makho.

'Reporting from Moscow on a special day': This passage describes Artemy Mikhailovich's memories of special Soviet events: space flights, important Soviet parades etc.

I think it's the followers of Cthulhu: Cthulhu was the invention of the American author of horror, fantasy, and science fiction H. P. Lovecraft.

Further Reading

There is much Russian literature in translation that is set in and around Moscow: the big Tolstoy novels for example, *War and Peace*, *Anna Karenina* or Bulgakov's wonderful *Master and Margarita*. Pasternak's *Doctor Zhivago* passes through Moscow. Ilf and Petrov's satirical Soviet novel *Twelve Chairs* is now available in translation and has plenty to say about Soviet Moscow. A cult Soviet classic *Moskva-Petushki* has been translated variously as *Moscow to the End of the Line* and *Moscow Stations*.

Pushkin's long poem *Eugene Onegin* is a good place to start reading poetry about Moscow. His heroine travels to Moscow for the season and Pushkin describes early nineteenth-century Moscow in witty, elegant, profound lines. Poetry by Pasternak with a distinctly Moscow setting has been published in numerous different translations.

Most of the stories in this volume are translated into English for the first time. Other works by the writers have been published elsewhere in translation. Tsvetaeva, Chekhov and Bunin are very well-represented in English translation. Karamzin's prose is also available and can be downloaded free of charge from the internet. Larisa Miller's poems and prose have been translated by Richard McKane. Maria Galina's novel *Iramifications* was translated by Amanda Love Darragh. All these titles are relatively easy to get hold of on the internet.

Publisher's Acknowledgements

1. *Musa* by Ivan Bunin. Taken from *Полное собрание сочинений* (Moscow: Khudozhestvennaya literature, 1988)
2. *A Couple in December* by Yury Kazakov. Taken from *Легкая жизнь: рассказы* (St Petersburg: Azbuka-klassika, 2003)
3. *Kashtanka* by Anton Chekhov. Taken from *Полное собрание сочинений и писем* (Moscow: Nauka, 1985)
4. *The Red Gates* by Yury Koval. Taken from *Солнечное пятно: рассказы* (Moscow: Vagrius, 2002)
5. *Transition* by Tatyana Shchepkina-Kupernik. Taken from http://az.lib.ru/s/shepkinakupernik_t_l/(2012)
6. *Poor Liza* by Nikolai Karamzin. Taken from *Moskva v russkoi literature* (Moscow: Ast, 2007)
7. *Scar* by Evgeny Grishkovets. Taken from *Планка* (Moscow: Makhaon, 2006)
8. *Lady with a Little Dog* by Anton Chekhov. Taken from *Полное собрание сочинений и писем* (Moscow: Nauka, 1985)

9. *From Lefortovo to Khamovniki* by Vladimir Gilyarovsky. Taken from *Москва и москвичи* (Moscow: EKSMO, 2006)

10. *My Pushkin* by Marina Tsvetaeva. Taken from http://lib.ru/POEZIQ/CWETAEWA/pushkin.txt (2009)

11. *Very Proper Nouns* by Marina Boroditskaia. Taken from *Телефонные сказки Маринды и Миранды* (Moscow: Drofa, 2001)

12. *Clean Monday* by Ivan Shmelyov. Taken from *Расс-казы и повесты* (Moscow: Ast Astrel, 2010)

13. *Tsar or Prince...* by Larisa Miller. Taken from *Золотая симфония* (Moscow: Vremya, 2008)

14. *Underground Sea* by Maria Galina. Taken from the journal, *Новый мир* 7 (Moscow, 2010)

ALTUF'EVO
BIBIREV
OTRADNO
VLADYKIN
PETROVSKO-RAZUMOVSKAYA
TIMIRYAZEVSKAYA
DMITROVSKAYA
SAVELOVSKAYA
MENDELEEVSKAYA

RECHNOY VOKZAL
VODNY STADION
VOYKOVSKAYA
SOKOL
AEROPORT
DINAMO
BELORUSSKAYA
TSV

PYATNITSKOE SHOSSE
MITINO
VOLOKOLAMSKAYA
PLANERNAYA
SKHODNENSKAYA
TUSHINSKAYA

2
3
7

MYAKININO
STROGINO
KRYLATSKOE
MOLODEZHNAYA
KUNTSEVSKAYA

SHCHUKINSKAYA
OKTYABR'SKOE POLE
POLEZHAEVSKAYA
BEGOVAYA
ULITSA 1905 GODA
KRASNOPRESNENSKAYA

MAYAKOVSKAYA
PUSHKINSKAYA
BARRIKADNAYA
ALEKSANDRO

4

MEZHDUNARODNAYA
PIONERSKAYA
FILEVSKY PARK
BAGRATIONOVSKAYA
FILI
KUTUZOVSKAYA
SLAVYANSKY BUL'VAR
PARK POBEDY

VYSTAVOCHNAYA
SMOLENSKAYA   ARBATSKAYA
SMOLENSKAYA
ARBATSKAYA
BOROVITS
KIEVSKAYA
KROPO

STUDENCHESKAYA
FRUNZENSKAYA
SPORTIVNAYA
VOROB'EVY GORY
UNIVERSITET
PROSPEKT VERNADSKOGO
YUGO-ZAPADNAYA

PARK KULTURY
OKTYABR'SKA

5

1

SHABOLOVSKAYA
LENINSKY PROSPEKT
AKADEMICHESKAYA
PROFSOYUZNAYA
NOVYE CHEREMUSHKI
KALUZHSKAYA
BELYAEVO
KON'KOVO
TEPLY STAN
YASENEVO
NOVOYASENEVSKAYA

NAKHIMOV
SEVAS
CHE

AK

6

ULITSA STAROKACHALOVSKA
ULITSA SKOBELEVSK
BUL'VAR ADMIRALA USHAK
ULITSA GORCHAK

(M) MOSCOW METRO

1   SOKOL'NICHESKAYA LINE
2   ZAMOSKVORETSKAYA LINE
3   ARBATSKO-POKROVSKAYA LINE
4   FILEVSKAYA LINE
5   KOL'TSEVAYA LINE
6   KALUZHSKO-RIZHSKAYA LINE

7   TAGANSKO-KRASNOPRESNERSKAYA LINE
8   KALININSKAYA LINE
9   SERPUKHOVSKO-TIMIRYAZEVSKAYA LINE
10 LYUBLINSKO-DMITROVSKAYA LINE
11 KAKHOVSKAYA LINE

TRANSFER STATIONS

LINES UNDER CONSTRUCTION

LIGHT RAIL METRO

L1   BUTOVSKAYA LINE   LINES UNDER CONSTRUCTION

MONORAIL TRANSPORT SYSTEM

M1   TIMIRYAZEVSKAYA - ULITSA SERGEYA EIZENSTEINA